Praise for the
Libertyport Mysteries

"Entertainingly captures that odd New England mix of cloistered town-ies and worldly intelligentsia living (and dying) side by side. ... These are men who bury emotions under sea spray bleached Red Sox caps and modern women with Widow's Walk personalities, who dream of ships long since set sail."

Boston Book Bums

"*Boston Globe* correspondent has cultivated a local cult following. "
Kathleen Downey, Newburyport Today

"It's a great read, a fun ride. It sucks you right in, makes you laugh out loud and will leave you guessing up to the not-so-bitter end."
J.C. Lockwood, Newburyport Arts

"Yes, there is a murder or two; a lot of local gossip... but it is the cap-turing of Libertyport's heart and soul that makes this novel outstand-ing. Joel Brown has given a special gift to Newburyport and its people and its visitors. By the way, he is one hell of a writer."
Dennis Metrano, Newburyport Today

For Rosemary, always

Also by Joel Brown

The Libertyport Mysteries:
Mirror Ball Man
Mermaid Blues
Revolution Rock

The Essex Coastal Byway Guide

www.mirrorballman.com
www.facebook.com/JoelBrownauthor

Cover design and photo illustration by Greg Freeman
Owl photo © Kim In Sherl
Author photo © Rosemary Krol, all rights reserved

First edition 2017
Printed in the United States of America

ISBN 978-1542978095

PLOVER ISLAND BREAKDOWN

JOEL BROWN

Author's note

This story arose from a random conversation in the produce section at Market Basket with a guy I'd met years earlier, when I volunteered as a Plum Island plover warden for a *Boston Globe* story. So you never know.

Islands are natural workshops of evolution.
Richard Dawkins

ONE

One winter night when I was fourteen, my parents dragged me to a party on Plover Island.

They argued about going, in their usual muted way. It had snowed heavily the night before and most of the day, and my mother said the driving was too dangerous. But she'd been hinting all week that she wanted us to stay home.

My father's friend Don threw the party to celebrate his divorce. People did things like that in the seventies. Don called it a housewarming, but my mother said his "sad little bachelor pad" wasn't worth the effort. She'd never seen it, she just didn't like the whole idea.

My father insisted we attend, because he'd said we would and because Don had brought a case of expensive imported beer to our own housewarming, two years earlier. Even I knew these were not very good reasons. Probably Don had teased him about being dull or missing out on the fun everyone was supposedly having in those days. That was the kind of guy Don was. He and my father were freshman roommates at college but hadn't kept in touch until we moved to Libertyport. We were definitely going to the party, though. My father was a soft-spoken professor, but when he made up his mind, that was that.

My mother retaliated by wearing her one cocktail dress and pumps, which my father pointed out would be terribly impractical in the snow. She said if she had to go to the party, she was going to look good.

The only thing they agreed on was that I was going with them, like it or not. Someone had to keep Don's kids company, they said. The real reason was that they no longer trusted me home alone with the liquor cabinet. Given the mood they were in, I didn't dare argue. None of us spoke as we tromped out into the frigid wind, got in the car and drove away from our nice, warm, safe house in town.

Snowbanks turned the road across the marsh into a narrow corridor, but the pavement was black and clear for long stretches. Once we reached the island, conditions deteriorated immediately. Island residents always complain that they never get the same services as people in town, despite paying the same taxes, and that night it seemed that they were right. My father swerved around clumps of plow leavings, muttering to himself. Our Volvo wagon had good traction but was light in the rear and tended to drift. I expected my mother to tell him to slow down, but she was still mad and said nothing. Let him kill us all, I guess she was thinking, it would serve him right.

The convenience store at the center was the only island business that stayed open year-round. The owner lived upstairs, so even a blizzard couldn't shut him down. Snowbanks took on a multicolored glow from the neon beer signs in the windows. A couple of pickups idled out front, their owners inside on cigarette or beer runs.

The island is nothing more than a giant sandbar, long and skinny, its margins changing with every tide. Only a few people lived there full-time then, artists and fishermen and other ornery loners. Most cottages got boarded up at the end of the season, but there were cheap winter rentals that appealed to men like Don, who needed a place they could afford on top of alimony and child support.

Snowdrifts filled the small beach parking lot. Darkness closed in as we turned onto Northern Boulevard. Streetlights were few and far between, and we passed block after block of cottages with no sign of life. The ocean roared, out of sight over the dunes.

"Not another car on the road," my mother observed, a not-so-subtle continuation of their argument.

My father responded by speeding up, perhaps to prove that the driving wasn't so bad. He looked over to see her reaction. She kept her expression neutral and her eyes forward, so she saw the danger in the headlights first. The giant snowball in the middle of the road was taller than our car and six or eight feet wide.

"Look out!"

My father swore and stomped the brake, a mistake on the snow-covered road. The car barely slowed. There was a seasick, out-of-control feeling as we slid, but I said nothing, trying for cool. My mother's arm shot across the gap between the front seats to protect me, but I'd worn my seatbelt tonight. I was a teenager, but I wasn't crazy. We braced for impact. At the last possible instant, though, the snow tires grabbed. The car shuddered to a stop and stalled, a foot short of disaster. We all breathed a sigh of relief.

"How did that get there?" my mother said.

My father, furious, didn't answer. He pushed his glasses up his nose and leaned forward over the wheel to glare at the icy boulder, mulling his options. *Bang! Bang!* We flinched and ducked as snowballs exploded against the car. *Bang! Bang! Bang!*

The roadblock was just the set-up for an ambush. Shadowy figures bombarded us from atop the bank on our right, older teenagers whooping and laughing, both boys and girls. Probably I knew some of them, but it was impossible to tell in the dark. My jealousy was immediate and intense. Instead of going to some stupid party with their parents on Saturday night, they were out having an adventure, undaunted by the cold and snow, probably drinking and making out. I hoped none of them recognized me belted in the back seat like a little kid.

Their ammo ran out quickly, and they turned and ran, disappearing into the darkness. A final pair of snowballs thunked on the car's roof, long-distance lobs launched to cover a strategic retreat. Silence descended.

"Shitheads," said my father, who seldom swore.

After several tries, he got the engine started again, and we squeezed through to the right of the boulder, the side of the car scraping the snowbank. He immediately turned up a side street – Lilac Lane, according to the sign – and I realized to my horror that he was in hot pursuit of our assailants. The street hadn't been plowed since the beginning of the storm, but his anger seemed to power the car through the snow. The teenagers had vanished, though, their footprints already erased by the wind.

There were six cottages, three on either side, before Lilac Lane dead-ended at the dune. The last one on the left was the only one with a light on, and he stopped in front of it.

"What are you doing?" my mother said.

"Someone could kill themselves running into that thing."

"And what are *you* going to do about it?" When she was worried, her tone sharpened. She must have heard herself, because she added, "Let's just go to the party."

"I'm going to tell them to get it out of the road. They put it there, they can move it. Baxter and I can't do it ourselves."

"They're probably on drugs," she said. Another reason for me to envy them.

"They'll listen to reason."

When he got out of the car, the wind howling off the ocean blew powdery snow inside. Waves crashed on the beach, just over the dune. He closed the door and marched away, leaning forward into the gusts, man against the elements. We watched as he climbed the cottage's unshoveled steps and disappeared into the enclosed porch. She sighed and shook her head.

"I don't want you ever throwing snowballs at cars. Baxter McLean, do you understand me?"

"I wouldn't do that," I lied.

"You better not."

She wasn't angry at me, but she had to get it out of her system, and I was the only one handy. We sat and listened to the rattling heater, the booming surf, the wind buffeting the car. I figured we'd be stuck there until the snow melted. I pictured a surfer discovering our bundled-up skeletons in the spring, his eyes bugged out and hair standing on end, like a character in one of my comic books.

Our silence lasted probably ten seconds, but it seemed like forever.

"I don't know what he's doing in there," she said. "Go tell him to forget about those kids and let's get going. I can't do it, not in these shoes."

I didn't want to go, partly because it was as cold as *Ice Station Zebra* out there, but mostly because I'd look like a dork in front of a bunch of cool kids. He was probably lecturing them about civic responsibility while they made faces behind his back. I wasn't going to win an argument with her now, though. I sighed at my burden – wonder where I learned that – and got out of the car.

The wind tore at my clothes, blasting my cheeks with a mix of sand, snow and icy salt spray. I yanked my wool hat down to my eyebrows and trudged toward the house, avoiding my father's footprints and struggling because of it. I hoped the roar of the wind would cover the sound of my entrance. Maybe I could get him out of there before they even saw me. I'd just stick my head in and beckon. He would know who sent me. It might work.

A faint snatch of a Led Zeppelin song carried from the next street as a door opened and closed, a wordless Viking howl torn to shreds by the wind. No sound came from the cottage in front of me, though, which was weird if those kids were inside. Maybe he had turned off their music before beginning his lecture. So uncool.

Cursing this humiliating errand under my breath, I climbed the spongy wooden steps, opened the aluminum storm door a crack and slipped onto the dark porch.

The door to the house hung open. In the weak yellow light of the room beyond, my father stood with his hands up, facing a man with a gun.

TWO

"I'll ask you again," the man said. "Who sent you?"

The gun was a snub-nose revolver, black with wooden grips. He pointed it at my father's chest with one hand. A smoldering cigarette dangled from the other. He had wide shoulders and a barrel chest, an oversized head with a Roman nose, and thick, wavy, dark hair. He wore a Bruins sweatshirt with the familiar black and gold logo. In the weak light from a table lamp, he looked low-class and tough, but also flamboyant, like a pro wrestler. A single beer can stood on the oval table, next to a pack of cigarettes. The beer was Carling Black Label. The cigarettes were unfiltered Camels.

You notice a lot, fast, when someone is pointing a gun at your father.

They were both six feet tall, but my father was slender, with the lean physique of the marathoner he'd been before I was born. In his top-coat and galoshes, he clearly wasn't the kind of guy who had guns point-ed at him very often. If he was scared, though, he didn't show it. He just looked serious, as when we discussed my increasingly disappointing re-port cards.

"No one," he said. "No one sent me."

"Why should I believe you?" the man said.

Before my father could answer, a gust ripped the storm door from my hand and slammed it shut behind me. They startled and looked my way, but the gun never wavered.

"Who the hell are you?" the man said.

"That's my son." My father put his hands down without permis-sion. "Go back to the car," he told me in his *I'm-not-kidding* voice.

He was trying to protect me, but a deeply teenage mix of fear and fascination froze me to the spot. I didn't want to leave him alone, either. Somehow I knew the man wouldn't shoot him while I was there.

"Mom says to forget about those kids and let's get going."

The man said, "What kids?"

My father answered calmly. "Some teenagers blocked the boule-vard so we'd have to stop, then bombarded us with snowballs."

The man snorted. "Little pricks."

My father nodded and sort of smiled, as if they were friendly strangers talking in a bar. "They ran up this way. This was the only place with a light on, so I figured they were here. That's why I walked in on you."

The man lowered the gun just a bit. "Probably the kids from the next street over." He nodded in the direction from which I'd heard "Immigrant Song." "Maybe you can still catch 'em."

My father nodded again and said something that might have been "thanks."

"You need to forget you were here."

"Of course," my father said.

The man looked at me. "You too, understand?"

"Forget I was where?"

The man smiled, but my father gave me a warning look – this wasn't the time for my smart-mouth act – and pointed at the door.

I sneaked a last glance back as we left. The man still held the gun, but he wasn't even watching us. He dragged on his cigarette, the coal burning bright. He was already thinking ahead to his next visitor, the one he was waiting for. Someone more dangerous than me or my father.

As we trudged down the walk, pretending not to hurry, my father's voice was barely audible above the wind. "Not a word to your mother," he said.

THREE

The Volvo was stuck, of course.

Our escape involved much revving of the engine, rocking forward and back with snow shooting up from the tires. I began to worry that my comic-book vision would come true.

"What did you say to those kids?" my mother asked, as my father yanked it into reverse for the third time.

"They weren't there. Wrong house."

She nodded as if she believed that's all there was to it. We had kept secrets from her before, of course, like plans for her birthday, but saying nothing about the man with the gun seemed to cross a line.

My father hit the gas, and this time the car broke free. He backed down Lilac Lane, gathering speed, and swung out onto the main road. Just before our rear bumper hit the giant snowball, he stomped the brake, slammed the shifter into first and gunned away. Slick move, but he just wanted to get the hell away from there, and I knew why.

We found the party a short distance up the boulevard. Cars filled the driveway and lined the road in front of a weathered, two-story house on the inland side. Atop a snowbank, a tiki torch guttered in the wind, inside a ceremonial circle of beer cans. My mother shook her head. Don was already living down to her expectations.

We each took one of her elbows as she tottered up the icy drive in her heels. The house next door was dark and probably would be until Memorial Day, but after the events of the last ten minutes, I imagined all sorts of sordid activity behind the curtains and wished that I was part of it. Beyond the deserted cottages across the boulevard, the surf roared in the dark.

The party was hot, crowded and smoky. Red light bulbs turned the living room steamy. Disco throbbed from the stereo, Donna Summer moaning her way to an orgasm, embarrassing to hear in a room full of parents. Even worse, some of them were dancing. My father's glasses fogged up. He grinned and shouted greetings to people he knew. Don appeared from the kitchen with a drink in hand.

"There they are! Better late than never."

He wore a red leisure suit and had grown out his moustache. My father handed him a gift-wrapped bottle.

"Thanks, amigo. Are you ready to boogie?"

"Always," my father said.

My mother looked at him as if he'd just grown a second head. Don said his kids were upstairs, and she nodded to me in a way that meant, *Go*. It was a relief, frankly.

I found them in the attic playroom. Pink fiberglass insulation lined the slanting ceiling. Carpet remnants haphazardly covered the splintery plywood floor. A chubby boy of eight or nine stretched out on a piece of olive-green shag in footie pajamas, chin in hands, staring open-mouthed at the snowy picture on a tiny black-and-white TV. He didn't look up when I stepped over him.

I plunked down on the threadbare couch, at the opposite end from a runny-nosed girl in a smiley face t-shirt. I vaguely remembered her from junior high. She was two grades behind me, no one that I could make out with. On a broken end table stood a box of store-brand cookies, a two-liter bottle of store-brand cola, and a stack of paper cups. "You can have some," she said, barely taking her eyes off *The Love Boat*. I was in enough trouble already (the liquor cabinet) that I didn't even think of sneaking downstairs for something stronger. But I promised myself that soon I would be one of the cool teenagers, at a party with rock music and beer and no parents doing the Hustle. Then I helped myself to cookies and soda.

I was the only one still awake when my mother called up through the hatch that it was time to go.

She drove. My father slumped in the passenger seat, muttering to himself. I'd never seen him drunk before, not like this, but I couldn't blame him. If someone had pointed a gun at me, I would have gotten hammered for sure. Or wanted to, anyway.

The wind had died down. The sky glittered with stars. A plow had broken up the snow boulder and pushed it out of the road. The lights were off at Island Convenience. I yawned.

In the morning, my parents acted as if there had been no argument, no party, certainly no man with a gun. Except for my father's hangover, which no one mentioned either, everything seemed normal.

On a frigid Sunday afternoon a couple of weeks later, I watched a Celtics game with him in the den. He sipped a highball, his first drink since the party. It was time to ask.

"Dad?"

"Yeah, pal." Eyes on the game.

"What about that guy on the island? Who did he think you were? Why didn't you call the police?"

He sipped his drink. "What guy? What are you talking about?"

He knew damn well.

"The guy with the gun, the night we went to the party."

He turned to look me in the eye. "I don't remember that. You must have dreamed it."

He looked back at the game and raised the volume. I stared at him for a moment, then turned to the TV in time to see Dave Cowens make a layup in traffic.

I don't know why he lied. Maybe he thought he was protecting me from a traumatic event. Or maybe he didn't like to think about the danger we'd been in. I never asked him about it again, and the memory slowly faded. As time passed, I tended to think I *had* dreamed it.

But I never quite forgot the burly guy with the Roman nose and the gun. He was ready for trouble when a stranger came through the door. I always wondered what he expected to hear when he asked, "Who sent you?"

FOUR

On a sunny Saturday morning in January, Zack looked out the kitchen window and said, "Hedwig's back."

My son had gotten up to put his cereal bowl in the sink, which felt like a triumph of parenting, although the credit for civilizing him belonged to Amy, my ex. He lived with her and her husband, the headmaster at Governor Willey Academy, during the school year. I got him for most of the summer, school vacations and every other week-end. He ate a lot of cereal. Cereal was expensive.

"Come look, Dad."

I was glad to put down the newspaper, with its apocalyptic headlines about economic collapse, but I stood too fast, and my back issued a warning jolt. Nothing like a couple of nights earlier, when I rose from a chair after an hour of guitar practice and nearly screamed, but bad enough. Zack, oblivious, made room for me at the sink.

The snowy owl perched on the roof peak next door, white feathers gleaming in the sun, a magnificent bird. Huge yellow eyes with black pupils glanced in our direction, blinked, then turned back to the ocean horizon. Foolish humans, living indoors when they could have had the sea and the sky, the whole world.

"She was there yesterday, too, when Mom dropped me off."

Hedwig was Harry Potter's owl. Zack had chosen the name as soon as he saw her, during Christmas vacation. He insisted she was female, although the gender-identification tips we found on the Internet weren't much help. I was just glad his love of the Potter books had survived his growth spurt. At seventeen he was suddenly as tall as me, but less gawky than I was at that age, less prone to maudlin self-examination.

"I guess she likes it here," I said.

"It's harder for the bird people to find her."

"Not hard enough."

An older couple in matching parkas walked into the yard. The man carried a spotting scope on a tripod, the woman a camera. Behind them, a Subaru, a minivan and a Jeep with out-of-state plates crept up the sandy driveway from Northern Boulevard. A regular parade. The crowd grew to more than a dozen people. I recognized a couple of older women as veteran local birders, with mud-encrusted boots, binoculars around their necks. The others were mostly city dwellers in spotless outdoor getups who had read about Hedwig in the paper or on the internet. I couldn't tell them to shoo, because I was only renting, and I had no idea who owned the crabgrass and sand beneath the kitchen window. The houses were packed so tightly on the inhabited part of the island that property lines were Byzantine and inscrutable, and few homeowners bothered with fences. The driveway served five cottages. Once my landlord told me where to park, I hadn't asked any more questions.

One couple looked like escapees from the cast of *Jersey Shore*, the guy a heavily inked steroid case wearing just a muscle shirt despite the cold, the girl in a fur-trimmed white ski jacket and gobs of makeup. They put their spray-tanned cheeks together to take a self-portrait with Hedwig in the background.

"I wish they'd just let her alone," Zack said.

"They're not hurting her."

"I know, but she doesn't like all the attention."

"A snowy is a life bird for a lot of people. We can't keep her all to ourselves."

Snowies spend most of the year up in the Arctic, then fly south in winter until they find a vacation spot resembling their native tundra. This year, three of them had chosen Boston's Logan Airport. That could end badly for birds and planes alike, so officials netted them and released them in the federal wildlife refuge on Plover Island. For most people, the refuge's viewing platforms offered the best chance they'd ever have to see one. Of course the owls didn't keep to the refuge boundaries. Wherever they went on the island, the birdwatchers followed, blocking traffic as they stopped to gape at one on a phone pole or rooftop. Hedwig, the largest and least shy of the trio, was becoming a star. She looked down at her audience, blinked and looked away. Was I imagining her disdain?

Zack pointed at a guy with three cameras hung around his

neck. "He had a show at school last year. Three hundred bucks for a stupid picture of a couple of swans."

"Maybe he'll give us a print."

"Can't you just buy one?"

"I'm saving for your college." I'm supposed to be, anyway.

A distinguished-looking man wearing a camel hair coat and dress shoes stood slightly apart from the group. He glanced at Hedwig but seemed more interested in eyeballing the neighborhood, the houses and the snow-dusted dunes.

He had wavy hair, broad shoulders and a Roman nose.

The image flashed immediately in my mind: my father with his hands up, the man with the gun. It was the same time of year, the same neighborhood. The memory had been knocking since I moved to the island, and now I let it in. I was transported back to that enclosed porch, looking through the doorway as gusts rattled the windows and chilled my fourteen-year-old self.

I shivered.

Which wasn't great for my back.

The spell evaporated when I looked closer. This guy had silver hair, a reserved expression and an artfully tied scarf. Classy. A retired academic or a wine broker, definitely not a pro-wrestler type. He pointed with a suede-gloved hand and said something that made the other birders laugh. The object of his joke was a large plastic owl nailed to another nearby roof, the Hong Kong factory version of a great horned owl, put up there to scare away pigeons and seagulls. The white-streaked shingles made clear that it wasn't working. The *Jersey Shore* couple thought this was hilarious and took another self-portrait. This time they stuck out their tongues and made googly eyes.

"People suck," Zack said.

Hedwig turned her head sharply to the west, at a signal only she could hear. Some distant prey had made the fatal mistake of poking its head out of its burrow. After listening for a second or two, she launched herself into the air toward the marsh, her stocky body unfolding into a graceful flying machine, wings sweeping the air under her, gaining speed.

The photographer fired away, but by the time the others raised their cameras and focused, she was out of range. They gazed after her with disappointed faces. The *Jersey Shore* couple consoled each other with a kiss that needed an adult-content warning.

"I hope she comes back," Zack said.

"Don't worry, pal, she knows you're looking out for her."

"I don't think she cares what humans think."

As the birders departed, he grabbed a Vitamin Water from the fridge and went to the living room to resume last night's *Call of Duty* mission. I held onto the counter with both hands and stretched my spine, trying not to whimper.

With Hedwig gone, the neighborhood gulls returned to swoop and swerve above the roofs. The plastic owl could only scowl at them, and they knew it. There was probably a song in his lonely, pointless vigil, but I didn't feel like writing it just now.

I was older than my father had been on the night of the party, older than he was when he died. I decided that I ought to find the man with the gun and ask him what the hell.

FIVE

Tuesday turned out sunny and warmish, a nice day for a stroll. I walked south along the sandy shoulder of the boulevard. I could have walked down the beach, but I wanted to approach the cottage from the same direction as the night of the giant snowball. It seemed unlikely that the man with the gun still lived there, but when I turned the corner of Lilac Lane, I tensed up anyway, and it wasn't just my back.

There were still just six houses on the street. A Dumpster and a portable toilet stood in the yard of the worn-looking Cape at the corner. There were no curtains in the windows, and the interior walls had been torn down to the studs. A building permit was stapled to the front door, but no tire tracks or footprints disturbed the thin crust of snow on the yard. The economy had derailed a lot of projects, and this one wouldn't be finished anytime soon.

A *For Sale* sign stood in front of the small ranch across the street. The shades were drawn and a realtor's lock box rusted on the door handle. *Price Reduced*, said a second sign appended to the first. Good luck with that.

The next two cottages had been battened down for the winter by absentee owners, storm shutters lowered, evergreen shrubs wrapped in burlap. I kept walking as the pavement rose to the dune. Straight ahead was a shiny new guardrail, to keep people from driving onto the beach.

At the top of the lane on the right, a brand new three-story McMansion rose above the sand on cement piers. Parts of the wraparound deck were unfinished and closed off with yellow caution tape. The corner turret still needed shingling, sheets of green insulation open to the elements. The owners must have torn down the original cottage on the lot but run out of money before completing this monstrosity.

A white Lexus SUV stood on the sand driveway. An overfed golden retriever with a white muzzle snoozed in a patch of sun on the deck, next to an empty baby stroller only slightly less imposing than the car. The dog opened his eyes, checked me out, and went back to sleep. Clearly I was no threat.

The last cottage on the left was just as I remembered, an unloved old Cape with a center dormer and enclosed front porch. The color was a surprise, a pink so faded it was barely there; in the dark, everything looked black and white. The cement steps to the porch were new and already crumbling in the salt air. Scraggly, leafless bushes guarded the corners of the house: the last lilacs on Lilac Lane. A black Cadillac Eldorado coupe from the seventies stood in the driveway, hood as long as a coffin. I didn't remember a car, but it could have been buried in snow.

I started up the front walk, a line of square pavers set shallowly in the sand amid thin, brittle grass. The inside door opened and a man came out of the house as if he'd been watching me approach. My heart beat faster as he crossed the porch and came out onto the top step.

"That's far enough," he said.

I stopped at the bottom of the steps. He was shortish, old and hunched. Maybe he had shrunk with age, but this couldn't be the robust thug who pointed a gun at my father.

"Whatever you're selling, we don't want any."

He wore black dress pants, a white shirt and shiny black wingtips, hardly typical island wear. His head was large for his body. He had a straight nose, small dark eyes, thin lips. His thinning grey hair was wet-combed across his head. A half-dozen dark, knobby growths dotted his forehead and cheeks. Moles? Tumors? One or two sprouted hairs. Somehow, I knew his breath would be terrible.

"I'm not selling anything," I said. "I'm a neighbor, sort of. I live a few streets over."

"So?"

The last couple of nights, staring out at the surf, I had imagined a very different scene in which the man with the gun recognized me immediately and invited me in for a beer. He told me why he had been on guard, apologized for scaring us, and praised my father's courage that night.

Clearly none of that was going to happen.

"I visited here once when I was a kid," I said. "I was walking by and thought I'd check it out, see if the same guy still lives-"

"He doesn't."

He glanced around the yard, looking over the Cadillac carefully, as if I might have vandalized it. It was a big, manly, Republican car, not a museum-quality restoration but recently washed and well maintained.

"Have you lived here long?" I asked.

"Long enough."

Whoever he was, this guy was buttoned down tight. I had to shake him up.

"The guy I was looking for pointed a gun at my father."

His eyes flashed with avid curiosity, quickly suppressed.

"Sounds like Dodge City."

"The island was a lot different then. Some crazy people lived out here."

"Apparently it's not so different now." The corners of his mouth twitched.

"I was with my parents. We were on our way to a party that night, and our car got stuck." Trying to explain the giant snowball would not improve his opinion of me. "They didn't plow very well out here then."

"Still don't."

"We needed help pushing us out. This was the only house with a light on, so my father went in to ask. When he didn't come out right away, my mother sent me in to get him. I saw this guy pointing the gun at him."

"Fascinating."

"The guy was big," I said. "Tough. Someone was after him and he thought it was my father. In the end, he figured out he had the wrong guy and let us go."

"Quite a story. What's it got to do with me?"

"I thought you might know something about him. Any idea who he was, or who might know?"

"That was before my time."

"Did you ever hear-"

"I don't understand why you would want a reunion with some-one like that, anyway."

"I guess it's just a mystery from my childhood that I'm trying to solve. Could I have a quick look inside to see if I recognize it? I'd hate to think I got the wrong house."

He weighed it for a moment. Despite himself, he was curious. "You can take a look, if you want. A brief one."

"Thanks, I really appreciate it."

He shrugged. My gratitude meant nothing to him. He held the door for me to pass inside. I was right about his breath. Liverwurst.

The porch smelled musty from cardboard boxes stacked on the mushy plywood floor. He had left the inside door ajar, just as it was that night. I stepped into the house for the first time with the weird sense of piercing a dream. I idly touched a piece of furniture, looked down at it and felt a jolt of recognition.

"This is the right place. The lamp was different, and there was no beer can or pack of Camels, but it was the same oval table. It held a beige pushbutton phone and a local phone book. I ran a hand over the polished wood. "This was here then."

"It came with the house."

The flat-screen was new, and a newish recliner sat by an end table holding a coffee cup and the remote. The rest of the furniture looked as if it had been there for decades. Other than the table, though, I didn't recognize anything. I hadn't seen much from the porch. When I ran my hand over the books on a shelf, he stepped forward to steer me away.

"Please don't touch anything." A note of suppressed alarm had entered his voice.

"Sorry. When did you say you moved in?"

"I didn't." After a second, he relented. "It was 'eighty-three, full-time."

"You've been here ever since?"

"Except for a week in Florida now and then, when I can afford it." He smiled, although I didn't know what was funny. "What's your name?"

"Baxter McLean."

No flicker of recognition. He wasn't the kind of guy who listened to Top Forty, even back in the day.

"You never heard any more about this man who supposedly had a gun?"

Supposedly? "No, we drove away and never looked back."

"Your father didn't call the police?"

"No."

"That seems strange."

"It was. That's one reason I'm curious."

My father had suspended the normal rules that night. It was more than just the *What happens on the island, stays on the island* mentality immortalized on bumper stickers and t-shirts at Island Convenience. A gun pointed at you changes everything. I knew that from more recent experience.

"You live here with your wife?" She might know more.

"I never married."

"No family?"

"No, none." His expression hardened. I was too nosey. "Have you seen enough?"

"Yes, thank you. At least I know I had the right house. Can I leave you my number? In case you remember something."

He frowned. He wasn't going to remember anything. But he pointed at a scratch pad and pen next to the phone. Anything to get me out of there. I wrote my name and number, tore off the page and handed it to him. He pocketed it without looking and gestured to the way out.

"Thanks again," I said from the bottom of the steps, but he had already closed the storm door and turned away.

I was halfway down the street when I realized he had one thing in common with the man with the gun. He hadn't introduced himself, either.

SIX

"So, I saw you sauntering up Lilac Lane this morning."

Ronnie Terwey sat in a rocking chair on my deck, drinking a Narragansett tallboy. My landlord was a tall, pear-shaped, slow-moving man who wore layers of rumpled clothing and a chinstrap beard. He was as grey and ramshackle as the beach house, as faded as the deck furniture. In the falling afternoon light, he might as well have been camouflaged.

Surprises were bad for my back. "Jesus, Ronnie, I didn't see you there."

"Sorry. I didn't mean to scare you."

"It's all right," I said. "Maybe I'm a little jumpy today."

"No, my bad." He took a long swallow of his beer. Since I'd rented the place, I'd noticed that people who lived on the island full-time tended to drink like they were always on vacation. "So, you know someone over there?"

"Where?"

"Lilac Lane."

"I did. Sort of. It turns out he doesn't live there anymore."

"Someone from a long time ago?"

"When I was a teenager."

"Back in the day." Ronnie sighed and drank more beer. He was in his seventies, a fan of Elvis Presley, Route 66, Worcester diner cars and other artifacts of the mid-century America of his youth. He loved renting to an actual musician.

Last year, the rapper Polio had sampled my old song "Mirror Ball Man" for a track called "Haterz Gotta Love," a sure hit featuring guest appearances by Mary J. Blige and 2 Chainz. I decided to use the anticipated royalties to renovate my house in town, converting the upper floors to two apartments and redoing the heating and plumbing. I needed to relocate during the project. My best friend Davey, who owned the Rum House bar in town, said he knew a guy who could rent me a place on the beach. I just wish I'd remembered that in the music business royalties often turn out to be less than anticipated. Much, much less.

I hoped Ronnie would change the subject to that new Sun Records box set, which had been his favorite topic lately. He liked talking about Elvis with me, as if I had known the King personally. But no such luck. "You moved to Libertyport when you were in junior high or something, right?"

"Seventh grade."

Ronnie's marriages had both ended in divorce, his children had scattered, and he was lonely. He told me this back in November, while I was still reading over the lease, pen in hand. I learned soon enough that his tenants were his surrogate family, and he wasn't big on boundaries. Avoiding him was impossible, since he lived in the walk-out basement and could hear me come and go. He was harmless, really, and in any case I couldn't just tell him to go away, since we would be living in close quarters until May first. So I answered his endless questions in as few words as possible, without volunteering any information, like a hostile witness, hoping he would wear himself out. It hadn't worked yet.

"So it was one of your school friends?"

"No, just someone my parents knew."

"Was it the Williamses? I used to play with those kids, back in the fifties, maybe early sixties. I think Jim, the oldest, had inherited the house by the time you came along."

"I don't remember that name."

"Maybe it was the Kirkmans. They were from West Liberty. They raised Dalmatians, nasty ones though, nothing like the ones you see riding on fire trucks. These dogs were pure-bred and they were biters. The Kirkmans kept themselves a little bit aloof from us year-rounders. They owned a lot of property in town at one point, sold it and made a nice buck. Thought that made them better than everyone else. But now that I think of it, maybe they'd retired to Florida by the time you're talking about."

"I never saw a dog."

He drained his beer and tossed the can over the railing, onto his own patio below. He pulled another one from his pocket and cracked it, meaning he planned to stay a while. Up here, he could see the beach and the ocean. Plus he had me to talk to.

"Just about everyone had dogs back then. Jimmy Williams had a Lab that was a helluva nice dog. We used to feed it hotdogs, raw out of the icebox. Which cottage was it, again?"

"The last one on the left before the beach."

"And it was a family?"

"No, just a guy. I think he lived alone."

Ronnie nodded and drank, eyes on the surf. "A lot of guys lived alone on the island then. I guess we still do, huh?"

"I suppose." I didn't want to be part of that demographic. But he wasn't wrong.

"Last cottage on the left, that was a pretty transient spot back in the day. I don't know who owned it, but they had a couple fellas who rented there, mostly short-timers. They kept to themselves, as I recall."

"That sounds like him."

"I'll see if I can remember some names and get back to you." That way, there'd be another conversation. "So, you knocked on the door?"

I nodded. "Some other guy lives there now. He was kind of strange."

Ronnie suppressed a smile. "He give you frostbite?"

"He's not the warmest guy I ever met."

"You got that right. And those things on his face." He pretended to shiver. "That's Mel Frost."

"You know him?"

"Not really. He's from Albany, I think. Somewhere up that way. Been here a long time now, retired. He keeps to himself, kind of a Mr. Wilson type."

"Mr. Wilson?"

"From *Dennis the Menace*? You don't remember the comic strip? That was a classic. They don't put it in the paper anymore, no wonder nobody's reading it. Mr. Wilson was Dennis's grumpy next-door neighbor. You know the type. 'Get off my lawn!'" He shook a fist.

"Mel Frost wasn't thrilled with me dropping in."

"I'm sure he wasn't. Don't take it personal. Way I hear it, he's like that with everyone." Ronnie paused and removed an orange plastic

prescription bottle from another pocket of his coat. He had many ailments and many such bottles. He popped a pill in his mouth and washed
it down with beer. "Me and my wife at the time stopped by when he
moved in, like the Welcome Wagon. We brought him a bottle of hooch,
figuring we'd tell him where to shop and so forth. He took the bottle,
said thank you very much, and shut the door in our faces. We haven't
said another word in all these years." Ronnie shook his head at the mysteries of human nature.

"I won't be hanging out with him, either."

"If you're looking for people on the island to hang out with, I
know some guys you should meet."

I should have said that I was busy writing songs and needed my
solitude. Maybe then everything would have worked out differently. But
Zack was with his mother for the next ten days. I wasn't writing, and I
had no gigs lined up. My search for the man with the gun had come to
nothing. So I did something crazy. I encouraged Ronnie to keep talking.

"What guys are these?"

"We play poker," he said. "They all live on the island, and we
have a game every Friday night. Do you play?"

"Not really."

"You seem like the kind of guy who would."

Whatever that meant. "Once in a while, when I was touring,
there was a game back at the hotel. But it's been years."

"This is low stakes. I never bring more than fifty bucks. Don't
bring more than you want to lose, though. Some of the guys are pretty
good. They'll try to convince you they're not, but don't believe them."

"These guys would be all right with a new player?"

"You'll be with me," Ronnie said, as if that settled it.

"Fine, then, I'm looking forward to it." Surprisingly, it was true.
"Where is this game, anyway?"

"John Ventana's place. It's the one with the big steel beams
holding up the deck. Down where all those houses went in the drink."

In recent years, storm surf had swallowed several homes along a
stretch of beach south of the center. I had helped rescue one woman just
before her cottage washed away. Letters to the editor blamed rising sea

levels resulting from global warming. Wealthy beachfront residents fought erosion with I-beams or cement seawalls or truckloads of rock. The letter-writers said they were kidding themselves, that the whole island was doomed.

"At least we don't have to worry about that here," Ronnie said, looking over the wide expanse of dune and beach. "How are you liking the place so far?"

"It's fine. It's great. Love the view."

"The house can be a little drafty."

"No, it's fine," I lied.

"You like the décor?"

"Very beachy." There were glass lamps filled with sea shells, nautical charts and seascapes on the walls, furniture upholstered with lighthouses rampant on a field of blue. A persistent salty dampness permeated everything. I hardly noticed it anymore. "I love it."

Ronnie nodded to himself, satisfied. "My first wife gets the credit. All the décor is her. She did those paint-by-numbers herself. And how do you like the lobster family?"

"It's great."

Four plastic crustaceans of varied sizes climbed the wall alongside the stairs to the second floor: Mommy and Daddy and Sissy and Bobby Lobster. Their bright red color indicated they were already cooked, but they seemed happy. The party animal on the logo of the Thirsty Lobster bar in town had a lascivious version of the same smile. I had decided he must be their ne'er-do-well uncle.

Possibly I was spending too much time alone.

SEVEN

"How are you, Bax?"

I recognized that husky voice immediately. Lily Ford called me once every year or so, just to check in. She appeared in my daydreams more often than that.

"I'm good. You?"

It was late afternoon, the day after my visit to Lilac Lane. I stood by the windows, watching clouds slowly take over the sky. I had been restless since meeting Mel Frost, and my back was tight.

"Fine. Touring. Nothing new. What's this I hear about you moving to the beach?"

"Just temporarily. They're doing some work on my house, so I'm living out here for a few months."

"Sounds nice. Are you swimming a lot?"

Rock stars don't have to know things like the temperature. They can always fly somewhere warm.

"It's too cold for that, but I take long walks on the beach every day. And Zack practically has a pet owl."

She paused at that but decided not to ask. "Are you making any new music?"

"I haven't picked up my guitar much."

"How come?"

"It's complicated."

"I thought you were going to rework that album Dormer turned down."

"They dropped me."

Lily sighed. "What was the first advice I gave you? The very first time we met?"

"'Record companies are the devil.' Junior Wells told you that, right?"

"Actually it was Don Henley, but the point stands. Find another label. Get those songs out there. We only get so much time, honey. You can't let yourself get in a funk."

"I've been in a funk since you left me." I brought it up occasionally just to level the playing field. I tried to make it sound like a joke.

Another sigh. I wanted to believe it was affectionate.

"You're still exasperating."

"That's me."

Lily began playing open mike nights when she was in high school in Amherst and chatted up the old folkies and bluesmen who came to town to entertain the college kids. She was beautiful and talented and smart, and the combination got her everywhere she wanted to go. There was a famous black-and-white picture of her at eighteen, getting a guitar lesson from Muddy Waters in the shabby dressing room of some basement club while Buddy Guy poured himself a shot in the background.

When we met a few years later, she was already a big star, a singer-songwriter touring behind her second hit album, a veteran road warrior with a tight band. Intimidating as hell at first, but we kept crossing paths and sharing laughs until my twenty-first birthday, which fell on a rainy night in Seattle. She asked me if I wanted to sing "Further On Up The Road" with her during the encore, and at the afterparty she invited me up to her room to blow out the candles. There wasn't any cake.

I became the opening act on the southern leg of her tour. We traveled as a couple and sang a song or two together every night. Her band and crew made clear that I wasn't the first lucky fella to enjoy this arrangement, but I didn't care. I was in love. Then I woke up alone in an Arizona motel room on the morning after our last show to find a note on motel stationery: *Sorry, honey, but I'm going to do this next leg by my lonesome. See you further on up the road.*

"So why'd you call me? Have I won a prize?"

"Actually, yes. I'm going to be in your neck of the woods next week. I thought I might come visit."

My pulse quickened like a teenager's, although I should have known better. "What's the occasion?"

"I have a couple of days off between Portland and Boston, so I'm playing a benefit in Portsmouth. You know the Music Hall?"

"Nice place."

"Nice people too. That's close to you, right?"

"Close enough."

"You're not busy that night, are you?"

"I am never busy these days."

"We'll have to fix that. This business has changed so much, but we still need Baxter McLean out there with his crappy jokes and his good heart."

"You mean good jokes and crappy heart."

"You never could take a compliment. Keep Wednesday open. I'll call you when we get in. Gotta go now, they're calling me for sound check. Bye, honey."

Click.

She didn't say where she was calling from – I could look up her tour schedule online if I really wanted to know. She gave no details of her plans, but if she had, they would change more than once before she arrived, if she showed up at all. Her level of fame was a centrifugal force that threw everyone else's schedule off track, bent their plans to her whims. She was on Rock Star Time. If you wanted to see her, you just had to roll with it.

I circled next Wednesday on the wall calendar that the loan officer at the bank had given me.

EIGHT

The next morning, a cold wind from the Gulf of Maine brought a cloud bank and ocean-effect snow. Fluffy, oversized flakes fell silently to the sand, whispering in the dune grass, grazing my cheeks as I walked down the beach.

Blue sky taunted from the west. It wasn't snowing in town. The island often had its own weather.

A couple of retirees sat side by side in their idling cars in the beach parking lot at the center, windows open so they could talk. Two gulls fought over a hamburger pulled out of the trash. The Dumpster didn't smell as bad as the Swisher Sweet one of the men was puffing.

I kept walking. I had a lot to think about. Money problems, for one thing. My career was no better. Those were easier to face than the death of an old friend, which still haunted me although it was many months ago. I had walked away just when he decided that he couldn't live with the things he'd done. What, exactly, had I made of my forty-odd years on this earth, except a mess?

The surf got louder south of the center, where the high-tide line came right up to the dune. Empty lots showed where houses had lost their battle with the sea. Ventana's place was easy to spot, with steel beams worthy of a skyscraper holding up the deck. Solar panels covered the south face of the roof. Only a cement foundation remained of the house next door, with a message for Mother Nature in orange spray paint: a cartoon hand with a raised middle finger.

Farther down stood Tru: The Place at the Beach. For decades it had been the Wayfarer Motel, a rundown seasonal lodging where island residents deposited their overflow guests. An out-of-town millionaire had bought the rambling, two-story structure and renovated it into an aspiring celebrity retreat, complete with pretentious new name. One of the lesser Baldwin brothers stayed there last summer while filming a low-budget movie in Ipswich. He spent all his off-hours in his room with a waitress from the Plover Island Grill and never appeared on the patio overlooking the beach. Other celebrities were so far theoretical, and guests of any kind were rare in winter. The curtains in all the rooms hung closed today, and the patio was empty.

A hundred yards beyond Tru, the federal wildlife refuge announced itself with a large sign listing the rules: No dogs, fires or alcohol. Don't pick the flowers. Don't molest the seals. Zack had a whole bunch of seal-molesting jokes. A second sign explained that the beach would be closed during the spring and summer to protect the nests of endangered piping plovers, the tiny shorebird for which the island was named. Surfcasters hated the plovers.

Beyond the signs, there were no more houses, nothing but sand and dune grass. The empty beach curved six miles to the south, a vast arc stretching all the way to the end of the island. I kept walking, trying to leave my troubles behind, waiting for my back to unknot. I didn't feel any better, though. All the piping plovers had migrated to Florida or maybe Bolivia for the winter, and I wished I'd joined them.

A short distance into the refuge, a weathered wooden staircase zigzagged down the face of the dune to the beach. A girl sat on the bottom step, hugging her knees, head down. Her shoulders shook with sobs.

Another girl appeared on the landing at the top and called to her. "Kayla, come on! Let's just get out of here!"

"I can't go back. I'm too freaked."

Pretty girls in expensive puffy jackets, but no hats or gloves. Both of them looked about Zack's age.

"Get your shit together. We've got to bounce before somebody sees us."

It was then, of course, that the girl at the bottom raised her head and saw me. "Too late," she said.

Her friend scowled at me and fled back over the dune without another word.

I stopped ten feet from the stairs, trying to seem unthreatening. "Are you all right?"

The girl wiped her eyes and looked at me with a resigned expression. "Did you do it? Did you kill that guy?"

"What guy?"

"The guy in the parking lot. In his car." She jabbed her thumb back over the dune. She was too upset or confused to notice that I came from the other direction.

"I didn't kill anyone," I said. "I'm Baxter. I live up the beach. Did you call the police?"

She shook her head. She had straight brown hair and intelligent, dark blue eyes. "We just ran. It was so-" She struggled for the right word. I expected her to say *gross*, but she said, "sad," which made me like her.

"I'll go back with you," I said. "We'll see what's up and then we can call someone. How'd you get out here, anyway?"

"Dakota commutes from West Liberty, so she had her car." She looked up the stairs and groaned when she saw her friend was gone. That got her on her feet. Her sweatpants bore the Governor Willey logo.

"You go to Willey?"

"Yeah, we skipped fourth period and came out here to smoke a jay. We thought it would be pretty or something." She looked me in the eye to see if she was in trouble. "I shouldn't have said that."

"Sounds like a good morning to me."

"Don't tell anybody, OK?"

"I don't think anybody's going to worry about it. Tell them you came to see the snowy owls."

"Owls?"

"Big white birds, like in Harry Potter."

Eyeroll. "I know what they are."

"They rescue them and release them here. It was in the paper."

"I never read the paper."

The snow had moved away down the beach as we talked, but her nose was still running from crying or the cold. I didn't have a tissue, but I found a Rum House cocktail napkin in my jacket pocket, and she took it gratefully. *Honk.* We started up the steps.

"You're Kayla?"

"Kayla White."

"My son goes to Willey. Zack McLean?"

"Sure. He's in my year." She stopped again. "Wait, I thought his father was the headmaster."

Aaargh. "No, that's his stepfather."

"Your ex married the headmaster?"

"Yep."

"That sucks."

"Truly."

At the top of the stairs, the low, brown hills of the mainland came into view across the marsh. Church steeples and water towers stuck up above the trees, along with the thin white spire of the new wind turbine, blades spinning fast against the blue sky in the west. Generating some serious electricity today.

The boardwalk crossed above the dunes on short wooden legs until it reached a parking lot surrounded by snow fence. There were only two cars in the lot, a silver-grey Audi and an old blue Volvo 240 wagon like the one my parents drove for years. The Audi was parked near the end of the boardwalk, but the Volvo was on the move. It sped toward the exit, passed the gatehouse and disappeared behind the dunes. Kayla's shoulders slumped.

"That bitch. Now I'll never get back in time for next period."

"We'll figure something out."

If the guy was really dead, and not just napping or passed out drunk, she was going to miss her next class anyway.

A faint, metallic sunlight glinted between moving clouds. The Audi was nosed up against the fence, facing the dune. The driver leaned against the steering wheel face-first, like a passed-out drunk in a cartoon. Kayla stopped twenty feet away and began biting her nails.

As I came up on the driver's door, the hair stood up on the back of my neck. Suddenly I was certain that it would be the man with the Bruins sweatshirt and the gun. But it was a yuppie in his forties, wearing black-framed nerd glasses, a French blue shirt and grey dress slacks. His spiked brown hair was frosted with grey. Silvery stubble covered his jaw.

He had been shot in the head.

He slumped forward with his chin on the wheel, head turned toward me, an exit wound making a grisly show of his right eye. The lens of his glasses was shattered. Dried blood and bits of him were all over the steering wheel, dashboard and windshield. I fought a wave of nausea. I didn't recognize him, although the car seemed familiar. There was only one road across the marsh, so I had probably seen him going in the opposite direction more than once.

The bullet had punched a hole through last year's Libertyport Compost Dump resident sticker in the corner of the windshield. My old Sunbird had the same sticker in the same spot.

"He's dead, right?"

"Afraid so."

Kayla stood with her arms crossed, trying to look angry rather than upset. She glared at the Volvo in the distance, speeding across the marsh toward the mainland. It was better than looking at the body.

I took a deep breath, pulled out my flip phone and dialed 911.

NINE

Few people visited the refuge in the winter, especially on weekdays, so the gatehouse was left unattended, and a skeleton crew tended its five thousand acres. I was surprised there was a refuge cop on duty. He arrived with the blue lights flashing atop his SUV and squealed to a stop behind the Audi.

"Who called?"

There were only the two of us. I raised my hand.

"Who are you?"

"Baxter McLean, I'm renting up the beach."

He looked me over with a slight grimace. He was handsome at first glance, with an angular face and cleft chin, but his nose was thin, his eyes a little too close together. A tag above his badge said *Ofc. Pilcrow*.

"How about you, miss?"

"This is Kayla White," I said. "She's a friend."

His eyes flicked back and forth between us for a moment, trying to decide how he felt about that explanation. He gave up and jabbed a thumb toward the Audi. "And who's that?"

"No idea. Kayla was walking by and spotted him."

He walked to the Audi and pulled a flashlight from his belt for a better look. His only reaction to the grisly sight inside the car was a slight curl of his lower lip.

"Guy must of topped himself," he said.

A good bet. Once every couple of years some broken soul would decide that the refuge's bleak winter landscape was the perfect setting to end it all. Looking around now, it was hard to disagree.

"Probably," I said, "but I don't see a gun."

"I didn't ask you, did I?"

Two police cruisers sped toward us across the marsh, lights flashing and sirens blaring. The refuge cops' main duty was busting speeders on the single paved road that ran through it. They also checked fishing licenses and handled parking-lot fender-benders. Local or state police took charge of any real crimes that came up, so he didn't have much time. He tugged a pair of blue latex gloves from a pouch on his belt. The girl backed away.

I said, "You're going to open the car?"

"Gotta check for vitals. Subject could be alive."

"I don't think so."

"You a doctor?"

Contrary to popular opinion, I do know when to shut up. He opened the unlocked door and felt for the dead man's carotid. I stepped forward for a better look over his shoulder and wished I hadn't.

Two Libertyport squad cars arrived, powering down their sirens, and stopped in a pincer maneuver. When the patrolmen got out and saw me, they looked suddenly queasy, as if that last oyster didn't taste quite right. They knew me from other scenes.

Pilcrow backed out of the Audi and waved them in, smiling as if locating the body was an accomplishment in itself. The tall one moved in for a look. The short one unspooled a roll of yellow crime scene tape to create a perimeter. When he looped the tape around the side mirror of the refuge SUV, Pilcrow's smile disappeared.

The tall cop herded me and the girl across the parking lot toward the visitor center, which was closed for the winter. He took out a notebook and pencil and asked Kayla her name and why she was there. She said she'd come with her friend to look for snowy owls, and he seemed to believe her. Before he asked me anything, an ambulance arrived with two EMTs. He waved them away. The driver switched off the lights and siren, turned a broad loop across the empty parking lot and drove away.

Ray Wankum, chief investigator of the Libertyport Police Department, came through the gate in an unmarked car with blue lights flashing in the grill. The tall cop went to meet him. Wankum stood by the Audi for a moment, looking in, then marched over to us.

"Another perfectly good beach day ruined, right, Bax?"

"That's terrible." Kayla looked like she might cry again.

"Sorry, hon. I didn't mean to sound like a jerk. I've been doing this job too long. Why don't you tell me what happened."

She made a face. *Fine.*

"My girlfriend and I came out here to look for the snowy owls. At first we just thought he was, like, sick or something. We were going to ask if he needed help, but then we saw the blood."

"Where's your friend?"

"She freaked out and left."

"I'll need her name and number. How close did you park?"

"Like, five spaces away? It would have been outside the tape."

"Did you see anybody else around the car? Touch anything?"

"No."

"So you saw him, and then what?"

"We, like, ran up the boardwalk. I don't know why. We were freaking out. And then *he* came along, and Dakota split."

Wankum turned to me. "And how did you come to the party?"

"I was walking on the beach, and I asked if they needed any help. When the other girl took off, I called 911."

"See anybody, touch anything?"

"Nope. Did you find the gun?"

"I don't see it, but it's probably under the seat or something."

"Do you know who it is?"

Wankum reached into his pocket and pulled out a driver's license the tall cop had handed him. "Philip Jonah. Age thirty-nine. Lives on the island. Either of you know him?"

We both shook our heads.

I said, "Where on the island?"

"Lilac Lane."

"No way."

"What?"

Now wasn't the time for the story. "That's close to me."

"But you don't know him."

"No."

"OK, so neither one of you repeats that name, until we can notify next of kin, got it?"

"We've got it." I said.

He looked at Kayla until she nodded.

"Well, I guess I have to go look for the weapon now."

"We'll talk later?"

Wankum squinted off across the dunes. "I really hope not."

"Guys are all the same," Kayla said when he left us alone.

"What's that?"

"You're trying to act like it doesn't bother you, but I can tell it does."

I shrugged. "I knew someone who committed suicide about a year ago. This reminds me."

"Why?"

"Why what?"

"Why did he kill himself?"

"He couldn't live with some things he'd done."

"That sucks."

"Yeah."

She looked off across the marsh, as if hoping that her friend was coming back for her.

"Why don't you call her?" I said.

"Screw that. I'm not going to beg."

"I'd drive you back to school, but my car is way up the island."

She bit a nail. "That's cool. I can call a cab or something."

It would take a long time for one to get here and it would cost a fortune. "Let me make a call."

I walked a little way off and dialed the headmaster's house. Amy answered on the third ring, out of breath. "Hi, Bax, what's up?"

"Zoomba workout?"

"Ha ha. Vacuuming. Tea sandwiches here with the board tonight before their meeting. Lawrence is hoping one of them will write a check for a new field-hockey pitch for the girls, so we stay in compliance with Title IX."

"Tell Larry I said good luck with that."

No one ever called him Larry to his face, because he hated the nickname. I only used it talking to Amy. As usual, she ignored it.

"I have a lot to do, Bax, so what's up? Zack's in class, if you're looking for him."

"No, this is different. I've got one of your students here, and she needs to get back to school."

Long pause. "Who is it?"

"Kayla White."

"I know her. Nice girl. Smart. Talented. What's she doing with you?"

"Well, she and a friend were skipping class and they ran into a problem."

"Such as?"

"Such as a dead body."

"Oh my god. What happened?"

I enjoyed shocking her, just a little. "They came out to the refuge to look for snowy owls, and there was a dead guy in a car right by the entrance to the boardwalk. Looks like suicide."

"Oh, the poor things. That must have been awful to see."

"Yeah, they were pretty shook up. Kayla's friend ditched her and drove back to school."

"That must have been Dakota. She's not so nice. Or so smart." Amy's voice took a wary turn. "How did you get involved?"

"I was walking down the beach, minding my own business, and I found Kayla on the stairs coming down from Lot One. She told me what happened. I called the police. Now they're done with her and she needs a ride back to campus. But my car is all the way up at my place, which is a hike."

"So you're hoping I'll come get her."

"Also, a little mothering might not be a bad idea right now, at least a sympathetic woman's voice."

"That makes sense."

"I was also thinking that, given the morning she's had, she could do without getting called on the carpet for skipping class."

"I'm not in charge of discipline."

"I know, but I thought you could put a good word in on humanitarian grounds."

Amy sighed. "I suppose. She must feel awful."

"She does, and her friend bailing on her didn't help."

"Tell her I'll be there in twenty minutes. Will I see you?"

"I think I'll take off." Seeing Amy today would be too much. "I've got a conference call."

"Rap stardom keeping you busy, is it?"

"Pretty much."

"Lawrence was watching Premier League soccer the other night, and they used 'Haterz Gotta Love' as intro music. He was quite impressed."

"I'm thrilled."

She ignored my tone, again. She got a lot of practice. "I haven't talked to you in a couple of weeks, how's the house coming?"

"Good I guess, except Billy Walston keeps trying to talk me into more expensive paint and tile and fixtures."

"Well, you can afford it, right? All that hip hop money?"

"I'll be fine."

"Some of the kids listen to that stuff all day long. You could only improve it. Are you writing any songs out there? I'd think the isolation would be good for that."

I wished everyone would stop asking. "A few things here and there, nothing finished."

"You should get to work, then."

Now that she didn't have to depend on me to pay the bills, Amy was an enthusiastic booster of my so-called career. I simultaneously welcomed and resented her interest.

"I'll tell Kayla you're on the way. She'll be right by the visitor center."

"OK, thanks. I'm glad you called. And I'll try to keep her out of trouble here."

"Appreciate it."

I resisted the impulse to tell her about Lily's impending visit. We said goodbye and hung up. I turned around to find Kayla watching me and chewing a nail again.

"I got you a ride back to campus. My ex will be here in a few minutes to pick you up."

"The headmaster's wife? She knows we were skipping?"

"I told her the owl thing. She'll keep you out of trouble."

"I'm going to be in trouble anyway when I punch Dakota."

"Harsh."

"She only thinks about herself, and she thinks that's OK, because she thinks everyone is that way. That's what she learned growing up. Her family is so messed up."

"There's plenty of that to go around."

"It sounds like you and your ex get along."

"She's just being nice to torture me."

She frowned. "I doubt that. You want me to say hi to Zack for you?"

"Sure."

"It's weird that guy lived near you, huh?"

"Yeah, it's weird."

By then, more cops had arrived. We watched in silence as they photographed the body. One climbed over the snow fence in front of the Audi and walked slowly across the dune, bent over, studying the sand between the waving tufts of beach pea and dune grass. He was going to have a hell of a time finding the bullet.

Finally my wife's car appeared across the marsh. It was also a Volvo – Libertyport was lousy with them – but a new, very expensive sport utility model. Headmastering paid well.

"I'm going to get going."

"OK, cool. Thanks for being so nice."

I accepted a hug, trying to think only paternal thoughts, then headed off across the parking lot.

Wankum knelt by the open door of the Audi, peering under the dead man's seat with a flashlight. "Got it!" He stood up, holding a black semi-automatic with two latex-gloved fingers.

I marched swiftly over the boardwalk and down the stairs to the beach. Fleeing the scene, but of what crime I wasn't sure.

TEN

"I've got to talk to you about tiles," Billy Walston said when I walked in the front door of my house in town the next morning. Multiple hammers pounded out an African polyrhythm as background music.

"What about tiles? Which tiles?"

"For the backsplash down here."

"For the kitchen or the bathroom?"

"The bathroom." Billy wore a paint-stained gimme t-shirt from Libertyport Paint & Paper, grimy jeans and three days' stubble. He had perpetual redeye and stringy hair in a seventies-rocker mullet. Except for the grey hair and crow's feet, he looked exactly the same as when we were teenagers. The cab of his pickup resembled a landfill after a tornado. All dogs loved him, because he carried treats. "Do you want to go with the Idaho Cornflower, or sub the Sedona Sky?"

"What's the difference?"

He rocked back on his heels as if absorbing a blow. "What's the difference?" He shook his head. "Two different colors."

I walked past him into my music room, formerly the front parlor. The work here was mostly cosmetic. The woodwork had been stripped, but no finish applied. All the furniture had been pushed into the middle of the room, and everything else, including my record collection and the pictures from the walls, was piled on top of it under a clear plastic tarp. The framed poster for the Boston No Nukes benefit, with Lily's name in big letters and mine in small ones, lay bubble-wrapped atop the pile, a framed gold record peeking out from underneath.

"You're saving about twenty percent with the Sedona, but I don't think the aesthetics are quite as nice, as far as the contrast with the paint colors and all that."

"Let's go with the less expensive ones."

He frowned, but I needed to cut every corner I could, his refined aesthetic sense notwithstanding. I'd bought the three-story Federal-style mansion with "Mirror Ball Man" cash when I was just twenty, filling it first with hangers-on and then my wife and son. Living there alone these last few years was not so much fun, the many unused rooms gathering dust and reminding me of the empty spaces in my life. Amy and my mother kept telling me I should downsize or subdivide, but I couldn't let go.

Then Polio called me, or rather his people called my manager. He wanted to use a ten-second sample of "Mirror Ball Man" on his new song. I had my doubts, but all he wanted was the bleeps and bloops of the drum machine track, which I'd never liked anyway. So I said sure.

In truth, I didn't know who Polio was. Zack showed me his latest video and his episode of *MTV Cribs*. Both featured Ferraris and gold chains, cash and automatic weapons, and a platoon of bikini-clad babes. Apparently there was a lot of money in rap music. So when his album finally dropped last summer, I took out a home equity loan and hired Billy to turn the house into a three-unit. I would live downstairs, paying the bills with the rents from the apartments above. That was the plan, anyway. And I signed the lease with Ronnie.

The first check from Polio's record company was smaller than I expected, but "Haterz Gotta Love" was blowing up on the charts. There had to be more money coming, right? Not so much, as it turned out. Each subsequent check was smaller than the one before. And with the economy crashing, the bank was unwilling to extend my credit any further, although my friendly loan officer made a sad-clown face when he told me. A graph of my finances would show the lines for revenue and obligations had crossed somewhere around Christmas, headed in the wrong directions.

Standing in the music room was too much, with my career – my entire adult life – heaped under that tarp. The graveyard of my one-time future. I walked through to the kitchen. The new cabinets were already in place, hardware still covered with plastic. Empty, unpainted, grimy spaces with hanging wires and missing trim showed where the appliances would go. The new veneer floor was coated with sawdust.

"So, how's the project going otherwise?"

"It's going." Billy didn't like giving clear answers, in case someone tried to hold him to a price or a deadline. "We need to talk about drawer pulls."

"Drawer pulls? What the fuck, Billy."

He seemed genuinely surprised. "What's the matter?"

"January's almost over, and look at this place. It's a disaster area. Nothing's finished. Am I going to be able to move back in on time?"

"We're doing the best we can." He tried to look offended but couldn't quite manage it. "It won't be too much longer down here. We've had a few unexpected challenges upstairs, though."

"Challenges?"

"Come on."

The back stairs featured more hanging wires, bare drywall, empty soda cans on the windowsill. Through a dirty window, I could see the wind turbine spinning over the industrial park.

"It was just the holidays, you know," he said over his shoulder.

"A month ago. I really hoped there'd be more done."

"Don't you like it out on the island?"

"That's not really the-"

"I wish I could afford to live out there. You're lucky." He hummed a few bars of "Haterz Gotta Love" and grinned.

I knew better than to explain the financial realities to a contractor, even Billy. Any hint of money trouble and he'd vanish, leaving my house a disaster area, no matter how many joints we'd shared while lounging in the high-jump pit during high school study periods.

When we reached the third floor landing, a cold wind blew around my ankles. He waved me in ahead of him. The interior walls had been ripped right down to the ancient studs. Electric wires of various vintages dangled from empty junction boxes. Naked pipes protruded in the bathroom and kitchen, and the old pine board floors had yet to be refinished. Here and there, sawdust and plaster had been swept loosely into piles.

All of it was illuminated in the sickly underwater light of the sun shining through the blue tarp covering the enormous hole in my roof.

"What the-"

"You had all those leaks you wanted stopped. And once we started looking, we just kept finding more and more rot."

"Jesus Christ, Billy."

"Hey, my roofing crew had a little scheduling problem, but they're going to be back here next week and close it up, so we can get started on the interior. You should be fine, as long as we don't have a big snowstorm."

"That never happens in New England in January."

"You'll be fine."

"I don't know what to say."

"The ceiling joists are good, and we only have to replace a couple of rafters. Those things have been up there for two hundred years, that's pretty good. Somebody sheathed the front slope with plywood once, probably in the seventies, went right over the old boards, and now some of the plywood is rotted too, so we've got to replace a few sheets before we shingle. And plywood the whole back slope, of course."

"How many sheets?"

"I don't know yet. Fifty? Not too bad compared to some of these old houses I've seen."

"And how much is that going to cost me?"

"Hard to say, really. I mean, you're talking high four figures without the structural work. But with it, hard to say."

"Seriously."

"The thing is, I'm going to need another check from you soon. A sizeable one."

My back began to seize.

ELEVEN

The white light moving steady and silent across the starry sky was the International Space Station, according to the weatherman on TV. Walking down the beach in the dark, I imagined the astronauts looking down and wishing they had a poker game to attend.

It's lonely out in space. Someone should write a song about that.

Lights were on in a couple of houses near the center, big-screen TVs tuned to the same basketball game. No one closed their curtains here, even at night. People never seemed to worry about who might be watching them from the darkness out on the sand. If they only knew.

Ahead of me, past Tru, the six miles of refuge beach were pitch black.

I had spent more than I could afford on the bottle of hundred-proof designer bourbon tucked under my arm, a gift for my host Ventana's deck used to rest directly on a dune, but now it stood twenty feet in the air on I-beams driven into the beach. To reach it, I climbed a clanking aluminum ramp that belonged on a wharf. *Thank you for coming on the Libertyport Whale Watch! Please watch your step!*

The booming of the surf must have drowned out my arrival, because the poker players inside didn't seem to notice me despite the wall of windows. Ronnie and four other guys stood around a marble-topped island in the kitchen area, talking intensely. One or two were vaguely familiar, as if I might have passed them on the road or stood in line with them at Island Convenience. I waited on the deck, not wanting to interrupt, especially if they were discussing the new player. Ronnie had said they would be fine with me joining, but I wondered. Part of me wanted to tiptoe back down the ramp and slink off home, but I didn't. I guess I really was lonely. After a couple of minutes the discussion ended, and they started filling plates from the spread laid out on the island. I knocked on the sliding glass door and they waved me in.

"Bax! What's this about you finding a body?"

"Ronnie, let the man get a drink." The speaker was maybe fifty, with a smooth handshake, arched brows and the brushy little salt-and-pepper moustache of a yacht-club commodore. Merino wool three-button sweater, unfaded mom jeans, deck shoes with no socks. "You must be Baxter. I'm John Ventana. Welcome to my home."

"Thanks for having me. This is for you."

He eyed the label on the bottle and said, "You're welcome here anytime, unlike these other cheap bastards."

"We're not cheap, it's just that you keep taking all our money," said a big guy in a Polo shirt and khakis.

"Play better, then. Baxter, this is Donnie Arsenault, he lives up island like you."

"A pleasure." Donnie was a few years younger than me, late thirties maybe. with sandy hair and a little goatee that somehow emphasized his extra chin.

I said, "My father knew a Don Arsenault who lived at the beach back in the seventies, any relation?"

"That was my dad. What's your father's name?"

I told him. "They were college roommates, freshman year."

"Of course, you're the singer. We met when we were kids, didn't we?"

"A couple of times. I came to a party at your house out here one winter."

"Oh, man, I don't remember that."

"You were little. How's your father?"

"He passed away a while ago."

"I'm sorry to hear that. Mine too. It's tough."

"It's been a while. That's wild that you knew him, though. Small world."

I didn't mention that I ran into his father one last time when I was a senior in high school, at a party on the island thrown by one of my coworkers in the Rum House kitchen. Don was boozy, loud, and at least a decade older than anyone else in attendance, cutting lines of coke on the glass coffee table in an attempt to impress a waitress half his age. I didn't stick around to see how it turned out.

"If you two can pause old home week, it's time to play some cards." Ventana had poured two measures of the bourbon and handed me one. "Cheers."

"Cheers." It was very good bourbon.

A poker table occupied one corner of the great room, surrounded by black-leather chairs. Autographed pictures of Bobby Orr and Larry Bird hung on the wall, along with a red-eyed snapshot of Ventana standing behind the 2004 World Series trophy. Everyone seemed to know their places. I took the empty seat.

"So you know Ronnie and Donnie. This is Chris Prather, he lives up island, too."

Chris reached across the green felt for a shake. He was about Donnie's age, also wearing a polo and khakis, but thin-faced and clean-shaven, with an eager smile.

"And Brian Quinn."

Quinn didn't stand or offer a shake, just an up-nod. He was Ventana's age or a little older, with short silver hair, hard eyes and a lean face. Flannel shirt with a pencil in the pocket. A townie for sure. I nodded back, but he didn't seem to notice. Or care. If anyone objected to me joining the game, it was him.

"We play mostly seven stud, but regular, none of that Texas Hold 'Em bullshit they play on TV," Ventana said.

"Got it."

"Whites are a buck, reds are two, blues are five. Ante's a buck." When everyone had a stack of chips, he slit open a new deck and shuffled. "So Baxter, Ronnie tells us you're doing over that big Federal of yours? You've been there for a long time."

When you're famous, people you've never met know all about you. I wasn't famous anymore, but my address was common knowledge in Libertyport.

"I'm turning it into a three-unit, and they're redoing the heat and plumbing, so I had to get out for a while."

Quinn spoke for the first time. "Who's doing it?"

"Billy Walston."

A nod. "He does good work, if you can deal with his bullshit."

"Quinn's a contractor too," Ventana explained as he dealt the first hand.

"And what do you do, John?"

"I run a solar energy company. We make and install panel arrays."

"Business must be good, with all the talk about climate change."

"You'd think. Even with the economy the way it is, we'd be fine, except for the Chinese stealing our patents and then undercutting us on price."

"That sucks."

"You got that right. What about you? What's it like being a singer?"

"Same as any other job, except no one thinks it's work."

He nodded and finished dealing. We picked up our hole cards. Quinn lifted his by the corner, just enough to see, like a player on TV. He grimaced slightly and pushed his hand away. I had jacks in the hole with a five showing.

"So c'mon, tell us about the body," Ronnie said.

It was reasonable to ask the new guy to entertain with a story, while the bet went around. I skipped over the gore, mostly, and I didn't mention the girls' names. When I mentioned Officer Pilcrow, Quinn said "asshole" under his breath, and the others chuckled in agreement.

"The cops think he topped himself?" Ventana asked, calling.

"There was a gun in the car."

"You don't sound like you believe it was suicide."

The game seemed to slow down. The others watched closely for my answer.

"It was a pretty strange angle to shoot yourself." I raised a finger gun behind my right ear to show them.

"Whatever happened, Phil was a good guy," Ronnie said, too loud, his voice a distraught bleat. Tears welled in his eyes. "Rest in peace."

The other guys looked embarrassed. "We all feel bad," Ventana said.

It took me a second.

"Wait, you knew him?"

"Ronnie didn't tell you?"

"Tell me what?"

Some odd looks went around the table.

"Phil played with us."

My jaw may have dropped for a second. "I haven't seen Ronnie since he invited me to play. He didn't tell me who was in the game."

They all looked at him.

"Sorry about that." Ronnie composed himself, wiping his eyes. "I was busy. The water's out at the place I own over on Skyline Drive."

"Ronnie invited you without checking with the rest of us," Ventana said. "It's fine of course, especially when you bring libations."

Ronnie popped a pill from one of his orange bottles. "I'm sorry. I should have mentioned it, Bax."

"You all let me tell the story without saying anything."

"We didn't want you to soften it up," Donnie said.

"You're pretty tight with that detective, Wankum, right? He'd tell you if they thought it was murder, wouldn't he?"

There were ways Ventana could have known that Wankum and I were friends. He might have been one of the spectators the night we rescued a woman from a collapsing cottage a couple of doors down. Still, it was odd. "We're not that close."

"I must have heard wrong. No worries." He offered a toast. "To Phil."

Prather crossed himself. We all drank.

"If it makes you feel better, Baxter, he didn't play last week," Donnie said. "He said he had something else to do."

"He was tired of losing, more like it," Quinn muttered.

"How did you guys know him?"

Ventana shrugged. "Donnie used to work with him. He lived on the island. He was around."

"Quinn was building Phil's house," Ronnie said. "You were the one invited him to the game, too."

"That was before he ran out of money."

"Phil and I both worked at Waltham Mortgage Technology," Donnie said, raising. "I was an IT guy. He was a founder or at least one of the first five employees, a lot higher up than me, but we got laid off at the same time."

"Me and Donnie used to have a few drinks with him at the Grill sometimes," Chris said. "That's how we got in the game. He invited us."

"Speaking of the game," Ventana said.

Chris folded. "I feel bad for their kids. They got the little one, and the other two, what are they, ten and twelve?"

"Nine and eleven."

"There's a jar for donations at Island Convenience."

Donnie shook his head. "Like they need it. Her parents will swoop in and take care of everything." To me he explained, "His wife, Rachel, has family money. Phil didn't like to use it, but when he got laid off they had to pay the bills somehow."

"She's the one who stopped work on the house," Quinn said.

Ventana flipped over his hole cards. "Kings, gentlemen. Read 'em and weep."

The conversation slowed, and the game sped up. More than half the hands went to Ventana or Quinn. Ventana took bigger risks and collected bigger pots, but Quinn won more hands, piling up chips slowly and steadily, as if he was working rather than having fun. Donnie and Chris tried to play the same way, as if they were pros, but they didn't have his discipline. Ronnie and I played for fun and got slaughtered. The talk drifted to other islanders and their finances, focusing on whose mortgage was underwater.

"Not literally underwater," Ventana said with a smile, "although we've had a few of those too."

"You've used that line before," I said.

"Once or twice."

"You look pretty well shored up here."

"Three houses went in the drink within a hundred yards of here. When the dune washed out, we had to do something. I've got fifty grand in iron in the sand. The beams go down thirty feet. I didn't need to spend so much, especially with the economy and the Chinese. Plus I just put out all that money hooking up to water and sewer. But it was either that or write the place off, and the kids love it out here."

"Where are they? Your family." A casual question, I thought, but suddenly the table got quiet.

"The kids are at school," Ventana said. "One's at Dartmouth and one's at Willey. Christine's at the house in West Liberty. She's not a fan of the beach in winter."

"Neither is Quinn's wife, but she's here," Ronnie said.

Quinn gave him a look. "She don't have a choice."

"Why's that?" I asked.

"Quinn sold his place in town," Ronnie said.

Quinn was annoyed. "Had to, the way business has been. Phil wasn't the only customer who ran out of money."

"I'm glad I'm just renting," Donnie said. "My water was off for two days last week."

"They've got big problems with that system," Ventana said. "Once again, the island gets screwed."

"Aces," Quinn said.

Everyone groaned and threw in their cards. I kept groaning when they stopped, though, and slowly straightened in my chair.

"Everything OK?" Ventana asked.

"Back spasm."

"From throwing in your cards? Hell. That happen a lot?"

"When I sit for too long."

"Chris is a chiropractor. He can fix you up."

Chris nodded vigorously. "I'd be happy to make an appointment for you, Baxter. You have insurance?"

"I do." For the rest of the month, anyway, until it's canceled for non-payment.

"The first one's free anyway. Just pick a date."

He already had his phone out, tapping on his calendar, beaming. Maybe the economy meant people were cutting back on chiropractic, too. At this point I was ready to try anything. We set it up.

Ronnie was the first to call it a night, pleading age and an early morning. He had a few one-dollar chips left and pushed them over to me rather than cash them in. A few minutes after he lumbered out, the rest of my stack was gone, too. I watched while Chris bet his remaining stake on an obvious bluff. Quinn showed his winning hand with a loud belch and smiled narrowly as he raked in the pot. It was the cheeriest he'd been all night. He'd been pounding the beers pretty good.

Ventana looked at his watch. "What do you say, gentlemen?"

He cashed out the survivors. Handshakes all around.

"It was a pleasure having you with us, Baxter," he said. "I hope we'll see you again next week. You don't have to bring a bottle every time, though."

"Good to know." I'd be lucky to afford a pint of rotgut after tonight.

Quinn said he was going to stay for a nightcap. I followed Donnie and Chris out the front door to the street. They each offered me a ride home.

"I'm going that way," Chris said.

"Me too," said Donnie.

"Thanks, but I'm good."

"You sure? It's cold out here."

"A walk will be good for my back. You guys OK to drive?"

"I'm fine."

"Me, too. There's no cops out here in the winter, anyway."

"Quinn's had quite a few," I said. "Should we take his keys or something?"

They chuckled.

"He doesn't have far to go," Donnie said and pointed across the street.

Quinn's house was a Cape with an attached two-car garage and multiple additions. Nice enough, but his view would always be the back of Ventana's house. A big Ram pickup gleamed silver under the garage light. A bumper sticker said, *Protected by Smith & Wesson.*

"We'll have to hang out soon, Bax," Donnie said. "It was great to reconnect after all these years."

"Sure."

"And don't forget your appointment," Chris said.

I started walking as they got in their cars. Down one of the cross-island streets, a constellation of orange trouble lights blinked atop sawhorses and barrels. Another broken water main? The flashes came as randomly as fireflies. Chris waved as he drove past me. It was after midnight, but Donnie honked. When their taillights disappeared around the corner, I cut through an empty lot and down to the beach.

On a summer weekend, the beach would have been busy with late-night dog-walkers and lovers curled in blankets, a covert bonfire or two. Tonight I was alone. I didn't mind the cold, thanks to the bourbon. The last flight to London moved across the sky, red light blinking. In the lulls between waves, I could hear its engines faintly.

I tried to empty my head, to just enjoy the moment, but I couldn't stop thinking about Philip Jonah. He and Mel Frost were neighbors. And his poker buddies didn't seem surprised that he'd shot himself, or even that he might have been murdered. I wondered why.

I kept looking behind me as I walked. No one was on the beach or in the deep, black shadows between the houses, but I couldn't shake the feeling that I was being watched. I kept up the pace until I got home and locked the door behind me.

TWELVE

Libertyport in winter has little to offer visitors once the Christmas lights and LED menorahs are unplugged and the big tree in the square has been cut up and carted away. A few stores and restaurants close for good, usually ones that we all knew weren't going to make it. The rest cut back their hours and payrolls, and everyone hunkers down to wait until the tourists return in the spring.

This year the slowdown was worse than usual because of the economy. My mother and I were one of only three tables for lunch at the Rum House. Day drinkers favored the Thirsty Lobster.

"I've been having some health issues," my mother said.

Instead of elaborating, she picked up her haddock sandwich and took a dainty bite. I drank my beer.

"Health issues like what?"

"Like none of your business. I'll be fine."

"Then why did you tell me?"

She shrugged. "I wanted you to know, in case something happens. How's the house project going?"

"The medical thing must be serious, judging by how fast you changed the subject."

Another shrug. Stonewalling me. Fine.

"The house is going well enough, I guess. I'm not good at things like picking colors." Maybe I wasn't particularly forthcoming, either.

"Few men are, although they seem to have lots of opinions once the woman has made a decision. Your father died hating that green in the living room, or so he said."

"Everyone hates that green."

"Well, you should have spoken up when I was choosing it." She sipped her white wine and looked out at the view, buoys bobbing on the tide, empty moorings, dirty snow piled in the shady corner of the deck where we sat in summer. "How is it, living at the beach? We didn't talk much about that over Christmas."

"It's nice. I like waking up every morning with that view."

"It's not lonely?"

"A little bit, but in a good way. I walk a lot."

"I can imagine. Maybe when things get a little warmer, I'll come out and stay for a few days."

"Come when Zack is there, we'll make it a family weekend."

"That sounds nice. How's your water situation?"

"A little cold for swimming."

"Good lord, that's not what I meant. Don't you ever read the paper?"

"I'm kidding. I know all about it. The pipes in that new system are breaking in the cold. The guys mentioned that at poker the other night. There were people without water for days, and it's getting worse."

"I wondered if you were affected."

"I think it's mostly on the inland side of the island. I haven't had any problems."

"Well, you're lucky. People paid thousands of dollars to hook up to the system. I'd be furious." Another tiny bite of her sandwich. Her appetite was definitely off.

"The mayor must be running for cover."

"The council asked him about it, and he made them go into executive session so they could keep it secret. This was all in the paper. You used to care about politics, what happened?"

"I never cared about the city council."

"You care about global warming, though. Well, this is part of it. How stupid of them to spend all that money running water and sewer out to the island, when those houses will all wash into the ocean sooner rather than later. I'm glad you're only renting. I'd hate to see you sink your life savings into a house out there and have it float away."

"You're cheery today."

She shrugged. "There are cheerier topics, if you prefer. Why didn't you mention that you found another body?"

"No reason to bring it up."

"You're not getting in the middle of something again, are you?"

"Someone else found it, actually, a couple of girls from the Willey school. They were pretty upset. I ran into them on the beach and called the cops for them, that's all."

"Things are going well for you now, you don't need any more trouble."

I wondered, how were thing going well for me, exactly? But I said, "There's no trouble, Ma. They think it was a suicide."

"So, you're gambling now?"

Sigh. "You mean poker? Just a friendly game with some other guys who live on the island. Very low stakes."

"I hope that's true."

"Ma, I'm forty-five years old, I'm not going to lie to you about playing cards." That reminded me. "Do you remember when we went to that party on the island when I was a kid?"

"What party was this?"

"It was the night after a big snowstorm. Dad's friend Don Arsenault had a bash."

"Oh yes. I couldn't stand him."

"Do you remember sticking me up in the attic with his kids?"

"I felt so bad for those kids, the divorce and then having to sit through things like that party. God knows what else they saw, being around their father."

"What do you mean?"

She sipped her wine and looked around to make sure we weren't overheard. The only people within earshot were a couple of drywallers who had hit a hundred-dollar scratch ticket and decided to blow off their afternoon's work for a few pitchers. They were having too much fun to pay attention to us.

"Don was into swinging. Do you understand what I mean?"

This was a conversation I never expected to have.

"Yes, Ma."

"Well, there was a bit of that on the island back in those days, or so Don claimed. After we went to that party, he asked your father a couple of times if we wanted to attend one of his 'special' get-togethers. Your father always said no, but I gather Don was quite persistent, to the point that your father started avoiding him. I just hope he had his fun on nights when those kids weren't there."

"Huh. I think I'll just finish this beer now."

"You're an adult, I thought we could talk about these things."

"I'd rather not."

"Oh, don't be a prude."

"It makes my story anti-climactic, too."

She rolled her eyes. "I'm sorry. Tell me your little story."

"I met Don's son the other night."

"Oh, that's a funny coincidence."

"One of the other guys in the poker game said his name is Donnie Arsenault. I asked him, and sure enough, he's Don's son. He didn't remember me at first."

"Small world. Whatever happened to his father, anyway?"

"He passed away a few years ago. Donnie didn't say from what."

"He outlived your father, then. Hardly fair."

"Do you remember what else happened that night when we went to the party?"

She shook her head and yawned. "No, what?"

"The giant snowball in the road?"

"Oh yes, and the teenagers who threw snowballs at us. They're lucky they didn't crack a window. What about it?"

"Do you remember what dad did?"

She pushed her plate away, sandwich unfinished. "He got angry and tried to catch them, but he had the wrong house. Is that what you mean?"

"Did Dad ever say anything to you about what happened in the house?"

"No, why? What happened?"

"I'm not sure exactly. You sent me in to get him, remember? There was a guy in there and they were having some kind of argument."

"I'm not surprised, the way your father barged in there."

"Dad never said anything to you about it?"

"Not a word, why?"

The waitress brought our check. Mom reached for her wallet, but I beat her to it and handed over plastic.

"Just wondering. My place is right near there, and I walked by that cottage the other day and remembered."

"The island is very transient. Probably ten other people have lived there since." Mom dismissed the entire subject with a wave of her hand. "Do you know there's a house out there that's on the market for a million and a half dollars. When we moved here, you could have bought every house on the island for that."

"Possibly a slight exaggeration, but I get the point."

My friend Davey, the owner, appeared tableside. With his white beard and large belly, he looked like a hard-living Santa Claus. His expression said there was nothing but coal in his bag today.

"Who died?" I said.

"There's some screw-up. Your card has been declined."

The drywallers glanced over, then looked away again quickly. Aside from my son, my mother and Davey were the last two people I wanted to know that I was broke. Their reactions were backwards, though. Davey looked worried about me, and my mother narrowed her brow suspiciously, as if she was holding my tab.

"Poker?" she hissed.

"It's got nothing to do with that."

"I can get this." She feinted for her purse.

"No need." I dug out cash. Davey looked relieved as he walked away.

"I'm sorry, but I don't have any money to loan you right now."

"I don't need money," I lied. "It must be some kind of billing screw-up."

"I thought you were doing well now, thanks to that disease person."

"Polio. And I am, yes. That song was number one for weeks. I only get a tiny percentage, but it's plenty."

"Well, I hope so. Especially if you're gambling. Of course I want to help you-"

"I don't need any help."

"-but with the economy the way it is, I really don't have any to spare right now. If you're in financial trouble-"

"I'm not in financial trouble."

"-I will do whatever I can. It's just not a good time right now."

"Ma, enough."

"Fine, fine. I wouldn't want to talk about it to my mother, either."

"There's nothing to talk about."

"All right, then. Now about this medical thing."

She looked so tired, and she hadn't finished her wine or even ordered her usual second glass. At her age it could be anything. My father's death had been such a shock that we had avoided discussion of ailments ever since. The most medical thing we had said to each other in a quarter century was *gesundheit*.

"You still won't tell me what's going on?"

"I don't know what's going on and neither do the doctors. When I find out, you'll be the first one I tell."

"Fine. Let me know."

"I may need you to drive me for some tests."

"Of course, Ma, just tell me when."

We made a plan, and she got ready to leave. I stood up to kiss her goodbye, moving gingerly because of my back. She didn't notice, another sign that she was off her game.

"You're staying?"

My jacket was still on the back of my chair.

"Yeah, I need to talk to Davey."

She looked dubious. "Don't drink too much."

"Bye, Ma."

I watched her walk across the room and out the door, a spring missing from her step. Rather than think about it, I picked up my jacket and moved to the bar.

Davey slid a coaster in front of me and set a pint on it. "Just as a precaution, this one's on the house."

"Thanks, I think."

"Nice chat with your mom?"

"She's got some health problem and she won't tell me what."

"She's at that age."

"I suppose."

"You tell her the truth about your finances?"

"You kidding? I haven't lied to her that much since I was a teenager. And by the way, the next time Visa rejects me, could you maybe be a little more subtle about it?"

"There's going to be a next time?"

"My point is-"

"Subtle, got it. You want me to use hand signals?"

"You've let me run a tab for a lot more than that in the past."

"In the past, I knew you were good for it. Now I'm a little worried about you. What's going on? I thought you were drowning in gold chains and sleazy ho's."

"Yeah, well, about that."

After a glance at the drywallers, I explained that my take from "Haterz Gotta Love" was considerably smaller than I anticipated. I was going to have trouble paying Billy Walston what I owed him already, much less the money for the roof. The obvious possibility was to sell the house, but it was my only remaining asset, aside from my car, my guitar, and the "Mirror Ball Man" copyright.

"So you fucked yourself, basically," Davey said.

"Basically, and now I've got bills no honest man could pay."

"Sorry, but I can't help you."

"I wasn't asking-"

"Look around this place. What do you see? Empty seats. I mean, January is my worst month anyway. But this year, with the recession or crash or whatever it is? I'm basically staying open just so you and I have a place to drink. And by the way, when was the last time you were in here? Are you that poor, you can't afford a beer now and then?"

"Well, I'm out on the island now-"

"And you can't walk here anymore, so you're doing your boozing at home. That's admirable, at least from a public safety standpoint."

"Thank you."

"The thing is, you aren't the only one. People are hurting. Everybody is doing their boozing at home these days, even my regulars. And in January, the regulars are all I've got. Normally I might be able to front you a couple grand to get Visa off your neck. But not now."

"I appreciate the thought, but I'm really not looking for help."

"So what are you going to do?"

"I don't know." I stretched until it hurt, which was not very far. "First I've got to fix my back.

THIRTEEN

Chris Prather's office was in a gambrel-roofed building on River Street with olive drab paint so faded that the grain in the clapboards showed through. The other tenants were a hypnotist who specialized in smoking cessation, a Thai massage studio, a shady college-prep counselor, and two CPAs. The foyer smelled of McDonald's fries, bleach and despair.

Chris buzzed me in and waited for me in the open doorway of his basement office, rubbing his hands in anticipation. He wore khakis and a golf shirt even though it was the middle of winter. "You're my first this morning."

"Lucky me."

He waved me inside. "Have you ever been to a chiropractor before?"

"I don't think so."

"You're not sure?"

"The eighties are a little hazy."

"I hear that." He picked up a clipboard. "Crazy thing about Phil Jonah, huh?"

"Yes it is."

His office occupied half of the walk-out basement. The building must have been apartments, originally. There was a sliding glass door and a small deck. A dying spider plant nestled in a macramé hanger that might have been part of the original decor. I stood looking out while he took my medical history and insurance information. Behind the small parking lot, a chain-link fence topped with barbed wire corralled a dozen or so boats that blocked most of the river view, cabin cruisers propped up and shrink-wrapped for winter. They looked like they'd been there for years, plastic wrap torn and flapping in the morning breeze, fixtures missing, paint jobs half-finished.

When he finished the history, he slid around me and closed the drape. "For your privacy."

"All right."

He stood hands on hips. "So, when you see a chiropractor on

TV, what usually happens?"

"I don't watch much TV."

"Well, what usually happens is that the chiropractor gives his patient a smackdown like a pro wrestler. They say they're cracking his back. That's what most people think happens here, am I right?"

"Sure."

"Well, it's not like that anymore." He must have intended his grin as reassurance. It didn't quite work.

"Good."

"Have you ever seen one of these?"

The object he held up looked like a ray gun in a 1950s science fiction show, with a plunger and a streamlined chrome body. But it had a hard black rubber knob on the end of the barrel.

"What is it?"

"We call it an activator. It activates your muscles to solve their own problems. It's what we do instead of smackdowns. Here."

He took my wrist and put the hard rubber knob against the back of my hand. Then he pressed the plunger. Thud.

"That's the worst thing I do to you. Can you handle that?"

"Sure."

"Good. So you've got a little back issue?"

I told him about the stiffness and occasional pain above my right hip and how it had gotten worse lately, to the point that I sometimes had trouble rising from a chair. He nodded.

"I can help you with that. Step over here."

In the middle of the room, a black padded massage table stood vertical. He tucked a piece of tissue paper across the top, where there was a round opening in the cushion. "Put your face in the hole and grab the sides of the table."

Against my better judgment, I assumed the position. "If I hear 'Dueling Banjos,' I'm out of here."

"I haven't heard that one before," he said good-humoredly, but in a tone that meant the opposite. "When it moves, let yourself go forward with it."

He pressed a button, and the table hummed and tilted forward.

My feet left the floor.

He said, "You've really never done this?"

"My wife was telling me to see a chiropractor for years, but she also tried to get me to do yoga and start running."

"Well, she'll be proud of you today."

"We're not married anymore."

"Gotcha. Well, here we go."

The initial exam consisted mostly of him gently poking and prodding my back. He asked me to raise one hand above my head, then the other, then both. Raise one foot, then the other, then both, and so on.

"Have you been here for a long time?" he asked, making conversation while he wrote notes.

"In this office?"

"In Libertyport."

"Since I was a kid. How about you. How long have you been here?"

"In Libertyport?"

"In this office."

"Fourteen years, since I got out of school."

The notion of coming here every day for all that time, walking into this building with its faded paint and smelly hall, filled me with a sort of claustrophobic terror. As often as I'd complained about the hardships of the road, I was grateful this was not my life.

"Now I'm going to use the activator."

Thud in the hollow above my sore hip.

"So how are you liking the beach?"

"It's nice, I like to walk."

Thud below. *Thud* to the left.

"Right, right. How is it, living upstairs from Ronnie?"

"He's pretty quiet most of the time."

"Except when he puts on Elvis, am I right?" *Thud* on the other side. "He's crazy about the King. Sometimes he'll drive through town with all the windows open and 'Suspicious Minds' cranked up so loud it would rattle your teeth. Is he talking your ear off, too?"

"Pretty much."

"He used to drive Phil crazy at games. I guess that's not a problem now."

"You and Phil were close?"

"Not really." *Thud, thud.* "I just knew him because of Donnie. They knew each other from work. They were at different levels of the company, but they commuted together a few times, mainly when Donnie's car broke down. Phil would give him a ride to Waltham."

"But the company went under?"

"With extreme prejudice, the way Donnie tells it. Here today, gone tomorrow, and there was some shady stuff going on I think. Like all those dotcom companies. The money isn't real until it's gone, know what I mean?"

"Like Monopoly money."

"Exactly." *Thud, thud.* "Neither of them talked about exactly what happened, but I got the feeling Donnie blamed everything on Phil and the other bosses. He had a bunch of stock options he was counting on to help after his divorce, and then – poof."

"Ouch."

"Did I hurt you?"

"No, I mean Donnie and the money."

"Oh, I know, right? What a thing. Stuff like that is why I'm glad I do this." *Thud, thud.* "It's hands-on, it's real, and I'm my own boss. I've got security, too. People are always going to have back problems, that's just the nature of the world we live in."

Security here sounded like a prison sentence. I changed the subject. "How do you like the beach? Is your water working?"

"Don't get me started. There was another break on Sunday, but it was only out for four hours. They've got half my street dug up. But at least they're trying to fix it, instead of ignoring it like they do everything else on the island."

"Well, if you ever need to throw in a load of wash or something…"

"Thanks, I'll remember that. Now I'm going to use the massager." He showed me another chrome tool with a retro look, this one resembling half a waffle iron. It hummed when he turned it on. "People call this the belt sander."

"Oh, good."

"Don't worry."

He put it on my lower back, a small weight like a dictionary. I heard a click, and it vibrated like the Sunbird that time right before it threw a belt.

It felt pretty good, actually. I began to relax.

"In the warm weather, when those boats go in the water, I've got a nice river view," he said. "If they go. Most of them stayed put last year, because of the economy, and the price of fuel. But maybe next summer."

"Sounds nice." Just a random mouth noise that barely qualified as a thought while the massager *vivivivibrated* across my back.

"The guy who built this place went into assisted living, though, and since then his son will rent to anybody."

"That's too bad."

"It's becoming a problem. The Thai massage place, upstairs? Oh boy."

"I saw the sign."

"The whole building smells like their incense." He switched off the massager. "That's not the real problem, though."

"What is?" I just wanted him to turn the machine back on.

"They're prostitutes. Two Asian women. Middle-aged and not all that good-looking, if you ask me. But their massages have happy endings. Hand jobs only, I'm told. But they're still whores."

"Here in our fair town?"

"I know, right? Grab the table again, please."

I held on as it slowly rose back to the upright position. When my feet touched the floor, I stood up carefully and backed away from the table. My back didn't hurt. Huh.

"They get their customers from the Internet. I've looked at the ads. Guys come from all over."

"Wow." What was I supposed to say?

"It's not a moral issue for me. I'm a libertarian. I don't care what anybody does in their personal life, you know?"

"They're really busy, too," he said, warming to his grievance. "Not this early, but it picks up around lunch time, and then again in the late afternoon. I'm sure it keeps going long after I leave for the night. And their customers take up the whole parking lot."

"I can see where that would be a problem."

"The worst thing is, the massage place is 2B. I'm 1B, and about three times a day I get some beer-breath carpenter or insurance salesman walking right in the door with a smile and a boner."

"Not good."

"I wish you could see their faces when they see me."

"Pretty funny?"

"Sometimes. Most of them are apologetic. Sometimes they think I'm the pimp and try to give me money, looking over my shoulder for the girls. But one guy saw the massage table and got pissed, like I was pretending to be a Thai chick on the Internet so I could get dudes. He was ready to beat the crap out of me."

"That's not good."

"It was tricky there for a minute or two. He was a big dude. but I talked him down. I don't want to go through that again. I'd like to call the cops and get rid of the women, but they pay their rent on time, in cash, and the landlord's kid would kick me out of here for making trouble. There's not another office downtown that I can afford, the way this town is gentrifying. I'd have to go to Seabury. So I don't know what to do."

I felt guilty, because I hadn't believed he could help my back.

I said, "I might be able to help you with that."

FOURTEEN

Ray Wankum grinned down at the badge the barista had drawn in the foam atop his cappuccino. "Did you see this? This is awesome."

"Yeah, I see it. So anyway, there's this poker game, every Friday night out on the island."

"I don't want to drink it, because I'll ruin it."

"Yeah, yeah, I got a G clef, it's great, but I'm still drinking it."

"Somebody's cranky."

"Are you listening to me?"

"There's a poker game. I heard you. But we don't care about poker games, unless it's big money and run by the mob."

"This isn't big money."

"Then we don't care. Hell, I play poker."

"There's something weird, though."

He raised the cup to his lips and took a sip. His eyes closed in bliss. His brow, normally furrowed by suspicion, lay smooth and untroubled. I had never seen him so happy.

"I always thought I didn't like this fancy coffee," he said, "but you may have converted me."

"I'll have to live with the guilt."

Normally Wankum and I met at Foley's on Main Street. The coffee shop was the central meeting place for the whole town. Billy Walston was always there, penciling changes on a bid or arguing with a subcontractor via cell phone, and Ronnie liked Foley's too, because it was a mid-century classic, with the original décor from a drug store and soda fountain that had occupied the space in the fifties. Tuscan Café, on the other hand, was the haunt of pet astrologists and kale-cleanse aficionados, ladies who talked about past lives as goddesses while they sank into the big, comfy chairs. I wouldn't run into any of the guys here.

"So what's weird about your poker game?"

"Guess who used to be in it."

"Who?"

"Philip Jonah."

Wankum winced. He set down his cup and folded his hands on the little round table.

"Please tell me this isn't another whodunit. We know whodunit. Jonah done it to himself."

"Yeah, it's just…"

"The guy had more than enough reason to top himself, from what we've got so far. He was facing legal trouble from the collapse of his company. Civil certainly, criminal maybe. And it looks like he was screwed nine ways to Sunday financially, which is why his new house isn't finished. So he had plenty of reasons."

"I guess." I drank some coffee. It *was* really good. "I live near him too."

"Well, the island isn't all that big. I don't think you've got anything to worry about. This isn't a stranger-danger deal. He shot himself."

"If you say so. What kind of gun was it?"

"A nine-millimeter Sig. Why?"

"Were there fingerprints on the gun?"

"Partials of Jonah's on the slide. The ones on the trigger and grip were smeared with blood."

"And nothing suggested he didn't kill himself?"

"Well, you were there. It was kind of a funny angle. I never seen a guy do it that way before. The forensics guys and the medical examiner will have the last word. But people do a lot of weird shit when they're ending it all."

"I'm sure."

But I didn't think Philip Jonah had shot himself. I pictured Mel Frost's creepy smile, the dead look in his eyes. I remembered my feeling of being followed after poker and shivered. But I couldn't tell Wankum about Frost, not yet.

"So Jonah was in this poker game?"

"I got invited to join the day before he turned up dead."

Wankum rocked back in his seat, eyes wide. "Whoa, that is weird. Why would they invite a guy like you to join their poker game?"

"Ha ha."

"Guy who's slightly famous, likes to drink, spends freely, probably isn't a very good poker player. What possible reason could they have?"

It was hard to choose one thing to complain about. "*Slightly* famous?"

"You've said worse yourself. But take heart. There's a guy over there trying to get your attention. I think he's a fan."

I turned. An elderly gentleman sat by himself at one of the tall bistro tables along the far wall, with an espresso and a thick book in front of him. He smiled at me. He had a white goatee and blue eyes so bright he looked stoned. He waved. I waved back. He opened his cardigan and showed me his Cape Ann Folk & Blues Appreciation Society t-shirt. I gave him a thumbs-up. He smiled and went back to his book.

"Why do you think I'm not a good poker player?"

"You're kidding, right?"

"There's something off about these guys, I'm telling you."

"Who asked you to join the game?"

"My landlord, Ronnie Terwey."

"Ol' Ronnie. He's a character. Kind of a busybody, but pretty much harmless."

"He's lonely. He talks so much that I've started ducking him."

"But he invites you to a poker game and you go. Who's lonely, again?"

"It gets quiet out on the island," I admitted.

"So, one more time, what's weird?"

"They weren't surprised."

"Who wasn't surprised?"

"The guys in the poker game. They weren't surprised that Jonah was dead. You'd think they would have been freaked out, that it would have made them sad, angry, whatever. But it was like they almost knew it was going to happen. They were matter-of-fact about it."

"They've been playing poker with the guy every Friday night. Maybe they knew he had problems."

"They didn't say anything, though."

"You're the new guy. They didn't want to air their friend's dirty laundry in front of you. That doesn't strike me as weird."

"Most of them weren't sad or upset, either. Even if they weren't shocked, they still should have shown *some* feeling. But instead it was just, 'That's too bad, whose turn is it to deal?'"

Wankum squinted as if trying to see the significance in this. "How many times have you played with them?"

"Just the once."

"You going back this Friday?"

"Probably."

"Well, maybe this week they'll tell you something. Guys get around a table, have a couple of drinks, they get talking eventually. I used to play every Wednesday night, upstairs at the Galton Club. You'd be surprised who was there. Judges and whatnot. It just takes a while to warm up to a new player."

"You don't play anymore?"

"After Jasper Tuthill topped himself in that room, nobody wanted to."

No one knew I had been in that room with him, or that I had walked away instead of tackling him or trying to grab the gun. I replayed that decision over and over as I walked on the beach.

I said, "That's not why I asked you here, anyway."

"You mean this is a two-fer? I'm going to have to start charging you."

"This is more like me giving you a gift."

"Now I'm frightened."

"I know somebody who wants to drop a dime, but they don't want to do it themselves."

"'Drop a dime?' You watch too many cop shows. Or maybe it's from hanging out with that rapper friend of yours. What's his name, Syphilis?"

"Polio."

"Oh, right. Would he call me 'Five-O?' Or better yet, 'the Po-Po?'"

"I wouldn't know. Never met the guy."

"I thought you had a hit record together. Don't you sit around and compare bling?"

"I've never even talked to him. Are you through?"

He smiled. "OK, what have you got?"

"Hookers, right here in Libertyport."

"No, really?"

"You know?"

"It's so cute when a civilian tries to shock a cop."

"They're in that green building on River Street-"

"Right. The 'Thai massage' place." Wankum sipped his coffee and frowned. Cold. He looked around, lowered his voice. "Of course we know about it. We've known since the day they opened. They had to get health department approval before they opened. They were up to code, the inspector cleared them, but he came back and told us something was hinky about the place."

"You haven't busted them, though."

"We can't, not yet."

"Why not?"

He leaned back in his seat. "Back up. You know that 'Pretty Woman' is all bullshit, right? Most of them are addicts, most of them were abused as kids, most of them get beaten by their pimps. Lately you've got some freelancers working off of Craigslist or whatever. But it's an ugly business. And the Asians have it worst. A lot of them are illegals, they come from poverty over there, China mostly, but also Thailand and Laos, and they pay thousands of dollars to these scumbag smugglers to bring them to America, where life is supposedly going to be better. The lucky ones fly. The unlucky ones come over in containers. But they figure when they get here, they're going to be free and get a job and live happily ever after. Instead these smugglers tell them they still owe more, and put them to work as prostitutes. And they keep them in line with violence and dope and by threatening their families back home."

"They're victims."

"Absolutely. You find them all over the Boston area and Worcester and Springfield, in these grim little strip malls. Buy a used massage table and a couple of bamboo shades, go to Costco for a jumbo box of condoms, and you're in business."

"So why haven't you-"

"I'm getting to that. The last couple of years, they've been coming into places like Andover and Libertyport. So some of the chiefs got together and decided they ought to form a task force, because the North County Narcotics Task Force has been so successful. The way that works is, a bunch of towns detail one officer to the task force, either full time or a couple of shifts a week. They can go undercover in towns where they're not known, make buys, make busts. The chiefs get on TV with a table full of dope and guns and cash. It works pretty good. So about a year ago, they figure they can do the same thing with sex trafficking."

"Makes sense."

"You'd think. But one chief started the drug thing, and he still kind of runs it, that's why it works so good. With the sex task force, they've got chiefs from a couple of dozen towns involved, and everybody wants to be in charge. They have meetings where they spend the whole night arguing about whose town gets help next. There's an actual written priority list, and you don't get your local issue taken care of until they get to you on the list. The problem is, the list keeps changing depending on who's up for reelection or whatever, and we're way down on the bottom. And local cops aren't allowed to bust any of these places on their own, which is bullshit in my opinion. But anyway, that's why your massage parlor isn't going to get taken care of anytime soon."

We sat quietly, contemplating the absurdities of modern law enforcement.

"Excuse me."

Goatee Guy stood over us, blue eyes twinkling, a smile still on his lips. Probably wanted an autograph. I felt for a pen, no luck.

"I wasn't eavesdropping," he said, "but I couldn't help overhearing you mention the massage studio. I can tell you they do *wonderful* work there."

He popped his eyebrows a couple of times, like Groucho. Face impassive, Wankum turned back the lapel of his jacket to show the badge clipped inside. Goatee Guy's smile only widened.

"Police get a discount, I'm sure," he said.

FIFTEEN

On Friday afternoon, Mel Frost's long, black Eldorado stood in his driveway, windows and chrome reflecting an overcast sky. The cottage's curtains were all closed, though. Pulse thudding, I walked to Philip Jonah's house across the street.

A white Lexus SUV stood in the driveway, but there was no dog or stroller on the deck this time. The yellow caution tape fluttered in the breeze as I knocked. I rehearsed what I would say if Frost saw me and came out to demand an explanation. *Just a condolence call…*

The front door swung open.

"Who are you?"

Rachel Jonah's black-and-white dress wasn't quite mourning wear. Something about the cut highlighted her figure too well for that. It matched her black hair and pale skin, perfect lashes and high cheekbones.

"I'm Baxter McLean."

"So?"

"I'm the one who found your husband."

"Two teenage girls found my husband." She began to shut the door. "I don't know what your game is, but-"

"I'm sorry, you're right. I was there, though. I called 9-1-1 for them."

The door swung back partway. "You're the good Samaritan."

"They were upset, and it seemed like someone should help."

"All right, thank you very much, Mr. McLean, I appreciate your efforts. Now if that's all-"

"I just wanted to talk to you for a minute. I play in your husband's card game."

That brought her up short. "Did his poker buddies send you?"

Who sent you? Another weird echo from that snowy night thirty years ago.

"No, I'm sure they'll send their own condolences. I'm relatively new to the game, actually."

"Did you even know my husband?"

"I only met him once." He was already dead at the time, but it was technically true.

She thought for a second, then said, "Please come in."

The door opened to a mudroom, with heavy woven mats underfoot and a bench along one wall, under a row of coat hooks. There were hardly any coats hung up, and only a couple of pairs of children's boots under the bench. Near the inner door was a stack of cardboard boxes each labeled TOYS. The floor was spotless.

I followed her through to the open-plan living area. The house was quiet in a way that made clear she was alone. A wall of windows offered a panoramic view of the beach, moody under the overcast. The light was already failing, and the sconces and pendants failed to push back the shadows under the cathedral ceiling. Vases of browning floral arrangements clustered on marble-topped kitchen island, awaiting the trash.

"I didn't hear your car."

"I live just up the beach, so I walked."

"Weren't you cold?" Her tone said only an idiot would have walked.

"It wasn't bad, although it will be worse going home, with the north wind."

"I suppose you could have some coffee. I just made a pot."

"That would be great."

I looked around while she fixed a tray. The bare white walls wanted art, and track lights were positioned to highlight it. But there were no paintings or photographs in sight, except for the children's watercolors on the refrigerator. Maybe Philip Jonah had to sell his art before he had a chance to hang it.

"I wouldn't normally have caffeine so late in the day, but I'm trying to keep my energy up." She poured into china cups and led me around to a couch facing the windows. "The children went back to school today, and Maisie, our youngest, is with my mother, so I can turn my attention to all the things that need to be done."

"I imagine there's a lot."

"No, it's unimaginable." Correcting me. "The will hasn't even been updated to include Maisie, and she's almost two for God's sake. What was he doing?"

"There's so much that's unexpected at times like-"

"Unexpected?" She laughed harshly. "Unconscionable, more like it. His business, our finances, it's all a disaster. If it wasn't for my parents, I don't know what I'd do."

I sipped my coffee. "He looked so successful."

"It was such a rollercoaster. Everything was going so well, and then the bottom fell out. The last six months have been hell."

"For a lot of people."

I was referring to the economy in general, but she misunderstood.

"Oh, yes. It was a small firm but everyone was hurt. Philip's death was just the last straw." A strange way to refer to your husband's untimely demise. "Our lawyer is beside himself, not least because he was an investor. They all had ambitions of getting rich, and put too much at risk. Gambling my children's future on the absolutely insane real estate market, where any fool off the street could get a mortgage for any amount with absolutely nothing down. Most of those people have no ability to handle money or even to understand what they were signing on for. Which of course is a recipe for disaster. And Philip invested everything we had and more."

She sounded more angry than grief-stricken.

"I would have thought a mortgage services firm was just paperwork or something. Title searches. Paid by the hour."

"Of course, that's where they started, with their software." Probably she learned that derisive expression from her mother. "But not Philip and his partners, oh no. They worked their way into the financing side. Started taking on subordinate debt from some of the banks they worked with. I don't really understand all the details, but they were getting their own little piece of the action, or so they thought. Actually the big guys were dumping their bad paper on my husband. And now it's all worthless." She took a sip, but it wasn't the coffee that fueled her bitter look. "He was a fool."

"What about the company?"

"Everything has been frozen while the lawyers and accountants go through the paperwork. The feds are poised to swoop in when they finish. If there's anything left, it will probably go to creditors, which if I understand it correctly are the same big banks that shifted their bad loans onto Waltham Mortgage. Too big to fail, and too crafty."

"What about personal assets?"

A strangled little laugh. "Philip 'repurposed' our savings to prop up the business. He made their monthly obligations for the last few months, payroll and so forth, by using our real estate equity in town and our retirement accounts, which are all gone now. I don't know where I'll be living in three months. We'll have to sell this place but even though my name is on it. I don't know how I'm going to pay for the children's school. I've barely got enough in the household account for food. And most of the kids' college fund is gone too."

For all the anger in her voice, she was barely holding back tears. They didn't seem to be for her husband.

"Was there life insurance?"

"Yes, that's the one thing he hadn't cashed out. But the agent claims there's some question about whether it was really suicide, which could void the policy. It's ridiculous of course."

"What do the police say?"

"They've been incredibly close-mouthed, except to the insurance agent, apparently. They say they're doing tests. My lawyer says not to worry, but it could be months. So here I am, destitute at the end of the world." She gestured at the bleak blue-grey vista outside. A single vagrant seagull rode a gust above the beach. "I'm selling this place of course, and we'll move in with my parents temporarily. It's a difficult time for the market, but I have no choice."

"I would think beachfront property would be worth a lot."

"Yes, but with the beach erosion and the water-and-sewer issues, it's a double-edged sword. And homeowner's insurance is beyond exorbitant. The little equity we have will go to satisfy judgments, anyway."

"I guess with everything going on, it's no wonder your husband missed the poker game."

She tipped her head to one side. "What do you mean?"

"The other guys said he missed the last game. Someone suggested he was tired of losing."

"He lost sometimes, I gathered from his mood when he came home. But the amounts were a drop in the bucket compared to what was going on at work. While he had work, that is."

"You didn't know he'd missed the game then?"

She brushed her hair back at the sides, fingered her necklace, thinking carefully about her answer. "He left here at the same time as every Friday night. But by then we weren't talking much, or he wasn't anyway. He was just obsessed with work and finances and the hole we were in. Are in."

"Did you ask him about it?"

She shook her head, looking down at her hands in her lap. "As I said, we weren't talking about much of substance the last couple of weeks. He did make a couple of stray comments about 'a cure for what ails us,' but I'm sure that was just wishful thinking." She stood up abruptly, dropping her cup on the glass coffee table with a clunk. "I'm going to have a drink. Will you join me?"

"Whatever you're having."

That turned out to be a lowball glass with two ice cubes overmatched by four fingers of gin.

A healthy swallow of Tanqueray put a small, sad smile on her lips. "Not exactly what you bargained for when you stopped by, I suppose."

"What do you mean?"

"You came by to give condolences, and instead I dump all my problems on you."

"I don't mind."

"Unfortunately, I don't have anyone else to unload on at the moment."

I tried not to be offended by "unfortunately."

"No family?"

"My parents are good at writing checks but not very good at talking. Except to remind me that they didn't want me to marry Philip in the first place. He didn't have much when we met. Needless to say, they now feel they've been vindicated. There's nothing my mother loves more than a good I-told-you-so. My sister lives in Hawaii, she got as far away as she could. I never fully understood why until recently."

"Friends?"

She scoffed. "What's going on with the company has made it awkward with a lot of Phil's work friends and their wives. Many of our other friends were investors. Half of them didn't even show up for the funeral. Most of the blame will be put on Philip now, since he isn't around to defend himself."

She took another deep dive into the gin.

"You must have your own-"

"Oh, all the best people." Her tone was mocking in a way made possible by alcohol. "Missy and Griselde and all the gals from Hamilton. We lived there for ten years, and I thought we'd formed bonds. Our girls rode together twice a week. And then when Philip and those guys started Waltham Mortgage, we moved up here. Everything was fine for a while, they came to our open house, they came for the Super Bowl party. But it was less than a year before the wheels started to come off. One story in the *Globe* business section and suddenly they weren't so good about returning my calls. And when I tried to talk to them about what Philip had done, they couldn't get off the phone fast enough. Failure seems so close for so many people these days, so if it happens to you, suddenly you're Typhoid Mary. They're terrified it's catching."

She emptied her glass and stared out at the swells rolling in on the sand. "I wish he'd stayed at State Street, and that we'd never come here."

"I'd better be going."

"Of course. I have Phil to thank for making me a bore, too."

"You're not-"

"Don't bother, Mr. McLean. I know what's what. Thank you for coming."

As she followed me to the door, I said, "Who's your neighbor across the street? That's quite the car he drives."

"Oh, that's Mr. Frost. He's a strange one. Kind of a hermit. Not unfriendly exactly, but – remote? He doesn't make small talk. Doesn't care about the weather. Doesn't say how cute our kids are, like everyone else."

I opened the door and stepped out onto the deck. "What did Phil think of him?"

A poisonous smile. "Phil called him 'The Troll.' They actively disliked each other. He complained about the house being unfinished. Once or twice we got his mail, and Phil took it over, but Frost wouldn't even let him in the front door. Phil had become a little obsessed with him, started keeping an eye on him. He said Frost was the kind of guy who probably has bodies in the crawlspace, and that I should steer clear of him. It wasn't like I wanted him to babysit anyway. I don't think I've spoken ten words to him since we moved in. And that's how he seems to want it."

She leaned her cheek against the door jamb, weighed down by alcohol and fatigue, and maybe grief. "Thank you again for coming."

"I just thought I should pay my respects."

"Poor Phil," she said and sighed.

I gave her my best funeral-home smile and turned to go. The caution tape whipped in the wind. The clouds to the west were outlined in orange from the setting sun they hid.

Mel Frost's driveway was empty. I hadn't heard him leave.

SIXTEEN

When I walked back into the beach house, an awful bray arose from the living room.

My singing voice, fresh out of the box.

I was only nineteen when I appeared on the *Tonight Show*. A momentous occasion at the time, but I hadn't watched this clip in years. I didn't want the reminder. Why in the world had Zack cued it up?

The girl from the refuge was the reason. They sat side by side on the couch, knees touching, the two of them watching my performance on the big screen. They looked happily fascinated with it, or each other, or maybe both. Zack turned wary when he saw me in the doorway.

"Hi, Dad."

"I see you have company. Why are you watching this?"

"I wanted to show Kayla." He had his laptop hooked up to the TV. "You don't mind, do you?"

"It's fine," I lied.

They grinned at the sight of me standing awkwardly on the *Tonight Show* stage, wearing jeans and a denim shirt, like I was Woody Guthrie or some other proletarian hero. A total fraud. I strummed my 1959 Berwyn D8 and sang "Mirror Ball Man" with an awkward upward tilt of my head, aiming my voice at the boom mike hanging over my head, just out of the camera shot. I was disconcertingly young, only a few years older than these kids, my face smooth and unlined, my eyes still full of something like optimism.

"This is amazing, Mr. B," Kayla said.

Apparently I already had a parental nickname.

"Nice to see you again," I said.

"You too." Her eyes remained glued to the screen.

"I haven't seen this in years," Zack said. "I forgot how awesome it is."

At the time, I didn't know that those three minutes at the tail end of the *Tonight Show* represented the highlight of my fame. And I had to share the glory with my nemesis, a first-generation beat box the record producer found in a studio closet on the night we recorded "Mirror Ball Man," after I had left. He used it to add a cheesy *bleep-bloop* rhythm to the track, the comic counterpoint to my earnest delivery of the downbeat lyric. I hated it; the record company loved it. Since I was nineteen and didn't know any better, they prevailed. And maybe they were right. The contrast somehow attracted America's ear and, more recently, Polio's.

On the *Tonight Show*, the beat box sat in the foreground. A spotlight glinted off its chrome trim and made star-shaped highlights for the camera. You'd think I was its backup band. Upstaged by twenty dollars of Japanese circuitry and four D batteries.

All these years later, I still hated that thing.

Johnny Carson seemed genuinely amused when I sat down at the desk. I still don't know whether it was my song that cracked him up or my faux proletarian getup and deer-in-the-headlights expression. He was kind, anyway.

So did you go to a lot of discos before you wrote that song?

I wasn't smart enough to have a joke prepared, and I was probably too nervous to deliver one anyway. *No, only one.*

Johnny's smile became a grin. *Only one? You're a real bon vivant, huh?*

I guess.

Well, you did a great job with the song. Very funny and a little sad, too. Great stuff.

I was thrilled that he had gotten it; most people didn't notice the sad so much. But before I could muster a *Thanks, Johnny*, he turned away to say goodnight to his audience. A stagehand with a headset ushered me away before we exchanged another word. The next day, the single zoomed back up the *Billboard Hot 100* to number two, its highest position ever.

"You look so young," Kayla said when the clip ended.

"As opposed to now?"

She pointed to the corner. "Is that the same guitar?" Smart girl, changing the subject.

"Yes. My father gave it to me when I was sixteen." It was the only one I'd brought to the beach with me; the rest were stored in my old room at my mother's house.

"Look at how many views you have," Zack said, scrolling down. "And look at the comments."

"That's because of 'Haterz Gotta Love,'" I said.

"You're on a roll, Mr. B."

"Yeah, dad, it's great for you."

They smiled at each other, their expressions full of secret meaning. Smitten.

"You want to see his video?"

"What do you think?"

He clicked a link.

My record company had spent copiously in their ill-fated attempt to make me into a star. They shot the video at a big disco in Cambridge that boasted three dance floors with mirror balls and strobe lights. This wasn't the Harvard Square part of Cambridge, but a place where young people came from triple-deckers and ranch houses all over the Boston area to get their groove on. Guys in skinny ties and girls in flashy dresses hanging on to a scene that was already passé everywhere else. The director hired a bunch of them as extras and put a DJ in the booth for the Saturday morning shoot. An actor in a white *Saturday Night Fever* suit played the Mirror Ball Man. He was older than all of the dancers, circling the floor like a wounded predator. I wandered in the opposite direction in my denim shirt with my guitar hung around my neck, mouthing the lyric while the DJ played the single over and over and the cameras stopped and started

The storyline became clear once it was edited together. The Mirror Ball Man went looking for love, but one by one, all the single girls rejected him and just … disappeared. The dancing couples popped off the floor too, until he and I were the only ones left. The strobes stopped flashing, the mirror balls stopped spinning, and the house lights came on. The Mirror Ball Man's time was over. Then he too vanished, leaving me alone.

"That's *awesome*," Kayla said.

"I wish more people thought so."

At the time, no one in MTV's target demographic wanted to hear any more about disco. The video aired only half a dozen times. It was another one of those things that hadn't quite worked out for me, another bullet point when the record company cut me loose a year later, after the profoundly disappointing sales of my second album.

"Zack says you know Lily Ford?"

I'd never wanted my son to capitalize on my celebrity. I had been around too many music-industry power trips, too many *don't-you-know-who-I-am?* scenes, to let him get caught up in that. But really there wasn't much left for him to capitalize on. If he could use me to make points with this girl, fine.

"I dated her for a little while," I said, as if she'd pried it out of me. Lily was a complicated topic.

"She's an awesome singer and her guitar-playing rocks. Total girl-power icon."

"We stayed friends. She's coming to visit next week, in fact."

"Wow, you're lucky."

I was afraid she was going to ask for a meet and greet, but instead she stood up and crossed the room to where my guitar stood in its stand.

"Can I try it?"

"You play?"

"A little bit."

"Go ahead."

"Be really careful," Zack told her.

She carried it back to the couch. A pick was tucked behind the strings, and she took it out and strummed a few random chords, listening carefully. She adjusted the tuning, then played the intro to *Mirror Ball Man* flawlessly.

"Wow," Zack said.

"Seconded," I said. "Did you practice that?"

"No, I just picked it up off the video. I can do that sometimes, hear something once and play it. I've only been playing for a couple of years. Before that my parents made me take piano and, like, flute."

"You're very good."

"Seriously," Zack said.

"I could play the whole thing, but I don't know the words well enough yet. I can't do the beat-boxing, but I don't like that part anyway."

"Zack, marry this girl."

"Shut up, Dad."

With my encouragement, she played one of Lily's tunes and "Blackbird." Her voice was lovely. Music was so thoroughly woven into Zack's childhood that he didn't usually pay much attention. But he was locked in this time.

"Thanks for letting me do that," she said as she eased the guitar back into the stand.

"No, thank you. That was great. Would you like to stay for dinner?"

"Only if we can cook," she said and looked at Zack, who never cooked. He nodded vigorously.

Amy had let him borrow her Volvo for the night, a rarity. They ran down to Island Convenience for hamburger and related supplies. They didn't even ask me money, which was good, because all I had was fifty for poker.

When they returned, I left them alone in the kitchen and watched the TV news, which consisted largely of terrifying stories about bank failures and mortgage defaults. Video of ghost housing developments out west reminded me of Lilac Lane.

"So how did you two, er, become friends?" I asked when we sat down to eat.

"When I saw Zack at school, I told him to thank you again for rescuing me, and we just kept talking. I asked him if he wanted to hang out."

"You asked him? Cool." Zack shot me a *Daaaaad* look. I showed mercy and changed the subject. "By the way, how did everything go when you got back?"

"It was all right. Amy was really nice. I don't know what she said, but nobody asked me where I'd been or why or anything. Dakota didn't even get caught for skipping."

"Glad to hear that worked out."

So she and my ex were on a first-name basis now. She had Zack surrounded. He seemed happy about it.

"Thanks for calling her. She said you're staying here because they're working on your house?"

"They're turning it into three units, with new kitchens and bathrooms. It wasn't going to be a pleasant place to live for a while."

"I'm sure it will be nice when they're done. But I bet you'll have a hard time leaving here. It's beautiful."

"I like walking on the beach," I said.

"Except for finding the occasional crying girl."

"I'm glad I did."

"And a dead body."

"That part not so much."

"Have you heard any more about what happened to him?"

The bright confidence had leaked out of her expression. Zack looked worried about how this was going to affect his evening.

I said, "They're still trying to be sure he committed suicide."

"He had really nice clothes and a nice car and stuff." She frowned. "I know you're not supposed to say bad things about the dead, but every time I think about him, I just picture this super-pushy business guy."

"The guys I'm playing poker with all knew him, and that was the impression I got from them, too."

"Maybe with the economy and everything?"

"He was having some trouble, they said."

Trying to change the tone, Zack said, "He doesn't sound like the kind of guy who kills himself."

Kayla shook her head. "I knew this girl at my last school, total Miss Popular, and then her ex sent everybody this naked picture she'd sent him, and she drank a bottle of vodka and cut her wrists in the bathtub. I'm sorry, that's pretty gross for the dinner table."

Zack said, "Don't worry. Dad talks about way grosser stuff all the time."

"Thank you, son. What happened to the girl?"

"She lived and everything, but she had to move away, and I think she changed her name. I guess what I'm saying is, there's not, like, one type of person who kills themselves."

"You're right."

"Everybody's in trouble with the economy. A couple of my friends had to withdraw from school because their parents can't pay the tuition all of a sudden."

Now I was the one who wanted to change the subject. "Maybe we should talk about something more cheerful?"

"So tell me about you and Lily Ford."

Before I could answer, Zack blurted, "She broke dad's heart."

"Thanks, son. How do *you* know?"

"Like it's not obvious? Every time one of her songs comes on, you get this look on your face, and either you change the station or you totally zone out listening to her, and then you're in a mood for the rest of the day."

So the secret I thought I'd been keeping all these years wasn't a secret at all. Anyone could look at me and see the truth. It was maddening and pathetic, and my heart sank along with my pride. But somewhere down in that twitchy, craven little part of my brain that writes songs, I sensed a juicy bit of material.

"Is that true, Mr. B? Did she break your heart?"

"Pretty much."

"That's heavy."

I asked Zack, "Is this what your mother thinks, too?"

He shrugged. "Sure."

"Terrific."

"Everybody gets their heart broken sometime." Kayla stood up, showing mercy. "Zack and I are going to do the dishes."

I sat at the table and listened to them while I finished my beer. She told Zack that she and Dakota were going to Bonnaroo this summer, or at least they were, like, planning to go. She didn't know what was going to happen now that they weren't speaking. It was, like, a ten-hour drive, and she didn't want to go to a festival alone. Surprising no one, Zack said he would be totally into going, maybe he could, like, borrow his mother's car. That wasn't going to happen, but I didn't interrupt to point it out. They talked about what they would need to bring and what bands were going to play. Kayla said she could borrow her brother's tent. Zack said that would be cool.

I stood up, put on my jacket, said goodbye and started down the beach. I didn't ask what time he had to drive her back to school. Someone should be happy.

SEVENTEEN

"We're all fucked," Ventana said as he dealt the first hand.

"Is that a reference to the economy?" Ronnie asked. "The election? Or just to Quinn taking all our money?"

Quinn didn't smile. No one did. The players were in a bit of a mood tonight. I'd only been able to afford a cheap bottle of bourbon, which Ventana had accepted without comment.

"I'm talking about the water situation."

"Mine's been out again the last two days," Donnie said.

"Mine was out the beginning of the week, and it didn't come back till yesterday," Chris said. "I got a room in Seabury for one night just so I could shower."

"And we're all glad you did."

"We haven't had a problem, have we, Baxter?" Ronnie said. "Seems like our part of the Boulevard is good. What about you, John?"

Ventana shook his head and sighed. "You can flush tonight, gentlemen, but it was on and off all week. Ask Quinn, we're on the same line. I keep calling City Hall, and they keep telling me everything's going to be fine. And I tell them, it's not fine if I'm flushing with club soda. Schweppes is expensive."

"Remember the old days, John, before they put the water and sewer in?" Ronnie loved the old days. "Everybody's well water was awful, and half of us couldn't even drink it because of the septic."

"I remember."

The houses crammed on the northern end of Plover Island had been a growing public health problem for most of the twentieth century. Small lots with no town services meant well water and septic fields side by side. Liquids percolated through the sandy soil. Tense neighbor vs. neighbor standoffs gave birth to lawsuits. After years of politicking, the islanders finally convinced the city council to fund water and sewer for the island. Fire hydrants were another bonus. The plan was approved over the objections of the town's many environmentalists, who said that, thanks to global warming, the island was going to wash into the sea sooner rather than later, so why spend all that money?

The islanders' victory was short-lived. They paid steep fees to hook up to the system and endured a year of construction detours on the island's narrow streets while the pipes were laid. The work had ended last summer. Just months later, with the first hard frosts around Christmas, bolts froze up, joints burst, and faucets ran dry. Residents were, unsurprisingly, furious. Some blamed the design, others said the contractors had used cheaper, substandard components and pocketed the difference. Still others said the whole system had been buried too shallowly. The town wasn't talking. Now the construction crews were back, closing streets and jackhammering. Town officials played their cards close to the vest, citing pending litigation against the contractor to keep the topic behind closed doors. In the end, no one was happy.

"Remember going and getting water at that hydrant they had with the faucet on it, over at the mainland side of the marsh?" Donnie said.

"It's still there," Ventana said. "People are using it again."

"My dad used to have me help him," Donnie said. "It was the only thing we ever did together, just the two of us. We'd load a bunch of those plastic gallon milk jugs in the car and go over there and fill them up. Makes me kind of nostalgic thinking about it."

"Screw that. It was a pain in the ass." Quinn flipped over his cards. "Full boat, tens over aces."

The rest of us groaned and threw in our cards. Ventana called a break. Ronnie got out one of his pill bottles. I went to fill a plate, and Chris followed.

"You ever have any luck with that thing we talked about?" he asked quietly. "In my building, I mean."

"I tried one guy. He can't help. But I have another idea. Give me a few more days."

"No problem. Whatever you can do, that's great." He looked around to make sure no one could overhear. "Don't say anything here, though, OK?"

"Sure. How come? Bad for business?"

"I think Quinn's a customer." He walked away.

Back at the table, the others were still bitching about money.

"Everything was supposed to get better after we paid all that money to hook up to the system," Ventana said. "Cost me seventeen grand. Between that and the pilings, I had to take out a second mortgage. I don't know where the hell I'm going to get my kids' tuition for next year."

"I got you beat," Ronnie said. "Between all my rentals, I was north of twenty-five."

"It was extortionate, as far as I'm concerned," Ventana said.

"Mine only cost five, but I'm glad I got the loan before the economy went tits-up," Chris Prather said. "I can almost make the monthly nut. Until my divorce goes through, anyway."

"I didn't pay anything. I'm renting, remember?" Donnie shuffled. "Like Baxter here."

I reluctantly met his high five.

"What about you, Quinn?" Ronnie asked. "How much did the hookup run you?"

"We gonna play cards or talk bullshit?"

"That much, huh?"

"These cards are what's brutal," Donnie said as he dealt, trying to smooth it over.

"I went to see Rachel Jonah the other day," I said.

That brought the game to a halt.

"What'd you do that for?" Quinn said.

"A condolence call, I guess. You guys didn't say anything about going over there, and I thought it was weird that no one from the game talked to her."

"You thought it was weird," Quinn said, drawing the last word out to three syllables.

"Kind of."

"It's nice you did that." Ronnie looked at his cards and failed to suppress a smile.

Ventana picked up his cards, looking puzzled. "You made a condolence call and you didn't even know him?"

"I found his body. Besides, we're practically neighbors."

Everyone kept their eyes on their hands.

"That's right, you live near Lilac." Ventana slid in a small bet. "Ronnie mentioned you went over there looking for someone?"

I had a seven and a jack in the hole, another jack showing. I pushed in some chips to call. "The guy I was looking for wasn't there, but I met Mel Frost."

Ventana frowned. Quinn looked at me as if seeing me for the first time. Donnie kept his eyes on his cards.

"Baxter felt the chill," Ronnie said and giggled.

"He's an interesting character," Ventana said.

"He's an asshole," Quinn said.

"We're not going to be best friends."

"Frost doesn't have any friends," Donnie said. "At least that's what I've heard."

"Mostly we know about him from Phil," Ventana said. "Them being neighbors and all."

"Frost is as cold as his name," Ronnie said, "but I am red hot." He made an unusually large bet with a queen showing.

"You think anybody's going to call now?" Quinn said, folding.

"Not me. He must have trips."

"Definitely trips."

"I sure can't afford it." I threw my cards in with theirs.

Ventana looked at his hole cards again and sighed. "Somebody should keep him honest, but the hell with it." He threw his in, too.

"Thank you, gentlemen," Ronnie turned his queen face down and slid his hand into the pile.

Chris picked up the cards and started a shuffle. Everyone sipped their beers. No one wanted to say any more about Mel Frost, apparently.

"So, Baxter, we've all bared our financial pain," Ventana said. "But you must be doing pretty good, right? Entertainment is recession-proof, or so I've always heard. Hollywood was big in the Depression."

"Actually, I'm about the same as the rest of you."

"Baxter got divorced a few years ago," Ronnie said.

Thanks, Ronnie.

"Sorry to hear that," Ventana said.

"It's pretty amicable, and she married the headmaster at Wil-ley, so Zack gets free tuition."

"And my kid's tuition pays for it." Ventana smiled to make clear he was joking, sort of. "But times are tough for musicians, too?"

"We don't get much for downloads."

"I hear those new streaming services are going to be great," Donnie said.

"Maybe. I make most of my money from performing now. And this time of year, I don't play much."

"What about the thing with that Pneumonia guy? I assumed you were very popular with the African-American community. There's big money there these days, as I understand it."

Quinn muttered something about "the yo's" that I pretended not to hear. I liked him less every time he spoke. But it wasn't the right time to call him out.

I said, "If I was rich, would I be hanging out with you guys?"

"I thought it was a number-one hit." Chris dealt.

"It was. You ever hear of Hollywood accounting? The music business is worse." I explained how little money I'd actually made from "Haterz Gotta Love." "I thought I was going to make a lot more. And I overextended myself."

Ventana nodded. "The big home renovation."

"Billy Walston found all this rot in the roof, so the price keeps going up."

"Of course it does."

"I've been robbing Peter to pay Paul." They didn't need to know all this, but once I'd started talking about it, it came out like a confession. "Including my kid's college fund."

A brief, respectful silence enveloped the table. It was that bad.

"He's a junior now, isn't he?" Ventana said, his expression sympathetic.

"Yes, he is."

"You are in a pickle."

I just nodded.

"Maybe you should bet," Quinn said, not caring.

"Yeah, you could win some of it back," Ronnie said.

I knew better, but I reached for my chips anyway.

EIGHTEEN

The broad patio in front of Tru had room for twenty tables. On Tuesday afternoon, a table and four chairs had been taken out of winter storage and placed near the edge. Lily Ford sat there alone under the grey sky, gazing out at the surf. A tall chrome heater stood nearby to keep her warm.

I stopped on the beach below the patio, wind-whipped sand lashing my ankles.

"Hello, Lily."

"Hello, yourself."

Her voice sounded slightly rougher than usual. She looked older than the last time I'd seen her yet just the same, in the way famous people do. She had more lines on her face, more tiny wrinkles at the corners of her eyes, but her star profile remained unchanged: High cheekbones, full lips, green eyes. The big mane of red hair made her petite figure look even smaller. Long legs, skinny black jeans, tall black boots with pointy toes. Bangles and rings, the ruffled silk top unbuttoned down to *there* as usual, even outdoors. Her only concession to the season was the puffy orange jacket draped around her shoulders like a shawl.

"You look good," I said.

"You too."

"Liar."

That got a small smile. She sat with her boots up on the chair opposite, ashtray and cigarettes at her elbow along with a half-drunk Bloody Mary. People were always surprised that she smoked. She never let herself be photographed with a cigarette, because she sang at benefits for environmental causes and women's health centers. But she had started playing nightclubs right after high school, and certain formative vices had stuck. Being a feminist didn't mean she gave up the boots or the skin-tight jeans or buttoned up the cleavage. She had made it in a man's world, and she stuck with the image got her there. She never let herself be photographed with a boyfriend unless he was famous, too.

"How long has it been?" she said.

"Too long."

"I know. I miss you."

She stubbed out her cigarette and immediately lit another. Maybe she was as freaked out as I was.

Instead of a railing along the edge of the patio, Tru had a row of clear-glass panels. Climbing up and over would be dramatic, but I would inevitably hurt myself in comical fashion. So I walked down to the end and took the stairs. Pulled out a chair and joined her at the table. Exercising an old lover's prerogative, I grabbed her glass and took a big drink.

I said, "You still like it spicy, huh?"

"Some things never change, like your lousy pickup lines."

Never mind that she had picked me up, way back when. We sat looking out at the ocean while I finished her drink. It didn't take long. The only sounds were the waves and the gulls.

"I guess we should get another round," she said. Star that she was, she simply raised two fingers in the air, knowing that she was being watched.

See you further on up the road had turned out to mean two years after that desert motel room. We met again when we both played a no-nukes benefit in Boston, and at first it was like no time had passed. We sat together backstage until it was time for me to go on, talking and laughing and drinking wine, my arm around her chair, her hand on my knee. I hung around after my solo set so we could sing "Mockingbird" during her encore, just like the old days. But when I went looking for her after the big finale, the bass player said, "Aw, she split already. Her new dude's waiting for her back at the hotel. Sorry, man."

A few years later, I met Amy, and then we had Zack. My career kept dialing itself back, until my only gigs were in coffeehouses and college-town bars. Lily's star kept rising. When she played Boston every few years, she left tickets for me at the box office. Amy could never come with me. Looking back, it's impossible to tell if I arranged things that way or she did, but I went alone. Usually Lily had me get up and sing with her, and then I made a gracious exit. I didn't hang around afterward.

"So what are you doing here? Plover Island in winter isn't exactly a hot spot."

"We were looking for a quiet place to relax. I'm not a spring chicken anymore, honey. Six weeks on the road, I'm beat. My manager is after me to write for a new album, and I thought I could get some work done here. Plus I could see you."

"We?"

"Me and Manfred."

"Manfred?"

"My boyfriend."

"Manfred. Seriously."

A little laugh. "I know, I know. He's German. Half-German and half-Malian, actually, but he grew up in Munich."

"And he's what, twenty-three?"

"Thirty-one. But given my current age, I think it still qualifies as robbing the cradle. I have a reputation to live up to."

"Where is he?"

"Up in our room, Skyping with his Swiss banker."

"So he's rich, too?"

She shook her head. "He's not after my money, if that's what you mean."

The waitress, a plump townie in a maid's smock and jeans, brought our drinks. Her hands shook as she set down the glasses, never taking her eyes off Lily. She curtseyed awkwardly before skittering away. To judge by the giant celery sticks and half limes stuffed into the glasses, she'd never made a Bloody Mary before. At least there were ice cubes. Tru had water today.

"So how are you, Bax?"

"I'm fine."

"The Polio thing is cool. It put a little cash in your pocket, I bet."

"For a while."

"And it got your name back out there. I'm surprised you haven't done any gigs with him."

"The hip-hop youth are not exactly my crowd."

"Everybody's everything these days. All the old categories are busted. As my manager keeps saying, we have to maximize our opportunities."

"All he sampled was the beat box. What am I supposed to do, go out on stage and press a button?"

"Still mad at that little piece of crap twenty-five years later?"

"The thing's more famous than I am."

"I don't think that's true, but if you do, why not change it? This is your chance. Polio's on every awards show this year. Call him up. I bet the producers would be thrilled to have you get up there and press the button. Then right in the middle of his song, they cut to you singing 'Mirror Ball Man.' You do a verse and chorus, then throw it back to him. And ten thousand people run to their computers to buy your song."

"You really think Polio would go for that?"

"He told me he would."

Beat.

"When was this?"

"Couple weeks ago, at the Music Cares benefit in Vegas. We got talking backstage. Your name came up."

"I don't need your help. But I'm glad you're still looking out for me."

"Somebody has to."

"What does that mean?"

"This island's beautiful and all, but it's kind of isolated. I hate to see you just quit."

"I haven't quit. Stuff happened. I had a new record all ready to go, and then Dormer dropped me."

"That label isn't what it used to be. But none of them are. Everything's money, money, money now. It's not about the music. And these streaming services they're all starting up, we're going to get like two-tenths of a cent every time someone listens to a track."

"At least someone's listening to you."

She frowned, sipped her drink. "And what have you done to make people listen? You've got to get over it, whatever's holding you back. Take charge of your own life. Call Polio and tell him you want to do something together."

"I'll think about it."

"Damn right you will. Now, so what about this benefit? You going to come sing with me? We can do 'Mockingbird' if you're up to it."

"I guess we should."

"Damn right we should." She slid a cigarette out of the pack and looked at the waves. "What have you got to lose?"

NINETEEN

Knock knock knock, urgent as a police raid. Donnie walked in without waiting for an answer.

"Can I use your-"

I pointed.

The bathroom door closed behind him. He wasn't gone long.

"You're a lifesaver. My water's been out for a day and a half now."

"Use the shower too, if you want."

"Thanks, but I don't want to impose. I didn't bring any clothes or anything, anyway."

"Come back later if you want."

"That would be great, actually. I've been wearing out my welcome everywhere else."

Donnie wouldn't have been my first choice of guest, but I was glad for the interruption. It was Tuesday night, I was washing dishes, staring into the darkness outside the kitchen window. He had pulled me out of a gloomy reverie about Lily and the slow-motion calamity that was my career and/or my life. "You want a beer?"

"That would also be great."

I rummaged in the fridge. "Guy at Island Convenience said the town is putting people up at a motel after twenty-four hours without water."

"Yeah, a motel over to Seabury Beach. That might be convenient if you could walk across the river at low tide, instead of having to drive all the way around. And have you seen those places? Crime-ridden shitholes, especially in the winter."

"So I hear." I had gone toe to toe with an angry dope dealer in a room at the Camelot a couple of years earlier, and the squalor had made a lasting impression.

"Not that this side of the river used to be any different. It hasn't always been yupped up like it is now."

"You spent a lot of time out here back in the day, right? With your sister. Was her name Jane?"

"Jan. We were out here with him for a few years, yeah. I must have been what, eight or nine when you came to that party?"

"I was fourteen. Your sister was two years behind me."

"Yeah, so I was nine. The divorce had just gone through. The old man was in a party-throwing mood."

"Not usually the case?"

He shrugged. "My folks had split up a while earlier. He lived in some crappy apartment near the city until the divorce was final, and then he got the place out here. He had me and Jan two weeks every month and for the whole summer. We were really psyched about being at the beach at first. Our friends would come out, and sometimes their parents would stay instead of just dropping them off. He was always happy to play host, mix up some drinks."

"Sounds like fun."

"Summers, sure, especially that first year. The rest of the time, it sucked. We were the last ones off the school bus. Out of season, there weren't really any other kids around, and there wasn't anything to do. I think it was harder on Jan than me. What did I know? I was a kid, I was bored, so what. But she was starting all that teenage stuff, and she hated being stuck out here. They had huge screaming fights. He was starting to drink a lot, and he used the belt. If she really pissed him off, we both got it."

Donnie washed away the taste of those memories with beer. I tried to change the subject.

"Were you out here for the blizzard of '78?"

"No, we were with my mother. I think my father got stranded in the city, but he was only renting out here anyway. He didn't have much to lose."

"I remember he liked disco."

"Oh yeah, he was the king, or at least he thought he was. I've been waiting for this to come up, you know. After we met at poker, I remembered your song. Came out in summer of '82, right? 'Mirror Ball Man.' I was still spending weekends with him then, although he had a different apartment by then, a dump out by the highway. You got another beer?"

"Not much beach out by the highway," I said from inside the refrigerator.

"Yeah, although being in town was handy. When he seemed like he was going to get out the belt, I could jump on my bike and go see my friends, get out of there. Jan had a car by then, it was her senior year, so she was hardly ever around anyway. And that pissed him off too."

"It sounds like pretty much everything pissed him off."

He laughed. "That's about right. I was really mad at him for a long, long time. I hated him, to tell you the truth. But now I'm in the same boat, you know? Divorced, broke, career in the tank, living in a rented shithole. I can understand him a little better, why he was such a frustrated, messed-up guy. I'm trying to be more charitable toward him, or whatever."

"That's good."

"I guess. He hated you, you know."

"I didn't think he knew who I was." I had been a wiseass, a kid that adults remembered, but I didn't think I'd ever smarted off to Don Senior. Or even talked to him, the few times we'd been in the same room.

"This was later, because of the song," Donnie said. "It was about a disco guy who was kind of a loser, right?"

"That's one way to put it."

"Well, it kind of hit my old man where he lived. He was still going to clubs and trying to pick up women. Getting some, too, although they were mostly skanks. He still kidded himself that he was this big Lothario. Your song was pretty much a kick in the nuts. He *hated* it."

"He wasn't the only one."

Disco was already on the way out when "Mirror Ball Man" was released. But a club DJ in Tarzana, California, organized a Smash The Mirror night where everyone who brought a copy of my album got the cover charge waived and a ticket for a free Tequila Sunrise. Inside they broke up the vinyl with a sledge hammer. All I cared was that the controversy sold a few more records.

"I guess it's funny now," Donnie said, "but he was really pissed off. To be honest, he probably didn't remember you before that. But when that song came out, people in town were talking about it, and he put two and two together, and decided you wrote it about him."

"*What?*"

"He thought you hated his guts and were getting even or something. Like you wrote it to make fun of him."

"I hardly even knew him."

"I know, don't worry."

"There was this guy at a bar in Amherst, it wasn't even really a disco, but he had the gold chain and everything, and he ended up with this girl I liked, so I was pissed off. That's what the song was about."

"I believe you. He wasn't exactly rational. Paranoia is common in late-stage alcoholism. One time the song came on and he threw a beer bottle at the stereo. Missed, of course. But it was all he could talk about for a while. He was telling people in bars that he was going to sue you for a million bucks. I think he actually used it to try to get over with women. Then my mother sued him for back alimony or something, and she became Public Enemy Number One again. But even after that, if 'Mirror Ball Man' came on the radio, he was off to the races."

I shook my head. "It's a strange world."

"No kidding. And then you and me meet at poker, after all this time. But I'm glad we did. It's nice to have someone simpatico to talk to. Someone who knows how he was, what it was like out here back in the day."

When he held out his bottle, I clinked it, and we drank a toast.

"You said he passed? How long ago?" I asked.

"Oh, it's been a while. It was a few years after your song came out. Like I said, I hated the prick at the time. I'm trying to forgive him, but honestly, if he walked in that door right now, I'd probably want to beat the hell out of him."

We drank some more and thought about that.

"How old are your kids?" I said.

"Eleven and eight. Now that you mention it, almost the same

ages Jan and I were when we met you. They're good kids, we get along good, despite my wife's best efforts to poison their minds against me. You've got one, right?"

"Yeah, Zack. He's going to graduate from Willey next year."

"Oh, right, you said your ex is married to the headmaster. Saves on tuition, right?"

"Zack wouldn't be there otherwise. He'd be at good old Libertyport High like his father."

"And me too, a few years behind you. I wish I could afford to send my kids to Willey. It'll help your boy get into a good college."

"That's where it will end up costing me. He hasn't got the grades for an Ivy, but he'll get into a next-tier school."

"Those aren't cheap, either."

"No. I committed to paying half of his college. I'm months behind now. Meanwhile my ex thinks I'm getting rich off Polio."

"The rap guy."

"Right. Thing is, there really aren't any more checks coming."

He shook his head. "What you said the other night, I never thought about it like that, I just figured, you're a rock star, you're doing OK."

"I wish I was a rock star. I'm just some guy who plays in bars. And there isn't a whole lot left from a Rum House gig after I buy groceries and beer."

"I'll bring the six-pack next time," he said.

"I didn't mean-"

"I know you didn't. But we're kind of in the same boat. We gotta stick together, is all I'm saying. It's funny, you're in the same mess as the rest of us, even though you're famous."

"Like I said, I'm not really famous at all anymore."

"Whatever you say." Bottle empty, he stood. "Hey, I think I'll take you up on your offer, run back to my apartment and get some clean clothes and take a shower, if that's still cool. I probably got a couple of beers left in the fridge, too."

"Sounds good. Sorry again about your dad."

"Really, don't be. I think he secretly kind of liked your song. I mean, he hated it, but at the same time, it meant he was famous too, you know?"

He had his father's laugh.

TWENTY

Convertibles suck in the winter. The cold streamed in as my old Sunbird sped up the highway to Portsmouth, and the rattling heater couldn't keep up.

Zack and Kayla huddled together in the back, supposedly for warmth, while I chauffeured. The cat was out of the bag about me and Lily, so why not bring them along? I'd felt a weight leave my shoulders when I picked them up at the headmaster's house. They would serve as a buffer, not only between me and Lily but between me and my tendency to focus on the dark side of things.

Kayla had Lily's *Greatest Hits* on her iPhone but there was no way to connect it to the old Sunbird's stereo. I saved the day by digging one of Lily's nineties CDs out of the glove box.

"Isn't that your song she's singing, Mr. B?"

"Why yes it is, Kayla, thank you for noticing."

Lily's cover of "Pressing My Disadvantage" had paid for Zack's first year of Montessori school. Now he was almost grown.

The music and road noise kept me from hearing more than snatches of their conversation, but they sounded happy. "Shut up, asshole!" "You shut up, woman!" They laughed a lot, in a way that I liked.

I found parking on a side street with no meters and took the kids for pizza at a nearby hole in the wall that I assured them was legendary for its thin-crust pies. It was also the cheapest place I knew in Portsmouth. I wasn't the only guy in the place with money worries, to judge by the faces of the other customers as they eyed the economic headlines crawling across the bottom of the TV screen. Zack ate as much as me and Kayla combined.

The Music Hall opened as a live performance venue around 1900, converted to movies in the twenties, closed in disrepair in the eighties, and became a big civic rehab project in the nineties. Now it hosted Richard Thompson and Ladysmith Black Mambazo, Irish step dance and HD opera telecasts. But an annual fundraiser was still necessary to keep the lights on and the furnace running.

Lily did benefits all around the world whenever she could, for anti-nuke groups, women's shelters and other good causes. It was silly to think she'd chosen this one just because I was near.

She left three of her comps at the box office in my name and turned the rest back to the organizers, because they were selling out, even at a hundred dollars a seat. She never played venues this small anymore, so it was a big deal.

I never played venues this big anymore. There was no Venn diagram in which our careers overlapped.

The tickets got us into the pre-show VIP reception, where we found her holding court with a circle of admiring locals. They looked drab next to her red mane, low-cut purple ruffled blouse, black jeans and spike-heeled purple suede boots. She fussed with her bracelets to keep her hands busy. She'd stopped drinking before performances years ago, along with the cocaine.

"Bax! Glad you made it." She put a hand around my neck and pulled me in for a kiss. "And is this Zack? Holy shit, kid, you got big and handsome just like your dad. Gimme some sugar, young man."

Blushing, he complied, then introduced Kayla, who got a hug.

"It's an honor to meet you," Kayla said.

"Oh, honey, the pleasure's all mine. It takes a strong woman to put up with one of these McLean men."

"No kidding."

"They're good guys in the long run, don't get me wrong. It's just – you know."

"I know, right?"

Zack and I exchanged a look.

"Well, hey, you three, thanks for coming to the show. It's a good crowd here but it's nice to have some people in my corner."

"Thanks for getting us the tickets," Zack said.

"You're always welcome at my shows. Just call up and I'll make sure you and your girl here get in."

She asked them about their favorite musicians. Kayla insisted Lily was hers, and Zack talked up some rapper that I didn't know because he wasn't Polio.

A young man detached himself from a nearby conversation and approached, smiling at Lily. He was blue-eyed and square-jawed with mocha skin, and a photogenic amount of stubble. He wore his hair in a close-cropped fade and dressed all in black and grey. He looked at me with mild curiosity as he put an arm around Lily's waist.

"This is Manfred." She introduced us and even remembered Kayla's name. "Baxter's the old friend I was telling you about, the one that lives on the island."

"Pleased to meet you," he said with a slight German accent. I figured he'd try to crush my hand on the shake, but maybe Europeans don't do that sort of macho crap, or maybe he knew he had nothing to worry about. He seemed utterly relaxed.

"So what do you do, Manfred?"

"I race bikes."

"Motorcycles," Lily said. "He's world class. He's in movies, too."

He shrugged. "Sometimes I do a little stunt work."

"A little?" Lily said. "You did the whole chase scene in the Tom Cruise movie."

"Wow." Zack said. "You met him?"

"I taught him to do the stunts."

"But half the time that's you in the movie," Lily said.

"I am not supposed to say that."

"I have a song on the soundtrack," she told us. "We met at the premiere, and the rest is history."

She gave him a squeeze, and he smiled down at her. The Lily I knew might go to the premiere of a Tom Cruise movie if she had a song on the soundtrack, but she would sneak out after the lights went down and go to a blues bar. Maybe she had changed.

"The movies are a job," Manfred told us. "Racing is my passion."

"Why?" Kayla asked. "Isn't it just going around in a circle?"

Love that girl.

"These are mostly road courses, but I understand what you're asking. It's the speed. The purity of it. The movies are tedious, a hundred people waiting around to shoot five seconds of film, everything calculated to within an inch. In racing, it is just you and your bike and your competition. There are no retakes. No one to catch you if you fall."

"Manfred's mother is from Mali," Lily said. "She was one of the first African supermodels. She was on a Fela album cover."

I was impressed, but the kids had no idea who Fela was or why they should care.

"She doesn't model anymore," Manfred said. "Mostly she shops. My father's an economist for Daimler."

So, he was rich. Even if he wasn't dating Lily, I would have hated him a little.

"Now that we've all met," Lily said, "are you going to sing with me tonight, Bax?"

Before I could answer, Zack butted in with the kind of grin that made parents hate teenagers. "I bet he put his guitar in the trunk before he picked us up."

A narrow balcony wrapped around three sides of the hall. Our seats looked directly down on the stage and the Persian rug that Lily's crew had been hauling around the country for at least a quarter-century. I recognized a few of the roadies too. Headlining a tour meant an entire organization working on your behalf, a little rolling army. I missed that, and the money that came with it. People noticed when they dispersed to the wings, and there was a murmur of expectation. The lights went out, and the crowd cheered.

Lily came out by herself with an acoustic guitar and sat on a stool at center stage, in a white spotlight. "Good evening, Portsmouth! It's great to be here in this beautiful theater. Thanks for coming out. Since this is such an intimate little get-together, I thought I'd play a couple unplugged for you to start. Does that sound good?"

Of course it did.

Dylan's "Don't Think Twice (It's All Right)" is one of the saddest breakup songs ever, in part because it tries so hard to seem matter-of-fact. Lily sang the hell out of it. There wasn't another sound until the last note, when the crowd roared.

As the applause died, she shaded her eyes against the light. "Hey Bax, you out there?" I waved, she pointed, everyone looked. "That's my old friend Baxter McLean up there. He's written a bunch of great songs, and this is one of them."

Kayla elbowed me in the ribs at the first notes of "Pressing My Disadvantage." Again Lily held the crowd in the palm of her hand, getting laughs in all the right places, and the applause went on for a while. When she was out there alone, you could still see the brave high school girl who had started showing up at church coffee houses with her guitar, her voice telling everyone what she already knew somehow – that she was for real.

The stage was washed in color as Lily's band came on. All guys. She sang at lots of benefits for women's causes, but she never had a woman in her band. The bass player had been around since the beginning, a tall, skinny guy wearing a faded Stones t-shirt, bald now, with tumbleweeds of grey hair at the temples and little round glasses. He looked more like a high school teacher trying to be cool than the band's cocaine procurer, which he used to be. The burly keyboard player had left a blues band beloved by bikers to join Lily on the road. His ZZ Top beard had turned white, and he had a hard time squeezing his gut in behind his Hammond. The rhythm guitarist and drummer were new; they looked to be in their thirties, pros she'd picked up somewhere along the way.

"So, Portsmouth, you ready to get funky?"

Of course they were.

She alternated rockers and ballads, originals and covers, hits and deep tracks. Her singing voice didn't reach quite as high, but it was as rich and effortlessly emotional as ever. Kayla seemed to know all the words, singing along softly. Zack watched her more than the stage. Before I knew it, ninety minutes had passed and the crowd was on its feet, applauding wildly as she led the band offstage. They stomped their feet and clapped in rhythm, demanding an encore. The stage lights never went off.

A roadie with cigarette breath put his hand on my shoulder and whispered, "It's time."

I followed him over to an exit and down a narrow stairway, along a short corridor and up more steps to the backstage area. We stopped in the wings, just out of sight of the audience. The guitar tech nodded and said, "Long time." Then he hung the Berwyn around my neck, as familiar as if he was still doing it every night.

Lily was talking to the audience. "When we toured together, we always did a number during the encore. Since he's here tonight, I thought maybe we'd see if we can find that old magic. Bax, come on out."

I threaded my way between the amps and guitar racks until suddenly I was standing next to her in the bright haze of every color of spotlight.

"Hey, baby, how you been?" she said, as if she hadn't seen me an hour ago. She pecked me on the cheek, drawing scattered applause and a couple of whoops. "You ready?"

I nodded. I couldn't see much beyond the lights, only a few rapt front-row faces and the red EXIT signs in the corners. Probably that was for the best. It let me sink back into memory. I stood on that same Oriental rug, next to the same beautiful woman, holding the same guitar. Suddenly it was the eighties again, somewhere in Hotel California, and I could imagine the rest of the night quite vividly.

Mock. *Yeah.*

The lyric came easily, although someone had helpfully taped large-type printouts to the monitors in front of us just in case. After the *a cappella* intro, the band rolled in behind us. It went pretty much like the old days, although a discerning fan would have noticed that we both avoided one or two high notes. The song was over before I knew it, and the crowd stood and cheered. I recognized Zack's piercing whistle from the balcony. Lily kissed me on the lips this time, then I waved good night and got off stage.

I drained a beer from the bucket while Lily closed the show with her song from the Tom Cruise movie, a lachrymose *I'll-be-there-for-you* ballad written by a team of Hollywood hacks, given dignity only by her heartfelt performance. For complex reasons, it made me want to drink a lot, but when the kids appeared at my side, I remembered that I was their ride. I could have all the beer I wanted if I had Zack drive home, but that wasn't the paternal image I wanted to project.

"You were awesome, Dad."

"Pretty impressive, Mr. B."

"Thanks, guys."

The guitar tech handed me the Berwyn, already in its case. Admirers swarmed Lily when she came off, and I felt a squirmy urge to flee. But the kids insisted we wait and say goodbye. Before long she came over, Manfred in tow.

"I think we gave them their money's worth," she said.

"We did indeed."

"It was great to share a stage with you again."

"You too. And nice to meet you, Manfred."

"The same."

The whole conversation seemed painfully awkward, although maybe that was just me. Kayla saved the day, asking rapid-fire questions about what tuning Lily used on one song and what had inspired her to write another. Manfred and I listened, politely ignoring each other. We were gradually surrounded by a cadre of locals looking at their watches. Eventually one coughed discreetly and Lily smiled to herself.

"We're going to dinner with the theater board," she said. "You all want to come?"

Manfred looked unconcerned, but if I were him, I wouldn't want me along. And "everybody shove down three" was not what the board members would want to hear. Dinner with Lily was their reward for all their hard work. There was also the issue of how much dinner for three at some trendy Portsmouth bistro would cost. Maybe someone else was paying, but I didn't want to take the chance. Or maybe that was just how I explained it to myself. An after-show dinner with Lily might be one memory too many, one toke over the line for my heart.

"I've got to get these two back to school. They're not supposed to be out this late on a weeknight."

Lily didn't seem surprised or disappointed, but she said, "Aw, party pooper," before hugging the kids and then me. "I'll call you for breakfast."

And then she was striding off surrounded by board members who turned toward her like flowers toward the sun. Manfred raised a hand to me with a wry smile – he was learning what it meant to date a star – and sauntered after them.

"That was awesome," Kayla said. "Thank you so much for bringing us."

"Yeah, Dad, thanks."

"My pleasure. Let's go."

On the way back to Libertyport, no one said much. The kids rode in the back again. I tried to keep my eyes out of the rear view mirror. I was less successful in keeping my head out of the past.

We dropped Kayla at her dorm first. Zack got out with her, but only to jump in the front, and there was no goodnight kiss. The ways of today's youth baffled me, but he looked happy.

At my insistence, we waited until she was safely inside, then drove to the headmaster's house.

"Thanks, Dad, really, that was great."

"You're welcome, pal. Any time."

He reached over for a fist-bump, then jumped out and slammed the door. I watched until the front door closed behind him, and for a little bit after. Maybe I had done a few things right in this life.

I drove through town and across the marsh out to the island. None of my neighbors were awake when I got home, their houses dark and quiet. I carried a beer up to bed, toasting the lobster family on my way up the stairs. When the beer was gone, I turned out the light and settled back against the pillow.

After a moment, a car started in the yard below and moved quickly down the driveway. I hadn't heard any doors open or shut, so someone had been sitting in the dark watching when I came home. I jumped out of bed and went to the window just as the car turned onto Northern Boulevard.

There were no streetlights nearby, and its headlights were off, so I couldn't be certain. But even through the gloom, it sure looked like a long, black Eldorado.

TWENTY-ONE

I tried not to notice how cold it was in the beach house before dawn, or the burnt, bitter taste of Island Convenience coffee, or how the frigid salt air leaked in around the ragtop as I drove. My mother needed me, so I went. I crossed the frozen marsh as the sun rose over the island behind me, painting the sky pink and blue.

She bustled outside before I came to a full stop. I'd intended to go to the door and take her arm. She was never one to insist on special treatment, which was why this request for a ride worried me.

"Brisk this morning," she said, buckling her seatbelt.

"Are you going to tell me what this is about?"

"Not till I know."

I nodded, and neither one of us spoke again as I navigated through town. The usual characters were up and about, despite the chill. Shimmy Jimmy rode his bicycle through Dock Square, looking a bit panicked at how thoroughly he had been bundled up by his mother.

The medical group occupied part of a renovated brick factory on the river, five stories on either side of a central clock tower that had once signaled to hundreds of workers when it was time to come and go from their labors. We arrived just before seven, when the lab would open, but we weren't early enough. A handful of the elderly and infirm were already lined up in front of the glass doors with the stoic expressions of refugees. No doubt one or two of them had worked on the factory floor back in the day, forging silverware that they couldn't afford. An ambulance idled at the curb, vapor curling from the tailpipe.

My mother said, "Poor souls." But she looked tired and pale.

We waited in the car, listening to NPR news, until the nice lady in SpongeBob SquarePants scrubs unlocked the entrance. The line shuffled inside, and the ambulance crew popped out their stretchered patient and followed. When they'd all gone in, my mother opened her door and said, "Come on," the same way she did when I was fourteen, as if I was dawdling.

The lobby was blond wood and old magazines and hand-sanitizer dispensers, murmuring receptionists and the soft clatter of computer keyboards. Fox News played on a flat screen TV, the sound muted, the closed captions blaring outrage. Signs offered flu shots (*It's not too late!*) and sternly advised those afflicted with a cough to ask for a surgical mask.

"You can sit," my mother said.

She marched forward to join the patients filing through a rope maze like an airport ticket line. Even now, she looked healthier and younger than most of the folks ahead of her. One rolled an oxygen tank along with him. Others bore that awful pallor of late-stage cancer. Check in for departure, indeed.

I found a seat as far from the TV as possible and grabbed a *Newsweek* at random. An older guy sat down next to me with a groan and a sigh, playing his infirmities for comedy. I did my best to appear engrossed in an article about foreclosure ghost towns in suburban Las Vegas.

"Renal failure," he said.

"Excuse me?"

"End stage renal failure. My Betty. That's what she's here for. Get the latest bad news. Then it's upstairs for dialysis." He had a red face, bulbous nose, lively eyes.

"I'm sorry."

"Not your fault. We're old, is all. Could have just as easily been me." He seemed good-humored about it, but he was fronting.

"How long have you two been married?"

"We're not, actually. Betty and I shacked up ten years ago, after her Frank kicked the bucket. Miserable prick *he* was. We both wanted to marry her right out of trade school, but he got the good job at GE in Lynn, so she chose him. I got the last laugh."

"Wow." I needed more coffee.

"No big deal. It was only fifty-two years I waited."

He'd used the line before, but I did my best to look surprised. "You waited all that time?"

"I didn't just sit around. I'm a sap, but I'm not dead. I was married twice, widowed twice." He patted the dark, straight hair on top of his head, which didn't match his wispy grey sideburns. "Good gals, both of them, but it was always Betty I wanted."

"Well, I hope she gets good news in there."

"There really isn't any good news to get, unless the space aliens bring down some magic cure, and even then those insurance pricks would probably find some way that she's not eligible."

"True enough."

"I'm Roger."

"Baxter."

"Nice to meet you. So you're kind of a young fella, what are you doing here?"

"It's my mother."

"What's she got?"

"That's what we're here to find out."

Under normal circumstances, that would have been a conversation ender. I returned to my magazine. But Roger really needed to talk. He reminded me of Ronnie in that regard.

"You live in town?" he said.

"I'm out on the island right now."

"The island is great. When I was a kid, my family had a cottage out there. Me and the first wife lived in it for a while. Got it all winterized and everything. This was back in the seventies, before it got all built up out there. Back when it was wells and septic."

"How did that work?"

"Pretty good," he said. "Better than what you folks are stuck with out there now, anyway. Ain't saying much."

"My part of the island, everything's still working."

"You're lucky, then."

"My friends come over to use the can, take a shower, get something out of the vending machine. I'm basically running a highway rest stop."

He laughed, and I wondered if there was a song in the water situation. What rhymes with "septic?"

"The island's quite a place," he said, pausing to blow his nose into a white hankerchief. "We used to have some good times out there, let me tell you."

"I bet."

"When I was a kid, we used to hunt and fish in what they call the refuge now. Twelve or thirteen years old, go out there with a .22 and shoot rabbits or squirrels, bring 'em home for dinner. Fished all the time, too. Mackerel, cod, big stripers practically jumping onto the beach."

"Sounds like paradise."

"Maybe. But that was the Depression, we needed the protein. Even after the war, money was scarce for most people in town, even some of the people in the big houses on High Street. Half the factories closed. Kids had to pitch in, help put food on the table."

I squinted at him. "How old are you?"

He puffed up slightly. "I'll be eighty-nine next month."

"You're kidding."

"Pretty good for an antique, huh?"

"Really. What happened to your family's cottage?"

"Oh, I sold it in the eighties. Prices seemed so high then. Could have gotten five times as much today. But hindsight is twenty-twenty, right?"

I could only nod.

"We live in the elderly housing now," he said. "Where's your place out there?"

"I'm just renting, actually." I told him where.

"We were not far away, over on the basin side, facing town. No beach, but nice sunsets."

I tried to slide it in without him noticing. "My parents had a friend out there in the Seventies, on Lilac."

"I knew people on Lilac. You had your Williamses there. Jimmy was a friend of mine. And then you had the Kirkmans and their damn dogs."

"Dalmatians, right?" Thank you, Ronnie.

"That's right. I don't know how many kids they bit, but the cops never did nothing because Kirkman was a big deal with City Hall."

"And there was a guy in the last cottage, kinda rough-looking, kept to himself. I forget his name."

Roger raised his chin, looked at the TV for the first time. "You don't know?"

"Know what?"

He glanced sideways at me, then back at the TV. "I don't know if I should to talk about that."

My pulse quickened. "It was a long time ago."

Roger rubbed his chin, thinking. "He told me not to say nothing."

"You talked to him?"

A nod. "He kept himself pretty aloof. He had for good reason. But one day, must have been the summer of seventy-nine or eighty, one of those Dalmatians was biting the hell out of a kid, and he chased it off with a two-by-four. Saved the kid's life, if you ask me. Kirkman got all high and mighty as usual, said the dog was just defending itself, the kid must have done something to provoke it. And the guy just looked at Kirkman and told him to keep the dogs tied up or the next time he'd use his thirty-eight."

He laughed. "Kirkman took the dog and went stomping back in his house. Biggest place on the street, but not nice enough for those yuppies who bought it last year. They tore it down and built that mansion that's there now, up on pilings. Looks like they can't afford to finish it though. Pride goeth before a fall."

"What did the guy say after he chased off the dog?"

"Not much. I figured somebody ought to thank him for standing up to Kirkman, so I told him I was going to write a letter to the editor about it."

"What did he say?"

Roger looked around again for eavesdroppers. "He beckoned me over by his cottage. He looked like he was just moving us into the shade, you know, 'cause it was a hot day. But really he wanted to talk where nobody could hear." He paused for dramatic effect. "He said, 'You can't tell nobody what I did, not the cops or nobody. You can tell people it was you that saved the kid, if you want.' I told him I wasn't taking credit for something he did, and he said he'd prefer it that way.

And I said, 'Are you on the lam or something?' You know, just joking. And that's when he told me."

He sat back and folded his arms across his chest. He was going to make me ask.

"Told you what?"

"That he was in witness protection."

Well.

Well.

That explained why he'd pulled a gun when my father came through the door without knocking on a cold winter's night.

"You said this was 1980?"

"Give or take a year, yeah."

"So he lived out there for a while."

"Couple of years, anyway. We left him alone like he wanted, till that day with the dog. He didn't exactly stand out. The island was a good place if you wanted to disappear back then. There was lots of transients, lots of weird people living there in the seventies. Still is today, you ask me. No offense."

"None taken. He tell you why he was in witness protection?"

"Not exactly. But he made clear the bad guys would have come for him if they knew where he was. He said his life might depend on me keeping my mouth shut. So I never told nobody. People were talking about calling the cops and making trouble for Kirkman over the dog, but I talked 'em out of it. Kept the whole thing off the radar like he wanted."

"He was right to trust you."

"I kept that secret a long time, except for telling Betty. Don't tell me your ATM code, though, or I'll spill it to the next guy I meet in the waiting room." Chuckle.

"He ever tell you his name?"

"Not his real name. His cover name was Edward Martin. Pretty John Doe, huh? That was the name people around the island knew him by, though not many even knew that."

"And he never told you his story?"

"No, but he must have ratted out some guys. Informed on them,

I mean. He kind of implied it was a big deal, but not around here. I always wondered, you know. Like maybe he was some famous criminal. You never know what your neighbors are up to, am I right?"

"Not on the island, anyway."

A snort. "You got that right."

"Do you know what happened to him?"

"No, me and the wife split up and sold our place not long after that. I still miss it. Can't afford nothing out there now. I'd like to take Betty out there in the summer, but even a week's rental is too damn much." He stood up abruptly. "Here's my girl."

Betty emerged from the end of the corridor where the nurses worked in little curtained cubicles. She looked very old and very tired, and her color was all wrong. She glanced around as if she didn't know where she was, until she saw him waving and relaxed.

"I've got to get her upstairs to her doctor," he said, beaming to see her. "Pleasure talking to you."

"You too. Have a good day, Roger."

"Hey, hush-hush on the witness protection stuff, OK? You never know when something will come back to bite you."

"No problem. Good luck to you both."

"Same to your mom, whatever it turns out to be."

I looked for her, but she must have finished checking in and been taken to the lab while I was pumping Roger for information. Something else to feel guilty about.

TWENTY-TWO

Heads turned in Raging Rosie's when Manfred swung a U-turn across Northern Boulevard and parked on the sandy shoulder out front. In summer, the canary-yellow Porsche Cayenne with New York plates wouldn't have attracted a second look. But this was the dead of winter, and any unfamiliar car on the island was an object of curiosity, never mind one this flashy.

A murmur went through the crowded dining room when Manfred and Lily started up the walk. A few of the lunchtime regulars turned and looked at me. Maybe they knew who I was, or maybe it was just that I was the only person sitting alone. When the door opened, though, everyone looked at their food, pretending not to notice the wealthy strangers, the star in their midst.

Manfred wore the orange puffy coat that had been wrapped around Lily's shoulders on the patio at Tru. She was draped in her usual rock star glad rags. She spotted me first and led the way to the table.

"How did you find this place?" she said.

"It's kind of an institution. And I can walk."

"I like it. It reminds me of New Orleans."

Manfred picked up a menu. "Breakfast all day, that's fantastic." It was almost one in the afternoon, but they were on rock star time.

Raging Rosie's started as a greasy spoon that opened before sunrise for fishermen and working stiffs. As the island changed, it had gradually acquired a funkier, more beach-centric personality. The owners painted everything turquoise, yellow and pink, even the furniture. They collected kitschy salt-and-pepper shakers, filled shelves with driftwood and shells, and covered the bathroom walls with snapshots of people wearing Raging Rosie's t-shirts all over the world, from Fenway Park to the Great Wall of China.

"I'm surprised it's so busy," Lily said. "It seems so quiet out here."

"The food is really good. And this is the only place to get breakfast or lunch on the island, unless you get HoHos from the convenience store."

"I went in there for cigarettes. How long has that place been open? The guy who runs it must be a hundred years old."

"And that's Hank *Junior.*"

The diners around us took sideways glances and sneak peeks. Women trying to play it cool but not quite able, not with a bona fide celebrity in the house. Lily seemed not to notice. Manfred got more attention anyway.

"You want something to eat?"

"Just coffee is fine." She hadn't even opened her menu. She never did.

"The omelets are good."

"I'll have a bite of yours."

"That's what you always say."

She smiled, shrugged, both of us remembering.

"The Hungry Man Special, this is for me," Manfred said, finally looking up from the menu.

He wasn't stupid, just uninterested in me or the part of Lily's past that I represented. The waitress was one of Davey's great nieces, a sturdy girl wearing a faux-vintage Lynyrd Skynyrd t-shirt. When he handed her his menu and said, "Thank you," with his slight German accent and the tiniest of smiles, she grinned, blushing wildly, and ran to the kitchen. He didn't react or maybe didn't notice. He took out his iPhone and began to scroll through his emails.

Lily rolled her eyes.

"He does look young," I said.

"He's not as young as you were. But then, none of us are. Say, I forgot to ask you before, how's Sol?"

"Sol passed away."

She teared up in an instant. "You're kidding."

"I wish I was."

Sol Greenspan was the only agent I ever had. He came up in the Cambridge folk scene in the fifties and had made and lost a couple of millions by the time he picked a college kid's demo tape out of the mail and heard something he liked. He changed my life.

"How did I not hear about this? When? What happened?"

"A stroke, about six months ago."

"That's awful."

"At least it was quick." I talked past the lump in my throat. "He was eighty. He drank, he smoked."

"He was a character," Lily said. "There aren't many of them left in this business."

"I didn't know he ever represented you."

"He didn't, but I saw him around a lot. The first time I met him, I must have been twenty. He'd booked Buddy and Junior into some club in the Back Bay." That would be her friends Buddy Guy and Junior Wells. "This was before you and I met. Seventy-nine or eighty, late disco era. Everything was synths and drum machines, no live musicians. Those blues guys couldn't get arrested then, except on the college circuit. They were touring acoustic, as a duo, playing real deep country blues. And he brought them into this place with mirror balls and brass railings. I don't know if he screwed up or did it on purpose. We walked in there, and they were like, what the hell is this? But Sol made the owner turn off the strobes and put chairs on the dance floor. Somehow he got three hundred people to show up for that gig. He was a sweetheart."

"He was that."

"I hope he was happy."

"Actually, he was. He believed he made the whole Polio deal happen for me."

"Nice."

Our omelets came, mine with bacon and toast, Manfred's with ham *and* sausage plus a stack of blueberry pancakes on a separate plate garnished with an orange slice. The waitress really liked him.

Lily stuck with coffee. "So who's handling you now?"

"Um, nobody. I haven't been gigging at all the last few months, actually, except for one night a month at my friend's bar in town."

Lily had a way of crinkling her brow when she was disappointed. "You ought to be making hay while the sun shines."

"How is the sun shining on me?"

"If you had a manager, they'd be wearing out the Polio thing. 'As heard on the #1 urban hit.' You could be busy."

"It's kind of a tough crossover, don't you think? AM Gold folksinger to Hip Hop Nation?"

"Well, you're not going to get more popular by hiding away out here."

"I'm not hiding, I'm just not chasing it." Putting myself out there meant being reminded of just how little of my popularity remained.

"If you're waiting for the world to come to you, you're going to be waiting a long time. You've got to put yourself out there."

"I'm doing fine. If I'd known how much getting sampled could pay, I would have done it a long time ago."

Lily saw right through that lie. "The checks are going to stop sooner rather than later. And then you'll wish you'd listened to me."

"Maybe I will."

"I could talk to my people, they'd rep you if I ask."

"Thanks, but I'm good."

We fell silent. She sipped her coffee. I ate.

Manfred raised his head from his plate and said, "This place is fantastic."

"I'm glad you like it, honey," Lily said.

He smiled at her and went back to eating. A nearby table of grandmas in appliquéd sweatshirts watched him as if he were a meal and they were starving.

"How's Tru treating you?"

"Well enough, considering it's not exactly the high season," Lily said. "Last night we made a fire. It was cozy."

"How long are you staying?"

"Our luggage is already in the car. Boston tonight, then Providence, New Haven and I think New Jersey. ConcertSquad routed me around New York this time. If I asked them, they'd have a good reason. But I've stopped asking. I trust them, and this is me talking. They're the best there is for people like you and me. They actually care."

"ConcertSquad?"

"My tour management. Seriously, they'll take you on if I want them to."

"I thought you said they knew what they were doing."

"I'm serious, Bax. You could open some shows for me. It would be just like the old days."

"Not *just* like the old days."

If Manfred was listening, I hoped the reference would go over his head, and apparently it did.

"I've got a run of theater shows coming up in a month," Lily said. "Baltimore down the coast to Florida. You could miss the end of winter, see some palm trees."

"I don't know." But I knew exactly what it would be like to tour with her, memories tugging at me every time she turned my way.

"You'd make some money, too. You know I'm always fair to my openers."

"They're working on my house, and I've got Zack every other weekend." It sounded lame even to my own ears.

"Fly him down. Tell him it's spring break. Bring his girl if you want. I liked her."

"I'll think about it."

"It would be good for you. And you must have some new songs. You were always writing, and there's not much in the way of distractions on this island."

"You'd be surprised."

"You can't tell me you haven't written something funny about getting sampled by Polio."

I'd thought about it, but that was all. Before I had to answer, Manfred pushed his empty plates away and sat back with a satisfied sigh. Lily said, "We should get going."

I reached for my wallet and Lily shook her head. "This is on ConcertSquad."

"Whatever. Thanks."

"Thank me by thinking about what I said."

I wondered if their visit to Plover Island was planned so she could give me this pep talk. Manfred waved for the check, gold card already in hand.

"It was nice to meet you," he said when they stood up to go. We shook hands, and he turned away to give us a moment. An annoyingly nice guy.

She kissed me, tasting of cigarettes and coffee, and held on. "I'll have them email you the dates for those shows. Just take a look."

I nodded, reluctantly, and she released me from her embrace. She followed Manfred across the dining room, weaving through the tables, not looking back. She'd always been restless, never settling down, always headed *further on up the road.* I had been too young to understand then. Knowing now didn't help. Still, I savored the ache as I watched her go.

They were at the door when the waitress ran over and handed them Raging Rosie's t-shirts. No one had ever given me one. They thanked her and posed for a picture, then got in the Porsche and drove away.

TWENTY-THREE

"A yellow Porsche. *Yellow*."

"That's rough."

"I had a hit record. Where's my fucking Porsche?"

"I hear you, buddy."

The Rum House bar was quiet. I sat in my usual spot, on the last stool near the windows, working on a pint of Ipswich Winter Ale. Davey leaned back against the beer cooler, keeping me company with a short one.

"I bet Polio has a Porsche. Hell, he probably has five of them."

"You'll get one someday. Hey, how's the house project coming?"

"Nice change of subject."

"You're welcome."

"It's coming. I don't know where I'm going to get the money to give him a check this week like he wants, much less pay the balance when he's done."

The harbor outside the windows was as quiet as the bar. The floats had all been taken out of the water before Thanksgiving and stacked in the parking lot. The only boats in sight were a couple of working draggers tied up to the bulkhead.

"You should be rolling in it after your big hit with Eczema, shouldn't you?"

"*Polio*."

"Whatever. That rap crap gives me a rash. Come in here on a Friday night, and you got drunk white chicks putting it on the jukebox and shouting along with the lyrics, the N word and everything. Drives everybody else out. Not your fault, of course."

"Gee, thanks."

"How much are you short?"

"If he stuck to the original estimate, maybe ten or fifteen grand. But now there's all this stuff with the roof. I figure I'm thirty grand in the hole. But it could be fifty, the way Billy's going."

"Can you get a second mortgage or something?"

"I'm a folksinger, not exactly the world's greatest credit risk. And with the economy the way it is, the only way you can borrow money is if you have money. That's what the nice lady at the bank told me, anyway."

"That sucks."

"It does. Hey, you knew some guys back in the day, right?"

"What guys?"

"Mob guys, like the Argentos."

When he came back from Vietnam, Davey worked the lobster boat he had inherited from his father and supplemented his income running bales of weed from mother ships offshore to secluded docks upriver. His employers were not the winking pirates of Jimmy Buffett songs but the famously humorless first family of organized crime on the North Shore. That was a long time ago, but he still got careful when the name came up.

"You're not thinking of going to a loan shark, are you?"

"No, nothing like that. Well, not yet, anyway."

"Then why are you asking?"

"I'm trying to find out about a guy, I think he was connected."

"Not another one of your curiosity-killed-the-cat deals."

"Not at all. This is from back in the day." I explained about the giant snowball, my father, and the man with the gun. "His place is just a couple of blocks from the one I'm renting. So I went over to see if he was still there."

"Of course you did. Was he there?"

"No."

"Of course he wasn't. The island then, nobody stuck around unless they had a family place."

"His situation was a little different. He was in the witness protection program."

"No kidding?"

"That's what I heard this morning. But somebody else lives there now."

"Do they know about him?"

"Not that the guy would tell me. He was kind of a prick. I'm not sure what to do next. I thought maybe one of your old, uh, connections might know something."

"From thirty years ago?"

"That's why I figured they'd be willing to talk."

"As far as I know, they never went to the island."

"Somehow I imagined them signaling you from the beach."

Davey snorted. "You got quite the imagination. This wasn't exactly the French Resistance. I'd motor out, pull alongside whatever old rustbucket the Jamaicans were using, some trawler with no running lights. I'd shout the password to the guy on deck, then we'd do a quick handover and get the hell out of there."

"What happened if you forgot the password?"

"Probably nothing. It wasn't big business like today, with the cartels and everything. But he usually had a gun. I suppose it could have gotten ugly."

"And you took the stuff upriver?"

"Not always. One time we offloaded right at the boat ramp in the state park on the Seabury side. Somebody must have paid off Ranger Rick. It was offseason, no campers, couple of guys backed up a box truck. That was the easiest. But usually we'd go to some rickety little dock in the marsh or up as far as Haverhill. This river used to be a lot more what I'd call work-oriented than it is now."

"You miss it?"

"Working the boat? Hell no. It was a ball-buster, whether you're talking lobsters or weed. But I do miss being out on the water sometimes. It was beautiful out there, and there weren't any beer salesmen or health inspectors or whiny goddamn Yelp reviewers."

"And you made a lot of money."

"Sometimes we did, and sometimes we didn't. That's why the extra cash came in handy. It would have taken me ten years to save up to buy this place without it."

"Why'd you stop?"

"I had enough money."

"Usually you tell me there's no such thing."

"Truth? Argentos wanted to start bringing in coke. Smaller packages, a lot more money. Weed was one thing, but I didn't want anything to do with coke. More guns, lots more paranoia, people getting ripped off and shot. Plus a lot more jail time if you got caught. So I told Carmine I was out."

"He was fine with that?"

He laughed. "Hell no. He knew I was buying this place, and he said, 'Fine, you're out, but I own thirty percent of the bar.' Which I told him, no way. I was young and full of piss and vinegar, I'd seen some shit in Nam and I figured he couldn't do worse. Which was stupid. I'm lucky he didn't have me clipped. But Carmine always liked me, I think because his kids were all screw-ups one way or another. I'd served. I was smart and worked hard, and he could trust me. So instead of having me clipped, he made me a deal. I'd bring in one last load for free and then I was done."

"Sounds fair."

"You don't know the crafty old prick. It turned out to be a double load, I had to make two trips, playing hide-and-fucking-seek with the Coast Guard in the fog all night. I would have made ten grand. Instead I got nothing but half a bale I stole. I figured it was only fair. At least I was out. But I could never go to him and ask for favors after that."

"Do you think he would have known about this guy?"

"If Carmine Argento had known about a rat hiding out here, he would have welded him in a barrel and dropped him in the ocean. Or more likely left him in a pool of blood somewhere public, as a message to all the other rats out there."

"Would he have been looking?"

"Depends where this guy was from. Witness protection, he was probably from out of the area. The feds don't want him running into somebody he knows at McDonald's. They'd want to keep him within a day's drive of whatever courthouse he was testifying at. So he was probably from New York or Philly or someplace. If one of Carmine's guys tripped over him, they would have called Providence, Providence would have called New York, and word would have come back what they wanted done. Argentos would have taken him out just as a favor to the Five Families. But I never heard about anything like that."

"Is there any other way I could find out who this guy was? Maybe by where he was living? Could I look it up at City Hall or something?"

Davey shook his head. "Most of the winter rentals out there were off the books then anyway. Most guys paid in cash, and nobody was reporting it to the IRS. That dough got a lot of people through some tough winters. At the least, they used it to fix up their cottages. There's probably still people who've got shoeboxes full of cash. I bet Ronnie doesn't report everything now."

"Oh well."

"Did you ask him about the guy?"

"He remembers him, but it's a little hazy. All I know is the guy's cover name, Edward Martin. It's not like I got a real name and address."

"If it was witness protection, you never will." Davey shrugged. "Why do you care so much, anyway?"

"I don't know exactly. But he could have killed me and my dad if he wanted to, and he didn't."

"You going to thank him? Is that why you're doing this, so you can send him roses and a card?"

"Maybe."

"Guy like that, he'd probably prefer one of them edible bouquets."

TWENTY-FOUR

Abigail pronounced the C-word with the ostentatious enunciation of a *Masterpiece Theatre* dowager.

"You'll have to come to my *condominium* if you insist on seeing me today. I'm feeling rather poorly."

Her tone made clear that my presence would be a horrible imposition. I pressed the button in the foyer of her building twenty minutes later.

"Yes?" Her annoyance came through even on the tinny speaker.

"It's Baxter."

A weary sigh came from the speaker, and the door to the elevator lobby buzzed open.

I'd taken high school English with Miss Marks, as I knew her then. Her sincere determination to impart to her students a rigorous understanding of grammar and literature came accompanied by a withering and strangely off-color wit. There were classmates of mine who, when they saw me today, still said, "Hold it like it hangs!" and laughed uproariously.

She also told us once that we should steal a million dollars if we had the opportunity, but anything less wasn't worth it.

Retired from teaching, Abigail debuted LibertyportGossip.com, a blog relentlessly highlighting the faux pas of our elected officials and other local notables, including myself. She made things personal there, too, enough that she'd been conked on the head by one errant local citizen and run over by another in his Prius. She recuperated from her injuries on Plover Island, where Wankum and I helped rescue her when her borrowed cottage was swept into the sea by a storm. She may have breathed a thank-you at first, but once she got her wits about her, she loudly blamed us for having "stranded" her there in the first place.

She was a piece of work.

Now past seventy, she had decided to run for city council. An at-large seat had opened suddenly, due to an embezzlement scandal at the peewee hockey snack bar, and she had gathered enough signatures to put her on the ballot for the special election. If she won, council meetings would be a lot more entertaining. Audiences for the local public access telecasts would soar into the double digits.

The building was a renovated shoe factory, where her parents had once scratched out a living on the shop floor. Her condo was on the third floor. She answered my knock instantly, as if she'd been waiting behind the door. "Come in, Mr. McLean, if you must."

She always addressed me the same way she had in class, as if to render me fifteen again and at her mercy. She turned and left me to follow her down the hall. She wore a purple paisley velour blouse, green corduroys, L.L. Bean slippers, a black crocheted tam and a tan fleece shawl. She still limped slightly from her confrontation with the Prius, but it was going to take more than an old man in an electric car to keep Abigail down.

"Thanks for seeing me."

"Quite."

Her unit had the exposed brick and hardwood floors legally required in all gentrified former factory buildings in the Commonwealth of Massachusetts. The walls were hung with Impressionist prints from the Boston museums. She led me to the dining room and an austere wooden table and chairs. Cushions were for sissies. One end of the table held a laptop surrounded by heaps of town documents and stacks of campaign brochures.

"So you're here to help with my campaign, are you?"

"Not exactly."

She blinked, a trifle annoyed. With her bug eyes and beaky nose, it had the quality of a moment from a nature documentary. "I thought you said you were. That's why I made room for you on my schedule. And Fridays are busy."

I thought she was under the weather and not planning to see anyone, but I let it go.

"I said it had to do with your campaign, not that I wanted to volunteer."

"Imprecision in speech was always a problem of yours, as I recall. Perhaps you would have had another successful LP if you managed to master the art of word usage as I advised. But that's water over the bridge. I'm very busy, so tell me exactly why you *are* here, then."

"Well, you have the water issue on the island in your platform."

"Yes, City Hall has been utterly incompetent on that project from the beginning, and now the people of Plover Island are paying the price."

"A lot of people in town were against that project from the beginning."

"That's true, and I was one of them. A ridiculous idea, providing permanent infrastructure to that shabby sandbar. It will all wash away someday. As you may remember, I have personal experience with the temporary nature of human habitation on the island."

"I don't think you'll be mentioning any of that in your campaign, though. It would sort of dampen the islanders' enthusiasm for your candidacy, wouldn't it?"

"You may be correct."

"So you'll be campaigning against the water mess when you're on the island, but what are you going to say back here in town? Most people here think the island never should have gotten water and sewer in the first place."

"There are a variety of issues with the way the tax levy is calculated-"

"Not exactly scintillating stuff."

"And of course there is the ever-popular issue of the leash law and the unhealthy preponderance of dog waste."

"On which you will inevitably tick off half of the town's population – either the dog people or the non-dog people – once you take a clear position."

"You've made your point, Mr. McLean. There is no single issue that offers as clear an opportunity to my campaign here in town as the water calamity does on Plover Island."

"What if there was?"

She looked at me for a moment, gauging the chances that I would tell her something useful. "Go on."

"Crime concerns everyone, correct?"

"That's true, but there's rather little of it in Libertyport, except for the lunatic affairs you seem to involve yourself in with some regularity."

"The police department is the single largest item in the city budget after the schools, isn't it?"

"It is."

"What if I were to tell you that there is a scandalous, ongoing criminal operation in our town, and that the police department is aware of it, but they're not doing anything."

She squinted at me. "If true, that would offer certain opportunities. What kind of criminal operation is this? I have had my fill of violence in recent years." This last came close to an admission of weakness.

"The kind generally referred to as victimless crime."

"Be more specific."

"It involves two consenting adults."

"A brothel?" She pronounced it like chicken broth.

I nodded. "Suppose I were to tell you the location and explain why the police have been holding back. Would you do something about it?"

She gazed into the distance for a moment, gears turning. "It would take a few days to organize, but I could make a protest in front of such an operation. And of course I would notify the media."

"That would get you some votes, don't you think? And you'd force them to close the place down."

"Yes, it would quite likely shame the constabulary into action. But what is your game, Mr. McLean? In my experience you are what I will charitably describe as a Libertarian, not inclined to interfere in the moral affairs of others. I hardly imagine you rushing to close down such an operation. You might even patronize it yourself."

I let this go.

"I have my reasons. I think this is a win-win situation for us."

"How I abhor that cliché."

Talking to Abigail was a grueling obstacle course, belly-crawling through mud, under barbed wire, climbing over fences and up ropes in the southern heat, all while being verbally abused by an angry drill sergeant. You just had to suck it up and keep going.

"You need votes. And I have a friend who wants this operation put out of business."

"I must insist on knowing why."

"He's a neighbor of this ... brothel. And it's becoming a real problem. For one thing, customers keep knocking on his door by mistake."

"That must be charming. I feel for your friend. I suppose you went to the police first. Detective Wankum, no doubt."

"You'll have to promise to leave him out of this. It's not his fault. The whole department knows about this place, but they're not allowed to do anything. It's politics."

Abigail sat back to think. Her cheeks were flushed, and she no longer looked ill.

"I have always tried to be a fearless truth-teller. Taking on law enforcement won't be easy or pleasant. And I am not sure how much benefit I'll get from it at the voting booth. But I will do it for your friend."

There was hardly a word of truth in her speech – she would love taking on the police, and she would only do it if she was sure it would help her campaign. But phony selflessness was good enough.

"Thank you so much, Abigail."

"One thing, Mr. McLean. If I help you with this, I'll need you to do something for me."

Damn. I'd forgotten about that.

TWENTY-FIVE

A cold wind sliced across the bay when I set out for poker. I had the beach all to myself. Surf ran hissing in on the sand, only the foam visible in the dark.

The chill and the solitude inspired a strange, bittersweet happiness in me that may be peculiar to New Englanders. We love nature and the outdoors as much as Californians, but we lack their facility for guilt-free enjoyment. We feel better when we have obstacles to overcome. I was alone in a beautiful place, sure, but having to walk a mile into that wind was what made it just about perfect. By the time I climbed the aluminum ramp to Ventana's deck, my cheeks hurt and my nose was frozen, but I was sorry that the hike was over.

The players nodded or said hey without interrupting their attack on the drinks and snacks. It was my third week in the game, so I figured it was OK to come empty-handed. I got a beer from the fridge. Nibbled pepperoni. We settled at the table, but no one spoke as Ronnie peeled the cellophane off a new deck. The sacred ceremony. I drank some beer.

When I lowered the bottle, they were all looking at me. Even Ronnie was quiet for once.

"What?"

"You've been holding out on us," Ventana said.

I felt a tickle of adrenaline, the beginning of the fight or flight reflex. "What are you talking about?"

"Well, we all knew you were this washed-up musician."

"Ouch."

"Am I wrong?"

"No."

"So we knew that. But apparently we didn't know everything. Donnie, if you please."

Donnie pointed a remote control. A familiar melody came from the stereo across the room, then Lily's voice. The guys around the table all smiled locker-room smiles. They couldn't have known how the song hit me. But as she sang "Don't Think Twice, It's All Right," sweet and low and sad, her voice took hold of them too, and the looks on their faces became less leering and more reflective. All except Quinn, who didn't seem to pay attention to any of it, staring into his beer as if waiting for this crap to be over.

As Lily rounded into the second verse, Ronnie began tossing cards across the green felt, and the spell was broken.

"You didn't tell us you were doing a gorgeous rock superstar," Ventana said. "We want details. The Portsmouth paper had a picture of you two smooching backstage."

"She's a friend, that's all."

"And she stayed at Tru. Or did she?"

"She did."

"We even hear you two had breakfast at Rosie's the morning after."

Smirks all around.

"It's not like that. There were three of us at Rosie's, actually, me and Lily and her new boyfriend. And it was lunch."

"Sure it was," Chris said, to laughter all around.

Sigh. I had to give them something.

"I went out with her for a while, but it was a long time ago."

I looked at my cards while they gave me the *oh-ho-ho*. My up card was a queen, but I had a pair of aces in the hole, the best hand I'd ever drawn at this table. I slid what I thought was a modest bet into the pot. Quinn folded immediately. It was like he could read minds. No one else appeared alarmed, though. They were too distracted by my history with Lily.

"How long ago was this?" Ronnie.

"Mid-eighties, when I had my hit."

"Didn't she have a lot of drug problems then?"

"That was mostly after."

"So losing you drove her to drugs?" Chris asked.

"I don't think there was a connection."

"You ever play with her?" Donnie asked, raising.

"I opened for her a bunch of times, and sometimes we'd sing together."

"She has a beautiful voice," Ronnie said.

"We're just friends now. Have been for twenty-plus years." I re-raised. I kept nudging up the pot, and, except for Quinn, they kept not noticing.

"So you really *were* a big deal," Chris said. "I never knew whether to believe Ronnie or not."

"You're too young. Baxter owned the top forty back around 'eighty-two."

"Long time ago," Quinn said impatiently.

"Can we talk about something else?" It was the only thing Quinn and I agreed on.

"How about the water situation?" Donnie said. "I am really getting sick of waiting for the town to do something."

"I talked to the mayor," Ventana said. "He just said the same thing the water commissioner said last week, which is that they're working on it."

"They're always working on it," Chris said. "I'd like to see them finish."

"We all would. It's egregious."

Ronnie sent the last hole cards around. I barely dared to look. It was another ace, my karmic reward for enduring the conversation about Lily.

"There's a crew digging on my street right now," Chris said, throwing in a generous raise without much thought. I re-raised him, but he was too outraged to sense danger. "It's like whack-a-mole."

"They're collecting plenty of overtime," Donnie said, calling. "Hell, it's probably double-time for nights."

"Our tax dollars at work."

"Right! But I still don't have water half the time. There's supposed to be a warm-up early next week, maybe it will thaw out the pipes so I can actually use my own shower."

"It's not the pipes, it's the bolts," Ronnie said, calling. "They freeze, and then when it thaws they break, and there's a leak."

"Maybe Baxter could write a song about it."

"Yeah, Bax, you should write a little ditty about the way the island always gets screwed. You'd have another hit record."

Little ditty? "I don't think so."

"Your loss." Chris turned over his cards. "Two pair, queens over jacks."

"Kings and tens," Ventana said triumphantly, leaning forward to gather the pot.

I stopped him and flipped my cards over.

"Great Caesar's ghost," he said.

"Pay more attention to the game," Quinn said.

While Chris shuffled for the next hand, I asked, "Any of you ever hear of a guy named Edward Martin living on the island?"

Head shakes all around. "Friend of yours?"

"He was the guy I was trying to find when I went over to Lilac Lane. I just found out his name from this old-timer."

"He lived near Phil?" Ventana asked.

"Right across the street. I was only there the once, but I thought it was funny I ended up living so close. So I thought I'd see if he was still there."

"And instead you met Mel Frost." Ventana folded.

"Those things on his face, they're godawful," Chris said.

"His personality is less than lovely as well."

"I told Baxter about the Welcome Wagon incident," Ronnie said.

"One bottle of wine, get over it."

"You all seem to have a pretty strong opinion of Frost. How do you know him?"

Shrugs. "It's a small island," Ventana said. "We run into him at Island Convenience and such."

"He'd give me the skunk eye whenever I went over to visit Phil," Donnie said.

"He does *not* like strangers."

"Who was this old-timer you talked to?" Ronnie wheezed.

I decided to keep Roger out of it. "I don't know. I ran into him at the doctor's office the other day. We started talking in the waiting room, and it turned out he lived here for years, across the Boulevard. He knew all the same stories you did, about the Dalmatians and whatever. And he knew Martin's name. But he didn't know what happened to him."

"I know a lot of old-timers on the island," Ventana said. "I can ask around."

"Me too," Ronnie said.

"That would be great."

Once again, Quinn and Ventana took the lion's share of the hands. Most of the money my aces had won trickled back to them over the rest of the evening. I still felt the dumb pleasure of having taken the biggest pot of the night, but that wasn't going to solve my problems.

TWENTY-SIX

Billy Walston looked like a man with many burdens when I pushed aside the plastic sheeting and walked into my house on Monday afternoon.

"Here I am, Billy. You said you needed to see me. What is it? Another backsplash crisis? Shower tiles just a shade too beige?"

He winced at my attitude, but I'd decided the best defense was a good offense. I trailed him to the kitchen, where we were alone. Still no dishwasher or range in sight.

He took a deep breath, squared his shoulders. "I need to know, have we got a problem?"

"What do you mean?"

"A money problem."

"Why would you-"

"I hear your credit card got rejected the other day."

"How did-" I remembered the drywallers at the Rum House. "Oh."

"This is a big job for me, Bax. I've got a lot invested in sub-contractors and materials, not to mention my own guys' time."

"I know, Billy, I know."

"I only asked you for a third upfront instead of the usual half, because you said you were waiting on some money from that Measles guy."

"Polio, and I appreciate that."

"Well, can I get a check now?"

"A check?"

"Yeah, a check. Piece of paper with writing on it, represents money."

"Har."

"If I could get a check for say, ten grand, that would be good."

"Ten grand?"

"Yeah, that'll cover my guys' time, plus the first tranche of materials for the roof."

"You want a check for ten grand."

"Yeah. Doesn't have to be today."

"Ten grand by tomorrow?"

"By Friday, let's say. A show of good faith. Just to let me know you've got it, and I'm not going to be left hanging here."

"That's a pretty big show of good faith."

"Hey, I hate to do it to you, Bax. But I hear a guy's credit cards are getting turned down, I gotta wonder, you know? Does he have enough scratch to finish the job?"

"I've got enough money, Billy. But I don't exactly have ten grand in my pocket. Like you said, I've got to get it from Polio, and he's not paying me directly, it's through his record company. A pain in the ass, but that's the way it is."

"I get it, totally. If you can't get a check that quick, we can talk to your guy."

"My guy?"

"Your financial guy. He can tell me the money's there and when it's coming, and I guess that'd be good enough."

My financial guy had gone to my wife in the divorce, and I hadn't replaced him. Before Polio sampled "Mirror Ball Man," I didn't really have enough finances to need a guy, and I figured there would be time to get one later. One mistake of many.

"The thing is, the end of the week, I've gotta pay my guys," Billy said, "and if I can't pay my guys, I'm probably not going to be able to get back here next week."

Which is pretty much the last thing you want to hear from the guy who has your roof torn open.

"I'll get you some money, Billy."

"Cashier's check would be best."

Driving back across the marsh, I came upon a line of cars parked on the shoulder. I knew what was up before I saw the cameras and spotting scopes. Hedwig was perched atop a telephone pole across from the Plover Island Grill, which was closed for the winter. The only familiar faces in the group were the two local women with the muddy boots. Several of the others had arrived in an Audubon Society van, and their guide was telling them all about snowy owls.

Maybe I could write a song about Hedwig and her followers. But that would not write a check to Billy Walston by the end of the week.

Back at the beach house, I turned on my old desktop computer and opened my emailed, hoping someone had remembered they owed me money. No such luck, but there was a message from Abigail. No subject line, just a link inside.

LibertyportGossip.com had been renamed *Abigail Marks for Councilor-at-Large News*, but the blog retained its atmosphere of juicy insinuation.

Sordid sex trade finds home in 'Port,
Right under nose of police
By ABIGAIL MARKS
Just when I thought nothing else could surprise me about the way this town is (mis-)run, from the soaring taxes to the calamitous incompetence behind the Plover Island water and sewer project, a local source whispers news of a new outrage.

Just a few short blocks from City Hall, you will find illegal immigrants from the Far East running what amounts to a brothel, although word on the street is that it's not quite a full-service facility. The women do all the work, you see.

I am told that area law enforcement officials are well aware of its existence, perhaps from first-hand experience, *ahem*. But they are postponing action until reaching the end of a standing queue of photo-op worthy enforcement actions, so as not to edge one another off the front page of the *Daily Liar* ...

If that didn't get the job done, nothing would. Ronnie knocked on the slider and walked in, can of 'Gansett in hand. At least he knocked, so I could close my browser before he saw what was on the screen.

He sat down in a chair that groaned almost as much as he did.

"I saw your son's owl hanging around again this morning."

"Yeah, Hedwig's over by the Grill now."

"Hedwig?"

"That's what Zack calls her. It's Harry Potter's owl. She was on top of a pole, with a bunch of birders watching her."

"How do you know it's a girl?"

"We don't, really. The Internet has some tips about size and color, but it's difficult to tell for sure."

"Look under the tail," Ronnie said, without a hint that he was joking. He finished his beer and exchanged it for the backup in his pocket.

"I can recycle that for you."

He shook his head. "Five cents is five cents." Just frugal, or were his financial problems worse than he let on?

"So, rent next week," he said. He'd never reminded me before. Maybe he'd heard about my credit card, too.

"I remember."

"Everything good? Washing machine working? Furnace hot enough?"

"Everything's good. Your first wife, was she the one who went with you when you brought the wine to Mel Frost?"

He frowned. "What about it?"

"You said he was kind of rude?"

"Took the wine and shut the door right in our faces. We expected to be invited in." He shook his head, then pulled out an orange pill bottle, extracted a white tablet and washed it down with beer. "Maybe Lancers wasn't good enough for him."

"Were you curious about him after that? Did you try to find out any more?"

"I don't know that I did. He was just another odd duck. There was plenty of them out here then. Still are plenty, for that matter, even with all the yuppies moving in."

"You didn't ask around or anything?"

"Not really. Why? You were asking a lot of questions the other night, too. What's up?"

"Promise not to tell the other guys?"

"Yeah, sure, what?"

"I hear that house was a witness protection site."

"You're kidding." He tried to look shocked, mouth hanging open, but it wasn't convincing. He already knew. Interesting.

"That guy I was telling you about, the one I was looking for? He was in the program."

"Golly! The things that happen right under your nose."

"I think Edward Martin was just the alias the government gave him."

Ronnie drank some beer, scratched behind his ear. "I seem to remember that name, but I can't remember why."

"He had a run-in with that guy Kirkman you told me about, over one of his dogs."

"Rings a bell. How did you find this out, again?"

"That old-timer in the waiting room at the doctor's office. And he was there the day this Edward Martin saved a kid who was getting bit by one of Kirkmans' dogs."

"I remember now. Those friggin' Dalmatians."

"Martin told this guy he was in witness protection, and implied he'd get killed if people knew where he was. So this guy kept his secret."

"Until now."

"Until now, right."

"Did this old-timer know anything about Mel Frost?"

"I asked him, but he got divorced and moved away from the island right after that summer."

"That's funny."

"What is?"

"Getting divorced and moving away from the island. Usually it goes in the opposite direction."

"Right. So, Edward Martin?"

"We might have met once or twice, coming and going. Or maybe getting water at the hydrant over on the mainland. Kind of a big guy, looked a little bit early Brando, like in *The Wild Ones*?"

"That's him."

"He was only here for a year or so. I didn't really notice when he left." He thought for a moment, then looked at me with a furrowed brow. "Didn't you say your parents knew him? He was kind of a blue-collar type, a little rough. I thought your dad was a professor or something."

"They met once, but they weren't friends or anything. It was a totally random encounter."

I told him about the roadblock, and the kids throwing snowballs. When I told him about Edward Martin holding a gun on my father, Ronnie raised his eyebrows.

"Guy was in witness protection, he must have feared for his life," he said. "You were lucky he didn't shoot you both."

"I know. I've never forgotten it. That's why when I realized it was only a couple of streets from here, I wanted to walk over there. I figured if the guy lived this long, he must have relaxed his guard by now. I wanted to thank him for not shooting us. That was all before I talked to the old-timer at the hospital, so I didn't know he was in witness protection. Now it makes sense."

"But instead of Edward Martin you found Mel Frost, who's a whole other kettle of fish."

"And he lives right across the street from Phil Jonah."

Ronnie nodded. "I see where you're going with this. But the cops still think Phil killed himself, don't they?"

"That's what they say."

"But?"

"But they're not sure."

"Have you told all this to that detective friend of yours?"

"Not yet."

"I wouldn't. If I were you, I'd just let it go." He levered his bulk out of the chair and stood. "Remember, it's a small island."

"What do you mean?"

"I've lived here most of my life. Everything out here is connected, except for the water and sewer. You poke something on one end, it might rise up to bite you on the other."

TWENTY-SEVEN

One night when Amy and I were first married, we drove out for a romantic dinner at the Plover Island Grill, which was still a funky little place where you could come in the door with sand on your feet and afford a meal and wine. After dessert, we walked over to the beach.

It was low tide, going on sunset. Early September, an unusually warm evening, but there were no people in sight, even though the sky was still bright. No TVs in the houses, no barbecues or music. It was as if the world had ended, or a wizard was about to appear. I decided to seize the moment. Amy turned her back to eye the sunset above the empty houses. When she turned back, my clothes were on a rock and I was in the water. She smiled but glanced left and right. *What if someone sees?* I gestured all around. There was no one. *Join me.*

No one appeared on the beach until we were dressed and walking again. A solitary dog walker came along, her black lab off leash and almost invisible in the gathering dark. The dog ignored us, weaving along a wrack line of seaweed and debris, nose to the ground. The woman smiled without saying anything or even meeting our eyes as they passed by.

A special night, but strange the way the beach cleared for us. Kind of a *Twilight Zone* moment.

It happened again on Monday night.

I was eating my divorced-single-dad dinner, a meatball sub from under the heat lamp at Island Convenience, and checking my finances online. Still a disaster. I needed a big check for Billy and a smaller one for Ronnie and I had nothing in the bank. When I tried to log out, the computer seized up, demanding I click OK to remove a virus. I started a reboot, then grabbed my jacket and headed out.

There were a few other people on the beach: a couple wrapped in a quilt near the center, a dog walker puffing the cigarette he wasn't allowed in the house while his Lab dug a hole in the sand. I walked on. The small waves coming ashore, one after the other, seemed like a metaphor for my errors and failures, financial and otherwise.

They just kept coming.

At Blu, Lily's table had been put back in storage, and the whole place looked empty. When I reached the refuge sign, with nothing but darkness ahead, I decided I'd gone far enough. The computer should be back up by now. And it was cold. I turned around to start for home.

I was alone.

Even though the western sky was still dark blue, there was no one else in sight. Even the couple in the blanket had gone. There wasn't so much as a seagull on the sand. In the east, violet shaded to a bruised purple at the horizon. The windows of all the houses were dark and blank. I felt a chill that wasn't entirely due to the temperature. But at the same time, I didn't want to go home yet. It was beautiful and strange. Darkness descended as I walked, and the first stars came out overhead.

I decided to look in on Mel Frost. See what the old creep was up to.

I crept up to the guardrail at the end of Lilac Lane. Lights shone from inside his cottage. The curtains were open, handy for snooping, but that meant he could see me too. Jonah's place was dark and still, the driveway empty. I circled around in the shadows behind it, picking my way through the dune grass and beach pea.

Behind the deck, which was about level with my chin, I had a sight line under the railing to the cottage across the street. Frost was watching television, a flickering light on the walls. Occasionally it glinted on the Eldorado parked outside. He must have been getting comfortable in his recliner, because I could only see the top of his head over the sill. Not exactly an imposing figure. It was difficult to understand how I ever thought he could be the man with the gun.

I rested my arms on the edge of the deck, and jumped out of my shoes when the world burst into brilliant white light.

The motion detector light was installed high above the front door. Protecting the house from the island's occasional off-season burglaries, now that Jonah's wife and kids had moved out.

Frost didn't get up to see what had triggered it. No doubt it had been going off now and then, whenever a stray cat ran across the deck, and he had gotten used to it. That was what I hoped, anyway. I let go of the deck, stood stock still and waited.

After a moment, the light blinked out again, and I exhaled. Frost still hadn't moved. It was getting cold fast. I flexed my fingers in my pockets and thought maybe I should learn to wear gloves. Or maybe that wasn't the problem at all. What kind of pathetic idiot stands out in the freezing cold by himself, in the dark, spying on someone for no good reason?

Of course, there was the mysterious car in my driveway. I wanted to believe there was something sinister about Mel Frost, that he was connected to the man with the gun and maybe to Jonah's murder too. But I had no evidence. Maybe it was all in my head. There was nothing to see here, nada, zip. I was wasting my time, shivering in the dark. Time to go home, drink a beer and crawl into a warm bed, where I could stare at the ceiling and think about money, old loves and absent friends until the wee hours.

I held my breath as I backed away, but the light didn't come back on. Apparently the sensor only registered as far as the edge of the deck. I looked around at the darkened houses and dunes, making sure no one would see me, then cut across the sand to the next street over. Beach Pea Lane was as deserted as Lilac, but slightly higher on the dune.

Donnie sat in his car in the driveway of the second house from the beach.

I recognized his silhouette immediately. No lights, no motor, just sitting there. Watching Mel Frost too.

I came up on the car in his blind spot. He jumped when I slid into the passenger seat.

"Hey Donnie."

"Hey Bax. You scared me."

He tried to sound leisurely, but he'd reached for the pocket in the door before he recognized me. Gun? Knife? Phone? It was too dark to see.

"You unscrewed the dome light."

"Yeah. I don't want to get spotted. He's pretty careful."

I nodded as if I understood what was going on here. He had a better angle on the cottage than I did from behind Jonah's deck. But Frost's view of us complicated by a shed and a dory between the houses, a few scraggly bushes. He still sat facing the TV, the light jumping on the wall behind him.

"What are you doing out here, Donnie?"

"Same thing you are." He sipped from an Island Convenience to-go cup. The coffee's burnt smell filled the car. "Watching this asshole. Too bad you didn't know about Phil's security light."

"Why are you watching him?"

"You tell me first. Ronnie says you've been interested in him since you got here. Why's that?"

I'd already told Ronnie, which meant everyone would know soon enough. So I told Donnie everything, almost, about the night he and I first met. The same story I'd told Ronnie, about the mystery that had been on my mind ever since I'd moved to the island.

"I introduced myself to Frost because I thought he might be the man with the gun," I said. "Now I think he might be the one the man with the gun was waiting for."

Donnie stroked his goatee a couple of times, staring at TV shadows moving across Frost's living room walls.

"You know, I figured out that party wasn't the only time we met." Interesting change of subject. "The next summer, we all went deep-sea fishing, just you and me and our dads."

A vague memory crept in. "On one of the party boats that docks up at the point, right?"

"I think it was supposed to be a father-son bonding trip, because of the divorce. You and your dad looked like you got along pretty good."

"We did."

"I was too young to understand what was going on with my parents, really, but I knew he wasn't around much. I was glad when he said we were going to do something just the two of us. I got pissed when I realized you were coming too."

"Sorry about that."

He chuckled. "We were just kids. It was stupid of me to be jealous of you."

"You were just a kid," I said. "The outdoors wasn't really our thing, anyway. I'm not sure my dad knew how to bait a hook. But when your dad invited us, he said we had to go."

Donnie nodded. "He took pity on us."

"I don't know about that."

"I hated the boat. All those guys, swearing and drinking, I felt like I was about to get stepped on half the time. And my dad trying to be the life of the party. I threw up like, four times."

"Sea sick?"

"Maybe. Or maybe it was the only way I had to show I didn't want to be there." He shook his head. "And then he tried to cook what we caught. Bluefish. He burned it on the grill because he was drunk, but he was determined we were going to eat every last piece. Christ, it was awful. I still hate bluefish."

"When we got home, my dad put ours in the trash before we went inside."

He laughed, then looked pensive. "Your dad died, right?"

"Yes, when I was seventeen."

He nodded. "I didn't tell you the truth before."

"About what?"

"My dad actually topped himself."

Jesus, this day.

"I'm sorry. I didn't know."

"It's a long time ago." Donnie chuckled, but not because anything was funny. "My dad was a messed-up guy. When he had us on the weekends, we saw all kinds of stuff. Girlfriends and whatnot. He used the belt on us a lot. When we were old enough, we just stopped going. He said he didn't care, but I knew he did. We hardly saw him for the next couple of years. Then my sister was getting married, a couple-three years out of high school, and he got hammered at the rehearsal dinner. Made an asshole of himself. She disinvited him from the wedding, right in front of everybody. And he went home and topped himself. A nice little wedding present for her."

"That's awful."

He nodded. "I found him. I was a senior in high school. He had another rathole over to Seabury Beach. I went over to see if I could get him cleaned up, so he could ask her to change her mind. I walked in the door and found him hanging from the railing on the stairs."

"I don't know what to say."

"It is what it is." He drank some coffee, frowned, and cracked his door to dump the rest in the sand. "It's nice to have somebody to talk to about this crap. Somebody who gets it."

I nodded, and we sat in silence for a while, watching shadows move on Frost's living room walls.

"Me and Chris and Quinn, we've been keeping an eye on Frost, especially since what happened to Phil."

"Really."

"Phil's the one who said something was weird about Frost in the first place. They got in some neighborhood scraps, whose trash cans were where, that kind of crap. Then Phil started googling him."

"You don't think Phil killed himself."

"No way."

"Then what?"

"We figure Mel Frost snuck up on him, made him drive over to the refuge, and killed him. Made it look like suicide."

"Maybe we shouldn't be sitting here with the doors unlocked."

He ignored this. "Phil didn't hide the fact that he was suspicious of the guy. I mean, he lived right across the street. He could just stand on his deck and watch him. That's the kind of guy Phil was. Type A, confrontational. We didn't know then that Frost was dangerous."

"But now you do."

"And that's not all. Phil found out something that's pretty interesting."

"What's that?"

"Mel Frost doesn't exist."

TWENTY-EIGHT

Donnie stroked his goatee and stared into my computer screen with a look of mildly horrified fascination. He looked like my accountant at tax time. "What the hell did you click on?"

"I don't know," I said, hovering. "Rebooting didn't work?"

"Not even close."

"Maybe my son did something."

"Blaming your kid, huh?"

"No, I just-"

"I thought you said he had his own laptop."

"He does, but-"

Donnie grinned without looking up. "Don't feel bad, parents do it all the time."

"People get a lot of viruses, huh?"

"Yeah. Usually from porn sites." He set down his beer and started typing.

"That their kids visited?"

"That's what they say, and I pretend to believe them." Torrents of code flowed up my screen in response to his rapid-fire keystrokes. "Don't worry, I can fix this. I do about ten of these a week, and I'm pretty good at it. This is nothing."

"You do mostly house calls?"

"House calls and small businesses. One-man shops and mom-and-pop operations mostly. Bigger places have their own IT people."

"How long have you had the business?"

"Nine months. Since Waltham Mortgage went belly-up."

"The economy is tough." Master of the obvious, I am.

"I think we would have tanked anyway. Most startups do. And I don't miss commuting to Waltham," he said. "I miss the money, though."

"Is that why you moved to the island?"

"Pretty much. Winter isn't so cheap anymore, but it's still cheaper than town. And I can stay close to my kids."

"Your family is here?"

The flow of characters down the screen stopped abruptly. He

thought for a second, then began typing again. The movement of his hands was economical, like a guitar player's.

"I got my ex and two kids still in the house in Seabury, the nice part, over the other side of the highway, which I bought two years ago, when the company was getting going and the future was bright," he said. "Now I don't have any of it. Well, I still have the two kids, at least to pay for. But Sandy keeps telling them what a failure I am, so who knows."

"Must be difficult." Master of the obvious, song fodder, right there in front of me.

"It's not easy." Donnie said as the indecipherable flow of letters and numbers resumed.

"That's your wife? Sandra?"

He shook his head. "Just Sandy. It's short for Sanibel, like the island in Florida. Can you believe her parents named her that?"

"Not really."

"They went there on their honeymoon and liked it so much they named her after it. Sanibel Pierzynski. They still go there every winter. We used to fly down and join them when the kids had school vacation. In fact, Sandy and the kids are going down next week. I maxed out my plastic paying for the plane tickets. I need all the house calls I can get."

"Yeah, about that-"

"Don't worry, this one is on the cuff. On account of my bathroom privileges."

"Thanks."

"It's just nice to have someone I can talk to. Doing this shit can be so boring. No offense, but everyone has one of the same three problems, and most of them are so easy to fix. I mean, it can be time-consuming and a pain in the ass, sure, but not really challenging, you know? I solve the problem, and most people make way more out of it than they should."

"They're impressed?"

"Oh yeah. Women more than men. The guys tend to be pissed they can't fix it themselves. They'll thank you in the end, though. It's the women who are really grateful. They'll tell you you're a genius. I've gotten action from a grateful customer more than once." I raised my eyebrows and he backtracked. "It's not like, *Letters to Penthouse*. 'I fixed her hard drive and then gave her a hard drive.' But a couple times, they gave me signals, so I got their number off the paperwork and called 'em up later. Took 'em out for a drink, and it worked out pretty good. Strictly one-time things, but still."

He took a big swallow of beer, maybe hiding the lie. It sounded like high school bragging. I wanted to keep him talking, though. "So there are fringe benefits."

"You bet. Once in a while. Usually, people back out of the room like I'm going to do surgery. Leave me alone with all their files. Sometimes I've thought about, you know, looking for account numbers and passwords or whatever, something I could use to get some money. It's just about that tight for me now."

"I know what that's like. It must be tempting."

He sat up straight, face close to the screen. "And *there's* your problem."

He fired off a final burst of keystrokes and stabbed ENTER. The letters on the screen scrolled up and away. My computer emitted strangled noises suggesting a garbage disposal committing suicide. Donnie sat back and folded his hands behind his head.

"Now we wait," he said. "I killed the virus, but we better flush the whole system and see what else is in there."

"Thanks a lot, really. You want another beer?"

"What else have we got to do?"

He followed me into the kitchen, stopping to eyeball the plastic lobster family in the stairway. I hit the fridge for beers, and we sat at the table.

"Ronnie lives downstairs, huh? He driving you crazy yet?"

"A little."

He chuckled. "Just wait."

"So, you want to tell me about Mel Frost now?"

He nodded, reluctant. He hoped I'd forgotten. He took a long drink, then stared down at the bottle as if he was trying to read the fine print. He spoke without looking up.

"Melvin Allard Frost was born in St. Elizabeth Hospital in Utica, N.Y., on Dec. 13, 1933.”

"So he's seventy-five. That sounds about right, if-"

Donnie held up a finger. I shut up.

"Melvin Allard Frost died in St. Elizabeth Hospital in Utica, N.Y., on Feb. 5, 1936, from a case of the croup."

"What?"

"The first time they talked, right after Phil moved in, Frost said something about being from Utica. When they started having trouble, Phil wanted to find out exactly who he was dealing with. So he guessed how old Frost was, roughly, and did a records search. There was only one Melvin Frost born in Oneida County in the thirties or forties. And he died when he was three years old."

"Explain."

"That used to be the standard way to create a false identity, get the birth certificate for a dead kid and build from there. It doesn't work as well now that everything's online."

"Phil told you all this?"

He nodded. "One night we were having a few drinks at the Grill, bitching about our wives, and he told me and Chris. He was wondering, like, what kind of psycho he had living across the street from his wife and kids. So we started looking into it, the three of us."

"And?"

"Mel Frost didn't exist between 1936 and when he moved into the cottage on Lilac Lane. No criminal record, no military service, no income taxes, credit record, nothing."

"You can find out all that from the Internet?"

"You can if you know where to look, and you have a few passwords. When we were at Waltham Mortgage, we had all the passwords. It wasn't like we forgot them when we left. I could find out anything about you that I want. Credit report is just the beginning."

"Don't look at my credit report, whatever you do."

"Right back at ya," he said and emptied his beer. I got him a replacement.

"So what about the cottage? Did Frost take out a mortgage?"

He shook his head. "It was bought for cash back in the early seventies by a real estate trust out of Schenectady."

"Upstate New York again. Who's behind the trust?"

"No way to find out. It doesn't even have a name, just a number. It was set up by an attorney, and the attorney is dead now. We've been trying to find open records, but so far no luck. I assume it's a shell and Frost is behind it. We know what his deal is, though."

The corners of his mouth turned up smugly. He wanted me to ask.

"OK, what's his deal?"

"He was a U.S. Marshal with the witness protection service. Retired about the same time he moved here. Real name, Harry Groener. Rhymes with trainer."

"I expected him to be some kind of crook."

"I know, right? But he was one of the marshals in charge of hiding government witnesses and other people who were in danger of getting whacked. He'd keep them safe until they were done testifying, and then get them a new life under a new name. Until finally he did it for himself." Donnie took a long, triumphant drink of his beer. "So, no wonder we couldn't find out diddly trying to trace back Mel Frost. This guy is a pro at changing identities. He got a little careless once, telling Phil he was from Utica, but that was the only mistake he made."

Roger had said the man with the gun, cover name Edward Martin, was in the witness protection program, and Ronnie had confirmed it. So maybe Harry Groener was in charge of protecting him? Which would raise as many questions as it answered. Such as, where was Edward Martin now?

"If Groener is so good at hiding, how did you find out who he is?"

"The Eldorado. It's registered to the same trust that owns the house. And Phil thought, he treats that thing like it's his baby, like he's had it for a long time. You should see him polishing it in the summer. So maybe he brought it from his old life – the one thing he didn't give up when he came here. So Phil crossed the street with a flashlight at two in the morning and got the VIN number, and we ran it online."

"And?"

"And bingo. Harry Groener bought the car new in Schenectady in 1976. Three years later he sold it to the same trust that owns the cottage, for a dollar."

"He couldn't let go."

"Exactly. Car's his Achilles heel. Once we had his name and DOB, it was easy to find out all about him. Utica native, served two years in the Army during Vietnam, in the military police, five years in the New York State Police, then joined the Marshal Service. We found a few old newspaper articles online. He gets commendations for tracking down some sixties radical fugitives, but then he goes quiet. There's not a word about him joining the witness protection division. But then, there wouldn't be."

"So how did you find out?"

"Another little slip. Harry bragged about it to his high school alumni association, who put it in their newsletter. Forty years of which were recently digitized and put online by a devoted alum. Chris found it on Google."

We clinked bottles.

"So what's he doing here? Why live under a new identity for all these years?"

"That's the really interesting part."

Headlights flashed across the kitchen windows, and we both sat up like we'd been caught. A high-riding pickup truck rumbled to a stop in the driveway.

"That's Quinn," Donnie said. "You don't know any of this, understand?"

"Why?"

Donnie spoke just above a whisper. "Quinn doesn't think we need another guy."

"Another guy for what?"

Before he answered, Quinn walked in.

"Hey, assholes."

"Quinn!" Donnie said, too brightly. "You're just in time. You want a beer?"

"Sure. What are you two talking about?" His expression was unusually cheerful, but his clothes were covered with a fine white dust.

"Not much, just hanging out. What are you up to?"

He talked too much, tried too hard. Quinn looked at him a moment longer than necessary, thinking.

"I came to ask Baxter a favor," he said finally, raising the gym bag in his hand. "Can I use your shower? I just got done work, and of course when I get home, my water's out. John's too."

It was nearly nine o'clock. A long day for a guy who used to be the boss. The economy was squeezing him too.

"Of course. There's towels in the closet."

"Thanks, but I brought my own."

"Then you're welcome anytime."

"Copy that." He nodded and walked to the bathroom, swinging the bag and whistling again.

When the door closed behind him, I said, "So tell me the rest."

Donnie shook his head, looking down the hall. "Later."

He went back to my computer and worked with his head down until Quinn reappeared. We drank my last three beers while making random conversation about the water situation and the weather and the economy. Quinn drank standing and it was clear he didn't want to be there. His good cheer had faded once he got his favor. Soon he was ready to go.

"You coming?" he asked Donnie. "We don't want to bother Baxter anymore."

"You're not bothering me-"

"I'm coming," Donnie said and stood up. "Thanks for everything, Bax."

He hadn't said another word about Mel Frost. He looked back at me from the doorway as if he hoped I wouldn't, either.

TWENTY-NINE

At first I thought it was a seal.

The breakfast crowd of seagulls fanned out across the beach ahead of me, foraging for crabs and edible trash under a blue sky. A front from the south had brought unseasonably warm weather in a rush of wind before dawn. Now dog owners trudged along, one layer less bundled-up than usual, bags in hand, their four-legged companions wandering happily off leash. Far down the beach, toward Tru, a jogger ran a weaving trail at water's edge, dodging the surf.

There was a purposeful splash just outside the break, and wet, black flesh glinted in the sun.

I figured it was one of the seals that come down from the Gulf of Maine at this time of year in search of warmer water. They form a lazy winter colony around the mouth of the river and leave when the boats return. The first time I saw one, from the boardwalk downtown, I wondered why a Labrador retriever was swimming in the river in January, until it disappeared under the water and didn't come up for nearly a minute. Then I figured it out.

This creature swam in a straight line, though, and never dove out of sight. As it got closer, I saw the arms churning and the feet kicking efficiently, barely breaking the surface. The sleek coat was a dry suit, and the seal was a person.

The temperature was warm for the time of year, but the water couldn't have been much more than forty degrees. Surfers occasionally braved it on a sunny weekend, but I hadn't even gotten my feet wet in weeks. The last time, New Year's Day with Zack, ten seconds was enough to give my ankles ice-cream headaches. This guy was crazy.

He switched from a crawl to a breast stroke, then veered to shore. He walked out of the water dripping, like the Creature from the Black Lagoon, and waved to me. I waved back, clueless. He flippered up to a knapsack on the beach, grabbed a bottle of water and a towel, and pushed his goggles up on his head.

"You're Baxter, right?"

"That's me."

"Perfect." He took off his gloves for a shake. "I was hoping you'd be out here."

His face was pale, almost blue. He was nearly a foot shorter than me, five-two at most. His eyes gleamed with the fervor of the true believer, or possibly hypothermia. He looked familiar, but I couldn't quite place him.

"You did all this just to see me?"

He laughed. "Hardly. I'm doing the Valentine's Day Polar Plunge for muscular dystrophy – or is it cerebral palsy? I can never remember. But anyway, it's such a nice day, I figured I'd test out the wet suit, and maybe run into you in the bargain. Otherwise I was going to come knock on your door."

"You have the advantage. I don't know who you are."

"Really? Oh, sorry, of course." He pulled off the rubber balaclava and goggles. "The cold is making me slow. I'm Miles Allgood."

Of course. An Eagle Scout as a teenager, he was often written up in the newspaper for his good deeds, although the senior citizens and needy children in the pictures never looked as pleased as he did. Two years ago, as a high school senior, he had run for city council on a platform of unfettered capitalism. Unfortunately for him, local parents were unconvinced that Ayn Rand was an education advocate, or that financial deregulation was a local issue, and he lost by eighty percent of the vote.

"I thought you went off to college after the election."

Mention of the defeat produced a flicker of annoyance. "I'm working on a dual major in political science and business administration, with a minor in philosophy." He'd be the one kid at the seminar table that everyone else wanted to kill. "I'm Abigail Marks' campaign manager now. I took the semester off to help her get elected."

He pulled off the top of his wet suit, toweled off his goosebumpy skin, and slipped into a sweatshirt. He had the aggressively unfashionable haircut of a Republican state representative or TV weatherman. "It's an independent study. I'm going to get a full semester's credit once I write the paper."

"Win or lose?"

"Yes, but we're not going to lose. I won't let that happen again. I think it's vitally important for the future of Libertyport that Miss Marks gets elected, so we can begin to get city government back on track. We need to bring back common-sense government and fiscal restraint, to reduce the burden on the taxpayers. If we make this a more attractive community for business, we can restore economic vitality beyond the tourist sector and create real jobs."

I marveled. Barefoot in the sand, dripping and shivering, he gave a flawless campaign speech.

"I understand you and the candidate had a conversation the other day," he said. "I just wanted to give you a progress report on your request."

"You know about that?"

"Abigail tells me everything. It was one of my main conditions for taking on the job."

"What did she tell you?"

"About the whores on River Street and your request that she take action."

I had been thinking more and more about those women, how miserable their lives must be. I felt guilty about dropping a dime on them. Miles calling them names made it worse.

"I don't really think they're that much of a threat-"

"Don't worry, it's taken care of. That's what I wanted to tell you. There's a plan in motion. Abigail and I have been working on it since your meeting. I think you'll be pleased."

"I don't want you to-"

He held a finger across his lips. "Best that we don't talk anymore about it. Preserve deniability." He wrapped his lower half in a towel and changed into sweatpants, balancing on one foot at a time, steady as any teenager.

"It's only a city council election."

"There are no small races, only small candidates. People's lives are affected every time they go to the ballot box."

"How do you know Abigail, anyway? She must have retired by the time you got to high school."

"When I was a junior, she came out of retirement to coach the debate team. We got to the state finals."

"Did you win?"

Another flash of annoyance. "We came in third. There were serious issues with the judging. I think I was targeted because of homophobia."

"You're-"

"Are you surprised?"

"Yes. No. A little. Your politics-"

"I always hear how progressive this town is, yet so many people cling to outdated stereotypes. For your information, I'm socially liberal and financially conservative."

"Sure."

"And I'm determined not to let antiquated bigotry affect the trajectory of my career."

"Helping Abigail run for city council is your big launch pad?"

His head snapped up at my tone. "I don't think you're the right person to criticize my career arc." Dressed now, he unwrapped the towel, and slipped his feet into a pair of Nike slides. "You had one hit song, what was it, twenty-five years ago?

"Something like that."

"And you've been going downhill ever since, if I'm not mistaken, until a member of the urban music community sampled your song?"

"Pretty much."

"This Coolio has quite a criminal record, as I understand it."

"His name is Polio."

"Whatever. My point is, your only hope of a career revival apparently rests with this African-American felon, and you've even failed to capitalize on that."

"I'm thinking about-"

"Meanwhile, your personal finances have reached a breaking point."

"How do you know-"

"I do my research, Mr. McLean. Before I let Abigail get involved, I checked you out thoroughly to see if there was an agenda. But it doesn't appear that you are organized enough to have one."

He smirked, and I had half a mind to throw the condescending little prick back into the ocean.

"We should talk when this campaign is over," he said. "Next semester I'm going to start a personal branding and image management firm. I could help you get back on track."

"I don't think-"

"There are plenty of areas you haven't explored. Webcam concerts. Online memorabilia sales."

"Thanks, but I'll pass." I started to walk away.

"Your loss," he called after me and laughed.

THIRTY

"You want to do something fun?" Donnie asked, when he finally returned one of my calls. "Something almost no one else gets to do?"

"Sure."

"Meet me in half an hour."

He gave me an address in the industrial park, which turned out to be a vacant machine shop that had been FOR LEASE since last summer. I parked next to his Corolla at the edge of the parking lot, which was large enough for a hundred cars. The temperature had shot up into the fifties under a cloudless sky.

"I knew you'd be up for this," he said, opening his trunk. "Maybe you can write a song about it."

The wind turbine stood in the middle of the field adjacent to the parking lot. It rose above us, sleek and white in the sunshine like a giant flower. The blades moved achingly slow in the faint breeze, attached to a white housing shaped like a shoebox. They seemed closer to the clouds than the ground.

"What exactly are we doing?" I asked, although I had an idea.

"You ever been inside one of these things?"

"No."

"Grab a hard hat."

"We're going inside?"

"We're going up."

"Seriously?"

"Seriously."

The turbine went up about the same time the machine shop closed, after many months of controversy. Libertyport residents loved alternative energy, just not in their backyards. Neighbors claimed its horrible whooshing sound and spinning psychedelic shadows would ruin their lives. None of the city councilors lived close by, though, so the project went ahead.

Raising the turbine was a major operation involving two giant cranes; it drew a little crowd and made the front page of the paper.

Since then it had become part of the landscape, visible all around town, blades spinning between changing leaves on a crisp fall afternoon, the blinking red aircraft warning light watching over me on late-night walks home from this or that bar.

I had never been this close before. It was big enough to mess with your head. Its shadow draped over a chain link fence behind it, crossed the field beyond and disappeared onto the flat roof of another industrial building on the next street.

I couldn't hear a sound.

"How come we get to do this?"

"The company that owns it, the VP of biz dev is one of the guys from Waltham Mortgage. He got out before we hit the rocks and joined the company that leases the land and puts up the turbine. They sell the power back to the grid, plus they get all sorts of tax credits because it's clean power. They lost their last computer guy, and they needed somebody to come up and take a quick look. He remembered me. Now I do regular checks here, and fill in at a couple of other sites."

"Interesting work."

"You're not afraid of heights, are you?"

"Not normally, but I've never, uh…."

"It's really cool up there, you're going to like it," he said, stuffing a laptop into a small knapsack.

"OK."

"You've got to sign a release." He handed me a photocopy and a pen. "It says that you're going up under your own accord. So if you die, you can't sue, basically."

I'd like to think my shaky signature was a result of writing on the uneven surface of the Sunbird's trunk and nothing else.

"Do you have anything in your pockets that could fall out?"

"Wallet and keys. Phone."

"Zip them in. We don't want them falling on somebody's head. Now let's get you into a safety harness."

He helped me into a canvas-and-Kevlar vest with D-rings everywhere and a heavy metal clamp on a strap dangling from the front. He adjusted the fit for me, then put one on himself.

"Let's do this."

The turbine rose from a square patch of crushed rock enclosed by a chain-link fence topped with barbed wire. Donnie opened the padlocked gate and beckoned me inside, then locked it behind us. At the base of the shaft, three corrugated metal steps led up to a heavy steel door with rounded corners, like the hatch of a submarine. I looked up again. The shaft tapered into the blue sky, the three blades hanging over us like mighty swords of judgment. The porch fan of the gods.

"How tall is it?"

Donnie worked the digital lock on the door. "Two hundred and fifty-two feet to the axis. Each blade is another seventy-eighty feet, so three-thirty to the tip."

I followed him through the hatch into the round shaft. The interior felt like a submarine too, riveted steel walls and floor, claustrophobic. Every sound echoed. Two small control panels with red and green lights winked in a glass-fronted metal cabinet. He unlocked the cabinet and began pressing keys on a keypad.

I looked up.

An aluminum ladder ascended the wall on one side. Caged lights ringed the cylinder at intervals. Opposite the ladder was a bundle of cables that presumably brought the power down from the turbine. The ladder went up to a landing. An open hatch revealed it continued to another landing beyond. And another one beyond that.

I felt the strange sensation of falling upward. Reverse gravity like in some sci-fi movie.

"Whoa."

"Yeah, cool, right?"

He locked up the cabinet and led me over to the base of the ladder. I grabbed a rung and he shook his head.

"Wrong side. Let me show you. I'll go up first, anyway."

He slid around into the narrow space between the ladder and the curved wall, facing me. A steel cable ran down the middle of the ladder. "Clip on," he said, attaching his vest to the cable with a heavy D ring. "This is your fail safe. It's a brake."

He climbed three or four rungs, then let go of the side rails and stepped off the ladder. He fell about a foot before the cable chunked to a stop and left him hanging. "You can't fall, so there's nothing to worry about. Except a heart attack of course." Dangling there, he adjusted his gloves. "There are three landings where you can get off and unclip if you need a rest. Just get off the ladder before you unclip."

"How long does it take?"

"For me? Twelve to fifteen minutes. But I've been doing it for a while. The first time took me like half an hour."

"How often do you do this?"

"Once a month, usually. The owners have a guy who goes up every week for maintenance, carrying a bag of tools. His record is four minutes."

"I can't imagine."

He started to climb again. "It is unbelievable. He's a gym rat, though. OK, I'll see you up there." He was already ten rungs up and climbing fast. "I've got water. Believe me, you'll need it."

People have the impression that folksingers are wholesome, outdoorsy types. They think of Woody Guthrie riding the rails and singing by campfires, amid redwood forests and Gulf Stream waters. People are sadly mistaken. Folksingers do not exercise or even go outside much. The dirty jeans and lumberjack shirts are a costume, shaped by bad laundry habits, not manual labor. We spend most of our time shut in our rooms with our guitars, except when playing in crappy bars and church basements. From Bob Dylan on, we've been faking it.

Now I was going to pay.

I watched Donnie till he was halfway to the first landing. Two hundred and fifty feet was what, twenty stories? I couldn't remember the last time I'd climbed anything higher than Billy Walston's stepladder. ("See that wire? Mice chewed that. That's all going to have to be replaced.") But I slid behind the ladder, my back against the outer wall, and clipped onto the safety line. The clinks and clanks echoed in the vast metal tube.

I went up a couple of rungs as a test and flashed back to junior high gym class, trying to shinny up a scratchy rope to a distant gym ceiling, the asshole coach yelling at me to pick up the pace. I hated that guy. I looked up. Donnie had already passed the first hatch. I took a deep breath, and began to climb.

I sprinted up the first twenty rungs and paused. I couldn't stop myself from looking down. The door and the control panels weren't all that far away, really. I looked up again and started to climb for real.

I reached the first landing in two or three minutes. Looking down again, I felt a slight tingle in my nether regions, the first sensation of real height. I was sixty or so feet up, more than high enough to kill me if the safety cable failed. But it wouldn't. Climbing was work, though. I thought about crawling out onto the corrugated steel landing for a quick breather, but I could feel the old gym class tremors trying to get their hooks in me. Not fear of falling but fear of failing.

I was only a quarter of the way up.

I started again. With the sun beating on the outside of the steel tube, it got warmer as I climbed, but there was no way to unzip my jacket without taking off the entire harness. By the second landing, I was sweating and wondering how much gas I had in the tank. Donnie had disappeared through the hatch at the top. Had it been twelve minutes already? I reminded myself that it wasn't a race. Just keep climbing. I looked straight down a hundred and twenty feet and felt no fear. I never thought that would have been easier than looking up and seeing how far I had to go.

One rung at a time, motherfucker. I am climbing you.

Up and up. Clink, clank.

It had to be eighty-five degrees at this level, a sauna. Sweat poured off my brows and into my eyes, but there was nothing I wanted to see anyway. Looking down was old hat now, just a good story I would tell at the Rum House. What mattered was getting to the top. Not quitting.

By the time I reached the third landing, I was drenched and panting. My middle-aged arms and legs were rubbery, and I could feel my hands beginning to tremble. Low blood sugar. I had used up all my energy and now I was eating into reserves. But if I stopped for a rest, I knew I'd be done for good, a failure, no way to go but down.

I began to notice a residue of grease on the ladder. My hands and sneakers slipped a little on the rungs. I held on tighter. Up and up and up. And then there were just. A few. More rungs.

I heaved myself through the final hatch and onto the greasy metal floor with a moan of relief, like a *Titanic* passenger flopping over the gunwales of a lifeboat. Panting, hands shaking. I lay there on my face for a moment, trying to get control of my breathing.

I've really got to get in shape.

When I looked up at last, I was in a narrow space under an enormous piece of machinery. Buried alive in a metal grave. Fortunately I didn't have the energy for a panic attack.

Donnie's face appeared upside down ahead of me. He looked calm and dry, breathing easily.

"There you are. Twenty-four minutes, though, not bad for a first-timer."

"Where am I?"

He patted the underbelly of the machine. "This is the actual turbine. Awesome or what? Crawl over here, and we'll go up top."

The close quarters reminded me of some grim European submarine movie I had seen at our little storefront cinema, sweaty men in filthy undershirts shouting in German as they realized they were about to die in their cramped steel coffin. The only difference was that we were hundreds of feet above the ground instead of deep under the North Atlantic.

I belly-crawled under the turbine, barely fitting with my coat and safety vest. The grease stains would never come out of these clothes. On the other side, I stood up carefully in a narrow slot, minding my back, but there was no pain. Maybe Chris had fixed me. Or maybe sheer adrenaline had taken over.

In front of me was another ladder, but this one was just three rungs. I climbed into another submarine compartment, this one slightly roomier. An influx of cool, fresh air came from a hatch above our heads showing to blue sky and sunlight.

"Welcome to the nacelle."

"The what?"

Donnie smiled and plugged his laptop into another set of control panels. "It means a housing, like an airplane engine rides in under the wing."

I was still panting. "Nacelle. ... Got it."

"With all the equipment and the blades, it weighs like seventy-five tons. That's why they needed two cranes." He clicked a few keys, and data began scrolling up the screen.

"Somebody been ... watching porn up here?"

He laughed. "No, I'm just doing a security update."

"Those controls ... are the same ... as at the bottom?"

He nodded. "Yeah, but what fun would it be, fixing it down there? I tell them it's important for me to make sure everything's working at both ends. You ready to go up?"

"Up where?"

He pointed to the free-standing aluminum ladder sticking up through the hatch. "There's no point climbing all this way unless you're going to get the view."

"I suppose you're right."

"Don't worry, I'll go first."

The ladder shifted bounced with every step as he went. He stopped halfway out of the opening for a demonstration.

"First thing you do when you get up here: You'll find two safety straps like these. Clip them to the rings on either side of your vest, just like this. That's all there is to it."

Now the fear of heights kicked in. This ladder wasn't attached to anything, and it stood on the greasy steel floor. I could see myself climbing all that way only to die in a moronic accident when it slipped out from under me.

"You're going to love this," he said. Then he climbed out the hatch and disappeared.

Well.

I grabbed the sides of the ladder. No time like the present.

I climbed fast, so there would be no time to think about falling. My head was in the fresh air, but I hooked on to the safety straps before I looked.

I was in the sky.

It was like I'd entered some magic Harry Potter attic, opening a hatch to another world. Cars like ants on the streets below. Libertyport and the river and Plover Island laid out below us as if on a map. The blue ocean stretching eastward until it vanished over the curve of the earth.

"This is cool, right?" Donnie said.

"Yeah, it's cool."

The nacelle was seven or eight feet wide and twenty feet long, with nothing to keep us from going over the edge but our safety harnesses. There was no railing around the edge, no wall, just the inch-high bar to which the safety straps were attached.

I climbed the rest of the way out of the hatch and slid over to join Donnie, who was sitting cross-legged on the smooth, white surface. It was like sitting on the narrow roof of a school bus, twenty-five stories in the air.

"The climb's a bitch," Donnie said, "but it's worth it."

The Boston skyline was visible on the horizon. Donnie looked around but kept glancing at me, as happy as I'd ever seen him.

A few feet behind him, one of the enormous blades rose from the hub on the end of the nacelle behind Donnie and towered above us, a giant white scythe. I didn't realize it was moving until it edged into the sun and a chill shadow fell over us. The only sound was a faint hum from the machinery below.

"Not generating much power today," I ventured.

"There's not much wind, but they'd move faster than this if I wanted them to."

"So you put the brakes on now?"

"There are no brakes, not in the way you mean. I could lock the blades in place, but that creates extra force, and then the wind makes this whole thing sway like a bastard. Not what I wanted when I was bringing up a guest."

"Thank you."

"You're welcome. So, what I did was angle the blades out of the wind. The blades are highly aerodynamic, less like an old windmill than the wing of a jet. The computer adjusts them, turning the nacelle and adjusting the blades for the ultimate efficiency. But each one weighs tons. Unless they're angled just right, they'll barely move."

"How do you know all this?"

"I spent a little time with the guy who designed it. He's a damn genius."

The air was noticeably colder up here, but it was one of those moments when temperature didn't matter. The sun was warm, anyway. I watched a handful of geese in a ragged V flying over the industrial park about a hundred feet below us.

"How are you with the height?"

I thought for a second. "I'm fine with it. I'm kind of surprised how fine. It's like being in an airplane."

Donnie nodded. "It's because you can't see your connection to the ground."

He was right. I could look down, but even if you leaned way out over the edge of the nacelle, which I wasn't about to do, you couldn't see the base of the shaft directly below us.

Behind me was a small array of weather instruments and the red warning light that I had seen blinking over the town on so many nights. Beyond it lay downtown and the river, the vast expanse of marsh with its maze of creeks and channels, and the island beyond.

"How fast do can blades go when they're generating power?"

"Wind speeds anywhere between seven and fifty-five miles per hour. We call those the cut-in and cut-out speeds. We're just above cut-in now, maybe nine or ten miles an hour. Below cut-in, the wind isn't fast enough to turn the blades. Cut-out is the point at which the turbine can no longer operate safely."

I wondered what it would be like to sit up here in a high wind, the blades whirling at the edge of self-destruction. I imagined grimy German submariners in the compartment below, racing about in increasing panic as the noise became deafening and the nacelle shook and smoke began to pour from the turbine.

"What about a hurricane?"

"We'd lock down the blades and turn the whole thing so they're out of the wind. The whole thing is built to withstand hurricane-force winds. Those bolts around the base go forty feet into bed-rock. It's not going to fall over."

"How long have you been doing this?"

"About a year."

"You're getting in shape."

"You'd think. I'm getting used to the climb, anyway."

"Do you ever get used to this?" I waved my arm around at the view.

"Sort of. I don't come up here every time. But once I get up here, it hits me all over again."

"Thanks for bringing me."

"Sure," he said, looking off toward the island. "Actually, I thought this would be a good place to talk."

The chill I felt wasn't from the breeze.

THIRTY-ONE

I tugged on my safety lines, a test. They seemed fine. For one brief instant I imagined going over the edge, that moment of weightlessness before the fall.

Maybe Donnie had brought me up here to get rid of me. Maybe he had second thoughts about me, or Quinn was mad that he'd told me about Mel Frost. A brawl atop the nacelle would be like a scene in a James Bond movie. I was taller, but he had ten years and fifty pounds on me. If he pushed me over the side, that would really put the *flight* in fight-or-flight.

If he knocked me out, he could unhook my safety lies and make it seem like an accidental fall. I was clumsy and liked to drink. It wouldn't be hard to convince people it was my own fault.

At least the news coverage of my demise would create a brief bump in sales of my music. Who said I wasn't a glass-half-full guy?

A gliding seagull rode a thermal up to our height to check us out and, finding nothing of interest, glided away. A birder could catch my last moments through a long lens, but they wouldn't look up here unless Hedwig came our way.

The gull continued on toward the Dumpsters at Market Basket, a mile to the northwest. The tiny cars in the parking lot glinted in the sunlight.

Donnie was still sitting cross-legged, a hard position from which to start a fight. "I figured, at least Quinn won't interrupt us up here."

Maybe he hadn't brought me up here to kill me. It would be a stupid move anyway. There would be all kinds of investigations. Wankum might not figure it out, but OSHA would. My heart began to slow toward normal.

"Quinn wants to keep you out of it. He says you're not hard enough. But I think you deserve to know the truth, especially since we're friends again."

"And the truth is?"

"Mel Frost, or Harry Groener, whatever you want to call him, is a seriously bad dude. He killed Phil to protect his secret. And I might be next. He saw me with Phil more than once."

"So let's call the cops."

Donnie nodded. "That's one way to go. Another way is we take down the prick by taking his money, his ill-gotten gains."

"His what, now?"

"That's what I'm trying to tell you. This scumbag is sitting on a million-four that he stole."

I may have blinked a couple of times.

"What?"

"That's what Chris and I said when Phil told us about it. I didn't believe him. I thought it was pie-in-the-sky bullshit, the same way he said Waltham Mortgage was going to make us rich."

"Pie in the *sky*? Really?" I gestured around us.

He giggled. "I get it. Funny. But here's the thing, Phil was telling the truth for once. He wondered, why would this Harry Groener go to all the trouble to become Mel Frost? Phil thought maybe someone was after him. Like some gangster one of his witnesses testified against. Groener knew a lot of bad dudes. So Phil did all this research. He started googling famous criminal cases in upstate New York in the year or two before Groener bailed. He found this."

He unzipped one of his jacket pockets, pulled out a piece of paper and handed it to me carefully, the corners fluttering in the breeze. It was a photocopy of a page from the Albany Times-Union in 1977. I scanned the headlines but saw nothing relevant until I looked at the black-and-white photo at the bottom of the page.

My stomach flipped.

"That's him."

"Yup, that's Harry Groener before he became Mel Frost."

"I'm talking about the other guy."

Donnie raised his eyebrows. "You know him?"

The photo was taken in a nondescript hallway. ROBBERY SUSPECT TO TESTIFY, said the caption. One of the two figures was Groener. He was closer to the camera, hurrying, with an irritated expression. He wore a brimmed hat, the kind men never wore anymore, and his badge was pinned to the lapel of his trench coat. The growths on his face were much smaller, barely noticeable. He gripped his prisoner's elbow with one hand and held up the other in a futile attempt to block the photographer's shot. The prisoner wore a windbreaker over a white t-shirt, and his hands were cuffed in front of him. He kept his head down, trying to avoid the lens.

He had wide shoulders and a barrel chest, a Roman nose and thick, wavy, dark hair.

"That's Edward Martin."

Donnie just nodded. "We found a bunch more stories once we started looking, but that was the only photo."

"They were trying to hide his identity. Witness protection."

"Sort of. Not exactly."

"What do you mean?"

"Groener had an idea, and worked it from the get-go."

"That's him, though. The guy who pointed the gun at my father."

Donnie pointed to the caption. "His real name was Mike Spano."

"Was?"

"Spano was a low-level mobster, Schenectady, Buffalo, Albany. Not a made member of the Mafia, just a guy who hooked up with different crews for things. A strong-arm guy, mostly. And then he joined a robbery crew for a big armored car holdup. You know they got the race there in Saratoga, the Travers Stakes?"

"Sure." Most of what I knew about horse racing came from old movies. Go Seabiscuit.

"They run it at the end of the summer, and it's the big weekend there. Lots of people go. And on the Monday after the race, five guys held up an armored car making its way down to Albany and got away with $1.7 million."

The success of the robbers made him smile. Donnie had not gotten away with a lot in life.

"The money from the racetrack?"

He shook his head. "That would have been a lot more dough,

but it also would have been guarded like Fort Knox. No, this was just a regular armored car that made the rounds in Saratoga Springs. Hotels, restaurants, places with too much cash to just send a clerk out with a night deposit. Remember, this was back before the Internet and ATMs and all of that. Plenty of people didn't even use credit cards. And a big weekend like that, people playing the horses, a lot of them were bound to be flashing cash. At the last stop on the truck's route, four guys jumped out of a van wearing Nixon masks and waving M-16s."

"They shot the guards?"

"Nope, the guards folded. One warning shot and they hit the deck, according to the newspapers. Guys grabbed five bags of cash, left about half a million in coins. Cops found the van abandoned behind a supermarket half a mile away."

"They got away."

"For a while. At first people said it was the Weather Underground or the Black Panthers. But one of them got caught spending some of the cash less than a month later. He flipped, and the cops nabbed two of the other guys off what he told them. They already had two strikes, they're still in prison. But less than three hundred grand was recovered between them. The last two guys were in the wind, and they supposedly had most of the money. They were never found."

"So there's still a million-four out there somewhere."

"Well, maybe. Guess who the flipper was."

"Mike Spano."

"Correct."

"And Harry Groener protected him during the trial and then got him into witness protection."

"Correct. And about a year later Groener quietly retired and just ... disappeared."

"And Mel Frost was born. Again."

"Now you've got the picture."

"I don't get it. The other two guys had all the money, and they got away."

"Maybe, but what are the odds we never hear from them again? Two bozos from Schenectady steal over a million and vanish into thin air? They're living a life of leisure in Tahiti or someplace like that? What are the odds they could pull that off?"

"You think they're dead."

"Yeah, I think your Mike Spano put them in the ground and took the money, and then he ratted out the rest of the crew so the government would take care of his getaway. He made one mistake, though. Trusting Harry Groener. Somehow Groener figured out he had the money. Or maybe he even told Groener about it. But instead of taking him to a government safe house, Groener brought him to this little cottage on Plover Island, off the books. Probably he told him it was the only way to keep him safe. And then Mike Spano disappeared for good, and Mel Frost showed up."

"Groener killed him?"

"That's what we think. You and your father might have been the last ones to see him alive. And Groener waited and put in his papers, and when the time was right, he became Mel Frost and moved into the cottage with all that money."

A faint buzz to the west caught my attention. It took me a moment, but eventually I spotted a light plane that appeared to be coming straight at us. I had almost gotten used to the height, but seeing the plane I felt it all over again. It would be ironic if I survived the climb and finally heard the true story of Mike Spano and Mel Frost only to be killed by an errant Cessna. The plane veered away before it got close, though, heading for New Hampshire. It was a couple of hundred feet higher than us, actually, a trick of perspective.

"Do you have any proof? This all sounds-" I groped for a word from TV cop shows. "-circumstantial."

Donnie smiled grimly. "Phil saw the money. Some of it, anyway."

"How?"

"He broke in. Well, he had a key. One time he saw Frost hiding his spare. He's got one of those fake rocks, can you believe it? So the next time he went to town, Phil took it and got it copied at Island Convenience, a couple of days before he was killed. Rachel was at her parents' house with the kids after another one of their big fights. Frost went off on his weekly trip to Market Basket, and Phil went over in broad daylight. That took some stones."

"He found the million or whatever?"

"No, but he found an almanac in the living room with the middle cut out and a stack of used bills hidden inside, all dated from 1977 or before. There was a Bible on Frost's bedside table, same setup. I'd say that's a little more than circumstantial."

"That's why Frost killed him."

"That's what we think."

"How did you find out?"

"Phil told Chris."

"And Chris told you."

A nod. "Me and Quinn."

"Ronnie doesn't know?"

"Not all of it, anyway. Ronnie or John. Phil talked about it at poker in the beginning, but they wanted no part of it. Ronnie would be no use anyway, and neither one of them has got money troubles so bad that he'd do something like this."

"Something like what, exactly?"

"Taking Mel Frost's money. His ill-gotten gains or whatever. Me and Quinn. And you."

The nacelle seemed to sway. Maybe it was the wind, or maybe it was my conscience. But whatever comfort I'd achieved with the height suddenly deserted me.

"I thought Quinn didn't want me to know."

"He doesn't. But you and I, we're buds again. You've got money troubles just like us. I figure you deserve a piece of the action."

"You're serious. You're going to rob him."

"What's he going to do, call the cops? He's a murderer and a thief. And if he did that, who knows what other stuff he's done."

"Why does he have any money left? It's been decades."

"He doesn't spend diddly, as far as we can see. He's not exactly a party animal," Donnie said. "Seems like he came here for a nice, quiet retirement. Say there's only a million left, though, or even half a million. That's still enough to get all us out of hock, right?"

Donnie sounded like a guy trying to convince himself that the scratch ticket he just bought at Island Convenience was the winner.

"And what do you do if he catches you?"

"We deal with him." Donnie looked off at the far horizon, then back at me.

"We-"

"We deal with him," he said, and I realized I was shivering. "We've been up here a long time. We should probably go. You go down first."

I crab-walked over to the hatch and paused for a last look around at the view. When I first came up here, it seemed life-changing, but now it was the second craziest thing that had happened to me in the last hour.

Donnie walked up behind me, safety gear clinking.

"I knew you'd like it up here," he said. He sounded like he meant it.

THIRTY-TWO

I hadn't actually said yes to Donnie's insane scheme, but I hadn't said no, either. What had I gotten myself into?

I blamed the island. I had been seduced by its rough beauty, when I should have been wary of the isolation, its effect on my judgment. *What happens on the island, stays on the island.* On some level, I had known it was different here since the night of the giant snowball. But I hadn't noticed it changing me until now, when it was too late.

Sitting on top of the wind turbine was awesome, though.

After getting home, I ate leftovers without tasting them and sat on the deck with my coat on, thinking and staring at the ocean, until late. When I went up to bed, I couldn't nod off for hours due to guilt, fear, back spasms and too much cheap wine.

This being New England, the weather sensed my sins and punished me, Puritan style. The pleasant, unseasonably warm air was swept away overnight by a cold front that shook the windows and made the wires hum and clatter.

All the noise didn't exactly help me sleep, either, and I woke up late on Tuesday morning. The temperature had plunged, and snow fell in random bursts, five minutes of every hour, without accumulating. I drank a pot of coffee while staring out at the sickly green waves pounding the beach. Even the seagulls were hunkered down.

When I'd read all the news online – the economy was in free fall too – I got my guitar out of its case. Handling it was familiar, comforting. When it needed work, I took it to an elderly luthier with a shop in Medford Square. He was always all over me about taking better care of it, even though it had survived my teen years and all those nights on the road. I wiped down the body and neck with the chamois he had given me. I used a toothpick to relube the tuning pegs with a little bit of Vaseline, with his voice in my head: *Not too much!*

I tuned up and spent hour or three working on "Master of the Obvious," but it was hard to get much done, with Mel Frost and Mike Spano and Donnie and Quinn in my head, circling a pile of misbegotten cash. Eventually I gave up, with the third verse yet unwritten.

Years ago, the luthier had convinced me to install a fancy humidifier in my music room in town. The notion that a 1959 Berwyn D8 would spend six months at the beach, curing in salt air and the dry blast from the rattling old furnace, horrified him. "That furnace will run full-blast all the time in cold weather and if it hasn't rot from the damp, that will dry it right the hell out." His voice rose in indignation. "It would be a sin to let that happen to that beautiful instrument." Now, belatedly, I followed his directions for making a homemade humidifier, slipping a damp sponge into an open ziplock tucked into the case before I put the guitar away.

One obligation met.

I bundled up, got in the Sunbird and drove across the marsh to town. The north wind off the river rattled the ragtop until I turned uphill at Dock Square. I went to the bank and took some walking-around money out of the account that held my contribution to Zack's college fund. Another month behind, and the college tours would start before long. I would never catch up, never make it right.

I parked across the street from my house. From that angle I could see Billy had a crew up on the roof, battening down rippling tarps over the gaping holes, in hopes of keeping the snow out. It felt like my whole life had been ripped open, its messy innards on display.

I told him right away that I didn't have his check yet. I made it sound like a minor inconvenience, that it was just some holdup with Polio's accountant, my money would be here any day. Like any liar worth his salt, I sounded completely confident.

"We known each other a long time," he said. "But I ain't screwing around anymore. You don't have a check for me by Monday morning, I'm sending these assholes home."

"I'll get you the money, Billy, really."

"If you stiff me, I don't know who you'll get to finish the job."

"Really, I get it."

"I just want to be clear."

And because I couldn't stand another second of this conversation, I said, "Hey, you know what I did yesterday?"

Billy looked to the ceiling for patience, frowned at something he saw there, then looked back at me. His expression said he was keeping his expectations low. "What? What did you do?"

"I climbed the wind turbine and sat on top."

"Bullshit."

"For real. This guy I met on the island is in charge of the computers that run it. He was going up for a maintenance check, and he took me with him."

"No way!"

I hadn't seen that boyish grin since we started talking about money. I tried to make the most of his good mood.

"I know you've got ladders," I said, "but you've never seen one like this."

He laughed at all the right parts of the story, his eyes big and round. He said he'd like to climb the turbine sometime and smoke a joint on top. I said I'd try to set it up. Then we argued about the pendant lights over the kitchen island. The ones he pushed for were almost four hundred dollars a shot, rich man's lights. He insisted they went better with the two thousand-dollar slab of granite underneath. But it was my house.

I had second thoughts while I ran errands. I almost called him and gave in, but I didn't want to give him another chance to press me about money.

The snow was steadier now, dusting sidewalks, yards, and the tops of parked cars. The street lights came on as I turned onto River Street.

Abigail and a handful of hard-core supporters picketed in front of the blue building, hunched against the wind and slanting snow. They looked like Christmas carolers, except that it was February and they carried signs that said END EXPLOITATION OF WOMEN, JOHNS GO HOME, and HONK TO STOP SEX CRIMES. The twilight and snow made the signs hard to read, but people were honking. In the first-floor windows, though, the red light still burned behind the bamboo shades.

I pulled over across the street and waited until Abigail saw me. She looked both ways and crossed while I was cranking down my window.

"Good evening, Mr. McLean, have you come to join us?"

"I don't want to ruin my reputation."

"For not getting involved?"

"Remember the last time you led a protest?"

"Of course, it was against that awful nude statue in the storefront by the square."

"She was only topless. And she was a mermaid. They're supposed to be-"

"The point is, acceptance of that sort of display only lowers the public morals. It leads to outrages like that one-stop sin shop over there."

Change the subject. "This should be good for your campaign."

"Perhaps, perhaps, but that is hardly my first priority, Mr. McLean. I am more concerned about the good people of this community and their right to-"

"You might as well save your voice for the campaign rally." Miles Allgood appeared at her side in a long camel hair coat that would have fit Richard Nixon, snow dusting his weatherman hair. "Baxter here doesn't believe in anything except himself."

I wanted to tell him that was a grossly inaccurate measure of my self-esteem at the moment. "I'm not going to dignify that," I said.

"Of course you're not."

"Gentlemen, I hardly think the people of Libertyport are well served by this discussion." It was the most statesman-like thing I'd ever heard her say. The weasel had annoyed her by interrupting. I'd known better since ninth grade. "Miles, I would appreciate it if you would give me and Mr. McLean a moment."

"Suit yourself," he said, still sneering at me. Then he turned to her and smiled. "I mean, of course."

She watched him cross the street, then turned back to me. "One makes compromises in a political campaign."

"Of course."

"He is an unconquerably efficient and determined organizer."

"And he looks good in a wetsuit."

She stared at me for a long moment and decided not to ask. "He'll go far, but I suspect he will have to be watched. I may not be around long enough."

"You're asking me to do it?"

"I am old enough to see beyond our petty differences to people with true values," she said.

I thought of the money in my wallet and the bills yet to pay, of what Donnie and Quinn had planned and the very real possibility that I would, against my better judgment and all common sense, go along. "You may be overestimating me."

"Perhaps. In any case, I think between the blog and our action this evening, either these women will abandon the location, or else the town will be forced to take action."

"I think you're right."

"Then I will consider this particular promise to have been met, and I will expect you to enact the quid pro quo, as discussed."

"Of course. I appreciate everything you've done."

"You seem preoccupied this evening, Mr. McLean, is everything all right?"

"Everything's fine."

She flared her beaky nose, then raised one eyebrow, the same look she gave in high school when I told her one day before the deadline that I would indeed finish my report on time. I was lying then, too. "If you say so, Mr. McLean."

Those might have been the exact words she said about the report, too. Suddenly I was back in high school, and I felt a trace of the same guilty panic, face flushed, stomach on alert. I'd pulled nearly an all-nighter to finish that paper. I didn't know what I was going to do now.

"Do you remember when that kid had to pull out of high school because his father got caught embezzling from the bank?"

"I do. A rather paltry sum, wasn't it, ten thousand or something? A shame to destroy your career and your family's life over so little. It reminds me of the councilor who has vacated the seat for which I'm campaigning. A small-time crime once again has major consequences."

"Exactly. Do you remember what you told us in class about the banker?"

It took her a second. "I told you that if you could steal a million dollars, you should do it, but that anything less wasn't worth it."

"Still believe that?"

"I suppose so, although with inflation-"

"Look."

I pointed across the street. The red light behind the bamboo shades had gone out. Abigail turned and saw it, then gave me a look of triumph.

"Quid pro quo, Mr. McLean."

I gave her the thumbs-up and drove away.

I joined the long line of taillights headed across the marsh, most of them people returning to the island from jobs on the mainland. It was only a couple of miles, but it felt like a true exile. The pavement was just wet, but snow filled in white among the brittle marsh grass.

I put the groceries away and put The Band in the CD player, because their old-timey, rural sound was just right with the wind whistling outside in the dark. My back throbbed as I eased into the desk chair. I looked forward to my appointment with Chris in the morning. I would tell him what Abigail had done and, grateful, he would fix my back again. Snow hissed against the sliding glass doors.

The first email I saw was from ConcertSquad, Lily's management company, offering the opening slot on a run of a dozen shows beginning in a month. No doubt Manfred would be back in Europe by then, or on some movie set. Zack would understand if I had to miss one or two weekends. There was nothing to stop me except inertia and fear of failure, nothing at all.

I deleted the email, stood up carefully and went to get a beer. Maybe I could finish "Master of the Obvious" before I went to bed.

THIRTY-THREE

"Oh, Abigail," I said, although I was alone in the car. "You really did it."

Four TV trucks raised their microwave masts into the cold, crystal-clear morning on River Street. Local and state police cruisers were parked this way and that, blocking traffic in both directions, lights strobing lazily. She must have goaded them into a raid.

I had to park a block away. The bright logos splashed across the trucks created a carnival atmosphere. Cameramen and reporters presumably huddled in their idling vehicles for warmth, but cables had been run and cameras set up so they could come running when the cops marched the women out in handcuffs. A good, old-fashioned perp walk, a classic New England shaming. But even Wankum thought the women were victims more than criminals, and I felt guilty about what I had set in motion. Lily would not have approved, or would my ex-wife.

But I had enough things to hate myself for already. I shook their voices out of my head, got out of the Sunbird and headed for my appointment. Chris would be glad to see me today.

The front door of the building was propped open with a cinderblock and guarded by a uniformed trooper who glared at me as I approached. Better use the back door. The snow had stopped in the middle of the night, and a crowd of footprints and tire tracks led down the unplowed driveway. No one stopped me as I went, trying not to slip.

A big, black truck took up half of the little parking lot. Why did they need the State Police Crime Scene Unit to bust a massage parlor? It must have been a bigger operation than I thought. One of the investigators was uploading fingerprints on a laptop in the open back of the truck. He wore a white paper jumpsuit.

A Libertyport cruiser was pulled up at an odd angle near the back door. They'd arrived in a rush. Why the hurry? Were the women even awake this early? And come to think of it, they didn't live here, did they? Why were they even here?

An ambulance stood nearby, back doors open. As I slid down

the last few feet of driveway, the EMTs walked out of the building with an empty stretcher. They loaded it into the ambulance, expressionless, got in and drove away.

Several people stood just off the deck of Chris's office, inside a loop of yellow crime-scene tape. Wankum stood next to the State Police homicide detectives I knew as Putin and O'Hurley. One real name, one not. Putin was small but deadly looking, like the Russian president. O'Hurley was a classic red-faced Irishman, tall and slow-moving.

"You are unbelievable."

O'Hurley seemed genuinely outraged at the sight of me. Putin just stared at me with those cold eyes.

I said, "What's going on?"

"Every year we come up here, and you're mixed up in it somehow. Today the cleaning lady finds this stiff, and you're the next person in his book."

I looked at Wankum, but he looked away.

"Chris's dead?"

"We didn't come by to get a neck rub," O'Hurley said. "Kudos for being on time for your appointment, though."

Putin spoke at last, ignoring his partner's attempt at humor. "It's Christopher Prather, yes, though we are not releasing the name until the family is notified."

The sliding door was wide open. I stepped around them to look inside.

"Don't go in there," Wankum said.

"I know."

All the lights were on. The massage table was tipped up so I was mostly looking at the bottom of it. Two techs in white paper jumpsuits dusted the edges of it for prints. A lifeless hand dangled off one side and two worn running shoes hung limply off the far end. I didn't remember what Chris wore on his feet during our appointment. But it was definitely his face pushing through the hole in the table. Skin a pale blue-white, eyes open and staring blankly out the slider. A single trail of blood from the back of his head had run across his forehead and dripped on the floor.

"How did he die?"

"We ask the questions," O'Hurley said.

"I thought you were here for the hookers," I said.

"What's that supposed to mean, smart guy?"

Wankum stepped up. "The Thai massage place in 4-B gives happy endings. There have been a few complaints, including one relayed by Baxter here that I believe originated with Mr. Prather. The sex-crimes task force was looking at it. Yesterday this local broad led a protest out front. But it looks like they cleared out last night. There's no one there this morning, anyway, and a bunch of their stuff is gone."

I kept looking. The massager was on the floor a few feet away from the table, unplugged and covered in blood. Someone had clouted him when his back was turned.

"*Was* Prather the one who dropped a dime on these hookers?" Putin asked.

I nodded. "He said the police weren't doing anything. I told him I knew someone who could help."

Wankum said, "Nothing had happened yet, though. If they left, it was because of the protest."

"They left because of Abigail," I said.

"Who's Abigail?" O'Hurley said.

"Abigail Marks," Wankum said. "Local gadfly and legendary pain in the ass. Currently running for city council and looking for ways to make trouble. She led a protest against the hookers yesterday out front. They had handmade signs, *Johns Go Home*, stuff like that. *Honk To Stop Sex Crimes* was my favorite. Plenty of people honked, too."

"Pain in the ass is right," O'Hurley said, sniffling.

"It's free speech," I said.

"Whoop-de-doo for her."

"So this is payback," Putin said. "Their pimp killed him, and then they got out of here. They'll set up shop somewhere else by tonight."

"Could be," Wankum said.

"Did your friend the chiropractor say anything about a pimp?"

I thought for a second. "No, he only saw the women, I think."

"So how would they know that he was the one who dropped a dime?"

"I don't know."

"Who knew that he was the one who complained? That would be you, this Abigail and who else?"

"Abigail's campaign manager, Miles Allgood. No one else that I know of."

"So it seems like you and this Abigail are our prime suspects."

Wankum said, "I don't think either one of them…"

Putin cut him off with a look. "We'll talk to this Abigail, but the hypothetical pimp is our starting point. Either that, or this Chris tried to extort a freebie from one of the girls and got more than he bargained for."

"He wouldn't do that," I said.

"You'd be surprised how often the one who complains is also a customer."

"I know one thing," O'Hurley said. "We're going to need an interpreter, we ever find these bitches. I don't know anything except Pad Thai extra spicy." He sneezed and wiped his bulbous nose with the back of his hand. "Where's the nearest coffee, anyway?"

"There's a Starbucks and about five other places downtown," Wankum said.

"No Dunkin'?"

"We've got three. One at the convenience store corner on Parker Street, one at the rotary, one out by the highway."

O'Hurley nodded and felt for his car keys. "I'm gonna make a run. Anybody want anything?"

We all shook our heads. "Fine, back in a jiff."

When he was gone, Putin turned to me. "So, you knew the suicide they found out on the island, too, right?"

"Never met him."

Wankum caught up with me as I was slipping and sliding up

the driveway to the street.

"Was the chiropractor in your poker game too?"

I nodded. He made a noise halfway between a moan and a growl. "This is just what I need."

"When was Chris killed?"

"Don't know for sure, yet. But Freddie the EMT said he'd bet it was eight or nine o'clock last night."

"The cleaning lady found him?"

"Yeah, and I'm surprised she called it in. She's Guatemalan, her papers are obviously fake. I think I've convinced our Statie friends to overlook that, though, because she did the right thing."

"I bet you anything it isn't the massage people. They were probably already gone because of Abigail's protest. They don't need the attention."

"Maybe. Was this Chris a good friend of yours?"

"We'd never met until Ronnie got me into the card game. I had one appointment before today."

"For what?"

"My back is messed up."

"When did you make today's appointment?"

"I had my first appointment last week, and this was my follow-up. We set it up then."

"You haven't seen him otherwise?"

"He came over a couple of times to use the shower or whatever. He's one of the ones without water."

"Yeah, that's a mess, huh?"

"And it gives Abigail another campaign issue."

"If she gets on the council, just shoot me. She'll have that pointy nose of hers in everything. Including the police budget."

"I'm playing at her campaign rally."

"Seriously? Should I draw up commitment papers?"

"It's payback for her picketing the massage place. Remember, I asked you to take care of it first."

"I hate politics." He rubbed his face. "It's too early for this shit. I need another one of those coffees with the picture on top."

"You really have changed."

He nodded. "You know what bugs me, though? He got popped after supper last night, lay there all night, and nobody missed him. Nobody reported him gone. It took the cleaning lady to find him."

"Yeah, it sucks."

But under the same circumstances, would anyone have reported me missing?

THIRTY-FOUR

"It's true?" Donnie asked, without preamble.

"It's true."

"He's dead?"

"Yes." I stood in the Rum House parking lot, just before noon. There were more seagulls than cars, several of them rooting in the Dumpster. The rest stood on the pavement, watching me out of the corners of their eyes.

"Shot?"

"Smashed over the head."

"No way. Bad?"

"He's dead."

"Right. Where?"

"In his office, sometime last night."

"Frost. It had to be."

"You're probably right."

"Are they going after him?"

"Who?"

"The cops."

"Not yet. The Staties think it was someone from the Thai massage place."

Long pause on the other end. "Why do they think that?"

"Because Chris complained about them. He asked me for help. He didn't want you guys to know for some reason."

"What did you do?"

"I told my friend the detective about them."

"He busted them?"

"Not exactly."

"Then why would they kill Chris?"

"Because I also told Abigail Marks about them. And she kind of held a protest last night out in front."

"You're kidding."

"Looks like they pulled up stakes. And the Staties think one of them hit Chris on the way out."

"What about your friend?"

"He's not so sure."

"How come?"

"He knows that Chris and Phil Jonah knew each other."

"Shit, how did he figure that out?"

Long pause on my end. "I don't know."

"Does he know about Frost?"

"I don't know. I don't think so." Why didn't I tell him? Good question.

"Well, we're going to have to move fast."

"You want me to call him?"

"Who?"

"Wankum, the detective."

"No!"

"Why not?"

"So we've got to get to the money before the cops get to Frost."

"You're still-"

"I've got to talk to Quinn."

He hung up without a goodbye.

"Apparently it was just anemia," my mother said. "I was taking too much ibuprofen for my arthritis. I was bleeding in my stomach without knowing it, and I became terribly anemic."

"I'm glad to hear you're OK."

"The fatigue was unbelievable. I thought for sure it was leukemia or some other blood cancer."

"I'm relieved, really."

"But you'll just have to wait for your inheritance."

"Jesus, Ma! I'm really not thinking about that."

"It's only human nature."

"I'm not. Really."

"Well, I wouldn't blame you."

She'd started on her wine while she waited for me. I signaled

Davey for a beer and to hurry it up.

"Truth is, there won't be much anyway."

"Be much what, Ma?"

"Are you listening to me? You seem preoccupied."

"I'm listening."

"There won't be much of an inheritance. Your father was the earner in the family, and he was only an associate professor. He had tenure of course, but you have to be a full professor to make the serious money."

"Why are we talking about this?"

"Because I want you to understand the situation."

"We have to talk about this today?"

"This was only a scare, thank goodness, but I'm not going to be around forever."

It was Thursday, so there were a few more customers than the last time we were here. Davey was busy at the bar, so a waitress ferried over my beer. I took a long swallow.

"Did you hear me? I'm not going to be around forever."

"I know, Ma."

"I got his life insurance, which paid off the house, but I had to go back to work to pay the taxes and the oil. I had security at the school department, but what they paid me wasn't exactly a princely sum."

"I *know*, Ma."

"So I have some small savings that I'm living off, and of course the equity in the house. Which is quite a bit, or at least it was before this godawful real estate crash."

"That's good."

"Prices will come back when the economy turns around, of course, this is Libertyport. And as soon as that happens, I am going to sell the house."

That one took me a second to absorb, even though I knew it was coming someday. We'd moved in more than thirty years ago. My old bedroom had been converted to a nice, generic guest room a long time ago, but I'd slept there briefly during the divorce. When I was lonely, I sat on my bed and played my guitar, just like thirty years ago. The view from the window was the same, South End tree tops and roofs, a vista from a mostly bucolic boyhood. To think about it belonging to someone else was not easy.

"That's your decision, Ma."

"I'm glad you realize that."

"I said you should do what you want."

"I am, dear, I am."

"And what is that? What do you want to do?"

She pulled a color brochure from her purse. "Beholden Farm, Elegant Retirement Living in West Liberty. It's going to take just about every dollar I have, but it's what I want. Independence, but I don't have to cook, and I have access to whatever kind of care I will need."

"That's fine, Ma."

"Are you sure you're all right?"

Davey brought the check then, looking slightly nervous about it. My mother and I both reached for it, but I got there first. I took out my wallet and put down some of my walking-around cash.

"I'm fine, Ma," I said and handed the little tray back to a relieved-looking Davey. "I'm fine."

THIRTY-FIVE

The Plover Island Taxpayers' Hall was a simple, clean-lined, shingled structure across the street from Island Convenience. Civic-minded islanders put it up a few years ago as a place to hold weddings, birthday parties and funerals. It was also the island's polling place. Membership in the PITH Association leaned heavily to year-round island residents with townie roots. The annual operating budget came from donations, hall rentals, and charging barefoot tourists $10 or $15 a car on summer weekends for beach parking. You'd see them toting their towels and coolers up the street to the beach, quick-stepping because the pavement was hot.

The PITHy COMMENTS Facebook page had become the go-to source for the latest island gossip. Lately it had been dominated by complaints about the water and sewer situation, and the hall had been used for several "town meetings" where the mayor and councilors were called to account. Their answers failed to satisfy. People were angry.

I carried my guitar case through a side door that opened right onto the expanse of metal folding chairs and fluorescent lights. Most of the chairs were already filled. The largest contingent was retirees, older couples who couldn't afford Florida and looked grumpy about it. I knew several of the men from breakfast at Foley's or lunches at Raging Rosie's. They were proud conspiracy theorists and dedicated Fox News viewers who wrote letters to the editor and put provocative bumper stickers on their Chryslers. There was also a substantial number of folks from the other end of the political spectrum, ex-hippies including the weird old guy from The Tuscan Café. No surprise he was an islander. Their distrust of corporations and government brought them into near accord with the Fox News viewers on such issues as fluoridated water, mandatory vaccinations and the secret meaning of vapor trails in the sky. A ten-million-dollar water system that froze in the winter was the most legitimate gripe they'd ever had, and they intended to take it all the way.

Three weeks without showers had left them all looking for someone to punch.

Because it was the middle of winter and the middle of the work week, the McMansion people were underrepresented. Maybe they just didn't care. Ventana and one or two others sat up straight in the front row like the important civic personages they believed themselves to be. He and I exchanged a nod.

Many of them were in line for the bathrooms. It was worth coming to an Abigail campaign rally to use a working toilet. The rest sat on folding chairs or stood against the walls of the brightly lit room, arms folded tightly across their chests.

Miles Allgood adjusted the folding chairs on stage to fit a precise plan that existed only in his mind. He wore the only suit and tie in the room.

"So glad you could make it, Mr. McLean."

Meaning, *Good thing you showed up.* The fervid glint in his eye creeped me out. I would not have wanted to run against her while he was in charge.

"I'm always happy to help out Abigail," I said. Odd to realize it wasn't entirely a lie.

"She's going to do wonderful things for our town." He looked out at the crowd with a hint of contempt. "These people have no idea."

I started for the kitchen, but he stopped me.

"Where are you going?"

"I'm going to go back and tune up and get ready. I need someplace to put my coat and my stuff."

He shook his head dismissively.

"The candidate is back there polishing up her speech. She needs her privacy. You can tune up right here."

"No I can't."

I pushed through the swinging doors to the kitchen. Everywhere I looked was gleaming aluminum and stainless steel, like the hall of mirrors in an old thriller. Hanging pots and pans were catering-size, and so were the double refrigerators.

Abigail stood back by an acre of sinks, wearing a for-her demure purple suit and cream blouse. She moved her lips while she read over her speech.

"In class you always told me not to move my lips when I practiced a speech."

Her head jerked back. "You practiced?"

"Touché."

"I would love to stand here and match wits with you, Mr. McLean, but I need to be ready."

For the first time I could remember, she actually seemed nervous. I found a folding chair near the dishwasher, sat down and began to tune up.

"Does it gall you, Mr. McLean?"

"Does what gall me?"

"Playing for an Abigail Marks campaign rally."

"It's unexpected."

She chuckled. "I'm sure. But it doesn't bother you? I gather we have rather different positions on a number of issues."

I stopped tuning for a second and thought about it. "I wouldn't vote for you for president, probably. But I think I understand why those people want you on the city council."

"Because they can't take a shower or flush their toilets."

"Because they believe you'll do something about it. And I bet you will."

"Thank you, Mr. McLean." She looked almost misty-eyed

We both turned away and went back to what we were doing, so we could pretend the moment never happened. In five, Miles stuck his weaselly little head in. "It's time."

We stood side-by-side behind the kitchen doors, watching through the little windows as he hopped up on the little stage.

"Ladies and gentlemen, we'd like to get started. If I could have your attention? Your attention please!"

Most of the crowd broke off their conversations and grudgingly returned to their seats, though a few took the opportunity to move up in the shortened bathroom lines. While they got settled, he reminded them of the election date, polling hours and the poll locations in each precinct.

"And now, before we bring out the candidate, we have a little entertainment for you. Most of you know Baxter McLean, and as I understand it, he's currently an island resident. So please give him a warm welcome. Baxter?"

I popped through the door, trying to simulate the eagerness of a game-show contestant, smiling my *How you folks doing?* smile. All contingents responded with dubious expressions and scattered applause, except for the weird old guy, whose wild clapping drew a few scowls. They wanted to get to the main event. They wanted Abigail, because she was going to listen to them. And they had a lot to say.

"Hey everyone, thanks for having me. I won't ask you how you're doing, because I know what a tough time some of you are having. Miles here is right, I am living on the island this winter. I'm lucky because I've had water all along."

A few sidelong glances, people looking at their spouses or neighbors as if to say, *So why are we listening to him?*

"Thing is, the water crisis has affected me too. Because all my friends on the island are in the same boat you are. About every fifteen minutes one of them knocks at my door with this crafty expression. 'Hey Baxter, what's up? Just wanted to drop by and see how you're enjoying the beach. Oh yes, I always bring a loofah and shampoo when I visit a friend.'"

That got a laugh, and I could see them relaxing.

" 'By the way, how's your towel supply?'"

I began to pick a few soft notes on the guitar.

"Sometimes I take pity on 'em and ask 'em straight up if they'd mind testing out my plumbing to make sure it's working. 'Take a shower? Well, if you insist.'"

More laughter. Miles grinned like he thought it was totally hilarious, but I could see the muscles in his neck clinching. If he was going to enact his plan for world domination, he would have to find a way to fake-smile with less effort, or he'd need a neck brace before he lost his virginity.

"I thought I would get a lot of work done while I was out here by myself, a lot of practicing, a lot of writing. But with all the people coming over to shower or use the can, I feel like one of those bathroom attendants places used to have. 'Would you like a hot towel, sir? Some cologne?'" A smattering of applause amid the laughter. "In between my valet duties, though, I have found the time to write a song or two."

My aimless tinkering on the guitar resolved into a chord and then another. "This is a new one called 'Master of the Obvious.'"

> *The island is cold in January-*
> *But you knew that, right?*

The song got a few laughs, but I still had work to do. Next I played "Mirror Ball Man," just to remind them who I was. Then "No Evacuation Possible," my island anthem from twenty years ago, when I played local rallies against the nuclear plant under construction just over the New Hampshire border. If there was a meltdown, the road across the marsh was going to look like *Mad Max: Road Warrior*, and no one was going to get to the mainland in time to save themselves. The ex-hippies remembered that one fondly, even though it hadn't stopped the nuke from going online.

Then, because I knew what islanders liked, I hit them with a cover of Jimmy Buffett's "Changes in Latitudes, Changes In Attitudes" that had them all thinking about summer and flip-flops and cold beers sweating in the sun.

That left them in a good mood for Abigail, who stepped up onto the stage as I stepped down.

"Thank you, Mr. McLean, I think we can now call it even for that paper you failed to hand in back in tenth grade," she said to laughter and scattered applause. "Now I would like to talk about the water situation."

There was a smattering of applause, and someone muttered, "Finally."

When the rally was over, I carried my guitar out into the darkened parking lot. I was reaching for my keys when Quinn appeared next to the Sunbird.

"Poker's canceled. It's a go for tomorrow night," he said. "Stay home and be ready."

I popped the trunk and set my guitar in, gathering the courage to tell him I was out. But when I turned around, he was gone.

THIRTY-SIX

On Friday morning, I turned on the bathroom faucet and nothing came out. I was still broke, and now my water was off too. I had become a Third World country. Did that mean I could steal Frost's money? I wasn't sure.

I couldn't think without my coffee. I used a bottle of Zack's vitamin water from the fridge to make a pot and told myself the funny taste was all in my head.

Unshowered, I spent hours trying to write songs but got nowhere. All I could think about was the night ahead, and what I should do. I was in, then I was out. Then I thought about Zack's college fund, and I was in again. I had screwed everything up, and if I went along with the heist, my problems would go away. In theory. If everything went perfectly. But I still had that sick, unmoored feeling of sliding on ice toward a real boulder, a slow motion car crash, trouble waiting to happen.

In the afternoon, I heard a sound as sweet as the first robin of spring: a jackhammer starting up. To celebrate, I put my guitar away and walked down the driveway to the boulevard. Birders and town crew alike had gathered at the corner of Lilac Lane.

The town crew had closed off the corner with orange cones and sawhorses. A curving tongue of sand showed where the water had flowed out of a jagged crack in the pavement and into the yards across the street, now covered with ice. At least they'd managed to turn off the flow. The guy with the jackhammer opened a long, thin rectangle of pavement that would end at the crack. Another guy followed him, guiding the pneumatic hose like a roadie wrangling the cord while a guitarist soloed. Back when guitars had cords. A yellow backhoe dug a trench in their wake.

The birders, eight or ten of them, clustered on the edge of the corner property, aiming their expensive German optics at Hedwig. The owl sat on the peak of the cottage roof, looking annoyed at all the noise. The town guys cast the occasional skeptical glance her way – You seen one snowy owl, you seen them all – but mostly they looked in the hole. Even as I watched them work, I couldn't stop thinking about the money.

It wasn't like we were robbing a bank or something.

We were merely repurposing some ill-gotten gains. Making off with the loot. Taking from the rich and corrupt and giving to the poor – us. Poor us.

We were robbing a guy who'd robbed a guy who'd robbed a bank. How could that be wrong? How could it be right? Had I forgotten the difference?

Or was Abigail right, that if you could steal a million, you should do it?

I could turn around, pack up, get in the car, and be out of town when it all went down. Or even in town. I could go sleep under a tarp on a couch in my own living room. I could work things out with Billy somehow. Go on a concert tour with Lily and pay back what I'd taken from Zack. Maybe if I did, the guys would see the light and call off their plan. Or maybe they would go ahead without me. Either way, I'd be in the clear.

Or maybe Quinn would kill me in my sleep with a linoleum knife.

I could warn Mel Frost. Walk right up there now and knock on his front door. He'd look thrilled as ever to see me, and I'd get another chance to enjoy his breath. I would tell him what was coming, and he would pack up his money and get away. They'd never know I had tipped him off. We wouldn't get the money, but nobody would go to prison, nobody would get hurt.

The jackhammer paused. *Take five everybody. Smoke 'em if you got 'em.* I walked closer to the excavation and stared down into the hole absent-mindedly, at the mint-green plastic pipes, the water and muck.

"You live here?" one of the town guys said.

"Just up the street."

"Water will be off till tomorrow," he said.

I shrugged. He nodded. Just the way it goes.

One of the birders edged closer, an older woman bent forward slightly, perhaps by the weight of her enormous binoculars. "Do you have to make so much noise with your tools?"

"Why do you want to know?"

"You'll scare the owl."

He blinked at her without expression. "We're almost done," he said, and walked away.

"They're going to scare her away," she said to me, her voice hot with outrage.

"I need water," I said.

She scowled, clucked her teeth and walked away too.

"I also need money," I said to no one.

I took another look at Mel Frost's cottage and the Eldorado in the driveway, then turned around and started for home. Hedwig was the only one who noticed. Her expression said she didn't approve.

Standing by the sliders, I watched the ocean turn pink and blue to match the sunset sky. Lovely, but it was colder out there than it looked. I called Zack.

"Hey, Dad."

"Where are you? Are you alone?"

"Yeah, I'm in my room, why?"

"You can't come out here tonight."

A brief pause, then a disappointed tone. "Whatever."

"Don't."

"Don't what?"

"Don't be mad."

"OK." Mad.

"I love it when you're out here."

"Hey, if you've got a date or something-"

"It's nothing like that. That's why I'm calling, to tell you, so you'll know."

"OK." Willing to listen.

"I just need to be alone here tonight. I'm not going to tell you exactly what's up, because it's none of your business."

He didn't say anything, and I couldn't blame him. I didn't exactly have the moral high ground. Was I doing this for him? Or was I doing it for me, so he wouldn't know what a failure I truly was?

After a long silence, he asked, "Is this another one of your shenanigans?"

"Shenanigans?"

"It's a word."

"I know it's a word. It's an old word."

"It's a Lawrence word," he said, and I realized he was offering a truce. Lawrence was the headmaster, under whose roof Zack now lived. Normally I hated him, but he wasn't contemplating armed robbery to meet his obligations to his son. "Some guys got caught smoking weed out behind the theater building, and Lawrence told them he was 'fed up with their shenanigans.' Now everyone's saying it."

"Yeah, well, then, I guess, it is another one of my shenanigans."

"Be careful." He sounded awfully serious all of a sudden. "Don't get shot again or anything."

I was shocked silent. I had never considered the effect that previous "shenanigans" had on him. Part of his anger was really worry, and that was my fault. Among so many other things.

So of course I add more lies to the list of my sins.

"I won't get shot. It's nothing like that. I'll call you tomorrow and you can come out then."

"That's cool."

"And Zack? Not a word to your mother." The words echoed in a way I couldn't quite latch onto. "Just tell her my water's off and you can't deal with no shower."

"That works."

"Good night, Zack."

"Good night, Dad."

After we hung up, I remembered when and where the echo originated.

THIRTY-SEVEN

That evening, I sat not watching *Jeopardy*, my mind elsewhere. Two dark silhouettes trooped onto my deck and opened the slider. Cold air rushed in, and the roar of the surf was suddenly louder than the TV. I turned off Trebek.

Donnie stuck his head in. "Are you alone?"

I nodded and stood up. He and Quinn came inside, dressed all in black. Quinn looked around as if expecting an ambush.

"You got water yet?" Donnie asked.

"Not yet, maybe tomorrow they said."

"That sucks."

"Why tonight?" I asked.

"Every Friday night, he goes to Giuseppe's for veal parm. Phil timed it. He'll be gone for at least an hour."

"This is crazy." That was the beginning of the resignation speech I'd been rehearsing in my head on and off all day.

"Maybe, but we're doing it," Quinn said.

Donnie pulled a box of purple surgical gloves from his knapsack and handed us each a pair.

"He's killed two people," I said. "Shouldn't we let the cops deal with him?"

"Say you call your friend Wankum," Donnie said. "They're going to question all of us. They're going to find out we've been planning to rob a retired FBI agent. How do you think that's going to go?"

"We'd be handing them the solution to one of the great unsolved mysteries. I don't think they'd be too unhappy. Or we can think up some other reason we knew about the money."

"So, say that works. We let them bust him and take the money. Where does that leave us? Quinn goes bankrupt. I go bankrupt and never see my kids again. You lose your house, and your wife and kid are pissed because of the college fund. You want that?"

"But if we get caught-"

"We're not going to get caught."

"He's already killed two of you – two of us. What if he catches us inside? What do we do then?"

"We've prepared." Donnie pulled a small semi-automatic out of his jacket pocket. He smiled down at it, his new toy. "Walther PPK, just like James Bond."

Quinn rolled his eyes. But he lifted his coat to show off the shiny silver revolver holstered at his waist.

I said, "We're going in armed?"

"Hopefully we won't need them," Donnie said. "We'll find the money and get the hell out of there. But just in case, we're ready."

"What if we can't find the money?"

"We wait for him to come home," Quinn said.

"You don't think he's just going to tell you-"

"I'm not losing my house while that scumbag sits there on a mountain of cash."

Donnie, playing peacemaker: "We'll get him to listen to reason."

"You wouldn't be trying so hard to justify it if you really thought it was right."

"We're doing it," Quinn said. "And you're coming with us."

Was this how my father felt when the snub-nosed revolver was pointed at him? He had stood strong under the gun, even though he was out of his element. I wondered if he felt the same dread that was making its way through my guts now. It made his behavior that long-ago night seem even more impressive. And now I was heading back to Lilac Lane.

"It's just a little casual breaking and entering among friends," Donnie said. "Reminds me of when we were kids. Remember? We'd break into summer people's houses all the time, steal their beer and empty their change jar. Half the time they'd leave the back door unlocked. Those were the good old days. Maybe that will happen again."

"I was never with you."

Donnie looked surprised. "You weren't? Are you sure?"

"It wasn't me."

"It's you now," Quinn said. "It's time."

Maybe, like my father, I could find a way to diffuse the situation. Maybe when push came to shove, they'd drop the whole idea. Or maybe we'd go in, find the money, and get away no problem.

    I grabbed my coat.

THIRTY-EIGHT

Out on the beach, the swirling wind whipped sand in my face and chilled me to the bone. All of the houses we passed were dark, and the sky held only stars.

At Lilac Lane, we stopped on the beach below the guardrail and squatted down to take stock. Dune grass thrashed in the wind. The lights were on inside Mel Frost's cottage. Across the street, Jonah's house stood dark and still, the driveway empty. Down at the corner, by the boulevard, a covey of yellow lights blinked randomly atop saw-horses, guarding the unfinished water main repair.

Donnie and Quinn took out their guns. Donnie pulled the slide to jack a round into the chamber. Quinn tipped out the cylinder of his revolver, spun it to check the load, then snapped it back in place.

"I thought the plan was that we'd only go in after he left."

Quinn scoffed.

"We'll wait," Donnie said, "but not forever. He killed Phil and Chris. He deserves whatever he gets."

I just shook my head. I was back in that slow-motion car crash, skidding toward catastrophe.

The light in Frost's kitchen went out. The living room lights went out next, and the porch light came on.

"He's going," Donnie said.

"You think?" Quinn said.

Frost came out the front door carrying two empty plastic milk jugs in each hand.

"He's getting water," Donnie whispered.

"No shit, Sherlock," Quinn said. "He'll stop on the way back from dinner."

Frost wore dress shoes and a long camel-hair coat. The man didn't have any casual clothes. He walked to the Eldorado, no more than fifty feet from us, popped the trunk, tossed the milk jugs inside and slammed the lid. The wind paused, so we could hear him whistling tunelessly as he walked around to the driver's door.

He fired up the big V-8, turned on the lights, backed out of the driveway and zoomed down to the boulevard. He barely touched his brakes before pulling out past the blinking sawhorses and onto the boulevard, the big engine growling. The wind picked up again as he accelerated out of sight.

Nothing else moved in the neighborhood except for the surf and a metal trash can cover that went skipping down the next street in a gust.

"Gentlemen, I'd say we have the green light," Donnie said after a moment.

They stood. Quinn stalked around the end of the guardrail, where summer beachgoers had worn a path, and Donnie followed. I still crouched behind the guardrail.

"You coming, asshole?"

"Don't worry about Baxter, he's with us, aren't you, Bax?"

"I'm up." My back suddenly locked tight, and not just because I'd been sitting with my guitar. But I moved anyway.

Donnie patted my shoulder. "Glad you're with us."

I should have said *Me too,* but I couldn't. "So what do you think we have, an hour?"

"Closer to ninety minutes if he's stopping for water."

We reached the edge of Frost's lawn. My last chance to bail.

"I'm going to hit the shed." Quinn headed down the driveway and disappeared into the shadows.

I looked at Donnie, who chuckled softly.

"Quinn has a theory. You ask me, no way it's out there. That much cash, Frost is going to hold it close. Of course, if Quinn finds it out there while we're inside, he'll take off on us. Then we'll be sorry."

We crunched across the lawn toward the front door. We were halfway to the steps when brilliant white light lit up Jonah's house and the whole street. We froze, caught.

Hedwig swooped down from Jonah's roof, huge and white, diving through the light she'd triggered. We must have startled her. She pulled out of her dive when she was almost to the deck, and rose above our heads. I could swear she gave me a stern look. She passed over Mel Frost's cottage, flapping her wings just once. We watched her go. When she was out of sight, the light went out, and we took a breath.

"That was *awesome*," Donnie said, as if he'd forgotten why we were here.

"I could have done without the surprise."

"At least it gets the old adrenalin pumping." He pulled on his gloves. "It's like when we were kids doing this and scared shitless."

"If you say so."

He couldn't let go of our imaginary friendship, the story he'd made up to convince himself that he'd had a happy adolescence and that I was part of it. And now didn't seem like the right time to argue about it.

We climbed the steps to the porch. When the storm door creaked, I felt the sense of having reentered an old dream. The inner door was closed, though. Donnie had a key. We stepped inside. The house had a faint mustiness, a tinge of that liverwurst smell.

"How are we supposed to do this?"

"However we want." Even in the dark, I could see his smile.

We walked around the living room, and I ran a finger over the side table again. He flipped open a music box on a shelf just long enough to show me the gun inside. No wonder Mel Frost hadn't wanted me to touch his stuff. Donnie started pulling down books, choosing the fattest hard covers. The third one he opened had been hollowed out for a stack of bills, twenties and tens, with a few fifties on the bottom. Donnie grinned and pocketed the cash, then put the book back. The next one held a similar stack, and he offered it to me.

"I'll wait for the big haul," I said.

"Suit yourself." He stuffed the bills into another pocket.

I joined him at the bookshelf. The first volume I opened held a small semi-automatic, almost a miniature. I showed it to Donnie, who wiggled his eyebrows like Groucho. Then I put it back.

"Let's try the kitchen," Donnie said.

Everything there was neat and clean and squared away, like the living room. Not a single picture or clipping hung on the refrigerator door. The only personal touch was a bottle of Early Times by the toast-er, a shot glass in front of it with a dollop of brown liquor in the bottom. Frost pre-gaming his trip to town. Everything else was so neat, I wondered why he hadn't washed and dried the shot glass and put it away.

Donnie unlocked the back door, then walked down the counter opening all the cabinets, then began taking down any container large enough to serve as a hiding place. He dumped oatmeal cans and cereal boxes and flour tins onto the floor, revealing nothing but oatmeal and cereal and flour. The mess felt like the first really bad thing we'd done. When he dumped the cornmeal, another small semi-automatic tumbled out and skittered across the floor. We froze until it stopped without going off.

"Check the fridge," he said, bending to look under the sink.

Frost used metal ice trays that had to be antiques, the kind with a lever you worked to crack the cubes free. Maybe they came with the cottage. There was nothing else in the freezer but a half-gallon of vanilla ice cream and a few packages of frozen vegetables. The ice cream looked normal, but a one-pound bag of frozen peas was suspiciously rectangular. I tore it open.

The money felt cold in my hand. That was when it finally hit me what we were doing, what a terrible idea this was. Master of the Obvious. The money wouldn't save me, only plunge me into much worse trouble. But it was too late. I put the bundle of bills back and closed the freezer while Donnie had his head in the cabinet. I was relieved to find nothing in the fridge, either.

Donnie dumped a box of dishwasher detergent on the floor. Nothing. "Don't look so worried. Frost's a bad guy. We're not stealing his money, we're liberating it. Let's try the basement."

He opened the door and flicked the light switch for the stairway down, grinning like a kid who was getting away with something, instead of an adult committing a string of felonies.

"Most of these dumps don't even have basements," he said.

I followed him down the rickety wooden stairs, stomach clenched. There was nothing immediately sordid about the basement. Bare bulbs on rafters lit a space with cinderblock walls and a poured-cement floor. Tools hung on a pegboard above a small workbench, their outlines drawn in magic marker. A lawnmower and gas can sat next to the workbench.

"What do you notice?" Donnie asked.

"It looks like pretty much every basement I've ever been in."

"What's different?"

Beyond the workbench, a few pieces of old furniture sat next to a mountain of dusty cardboard boxes. There were other containers mixed in with the boxes: old luggage, a steamer trunk, white plastic drywall buckets, a bag of rock salt for the driveway, a couple of big plastic storage bins, one with Christmas tinsel caught in the cover and hanging out. Under the harsh light of the bare bulbs, everything showed a patina of dust. Almost everything.

"It's dusty as hell. Except for those."

"Exactly."

Five drywall buckets sat close together in the middle of the mess, clean but not new. Donnie grabbed a metal handle and lifted one out with a grunt. "Heavy," he said with a grin. He lowered it to the floor at our feet and popped off the plastic lid. The bucket was full of rough grey powder – cement – but Donnie plunged his hand in, felt around for a moment, then said, "Yes!"

He pulled out a heavy black garbage bag, cement dust falling everywhere. The bag was thick contractor-grade plastic, like Billy used at my house. Donnie loosened the twist tie with an effort, reached into the bag, and came out with a brick of bills.

"Hiding in plain sight," he said, grinning down at the money stacked by his feet. "I bet when we get all these buckets open, it's a million-plus."

He reached for another bucket, but then we heard the kitchen door close, and we froze. Heavy footsteps crossed the floor above our heads, and Donnie drew his gun. When Quinn's boots and jeans appeared on the top step, he put it away quickly.

"Nothing in the shed. How are you assholes doing? Whoa. Hello, beautiful."

Quinn crossed directly to the money, picked up packages with both hands and stuffed them in his jacket pockets. I could see Donnie wanted to object but didn't dare. "How much?" Quinn said.

"Five buckets, could be all of it."

"Don't you want any?" Quinn asked me.

"I can wait."

"Suit yourself."

I watched him fill his jacket to bulging from the first bucket, while Donnie opened a second bucket and pulled out another garbage bag. He was about to say something triumphant when the kitchen floor creaked. He and Quinn exchanged a look, then Quinn backpedaled silently into the shadows near the stairs, his big silver revolver already in hand. He flapped his hand at Donnie: *Keep talking.*

"It's all here," Donnie said, a little louder than necessary. His smile was gone. "All the money we'll ever need."

Suddenly Mel Frost was there on the stairs in his camel-hair coat, with a large black gun in his hand.

"Don't move," he said mildly. "Especially don't go for that gun in your belt, Mr. Arsenault."

We both raised our hands without saying anything, trying strenuously not to look at Quinn in the shadows.

"Congratulations to you both," Frost said, stepping slowly down to the floor.

"For what?" Donnie said.

"For surviving the elimination round. Mr. Jonah did not, nor did Mr. Prather. It's been amusing watching you turn on each other before even reaching your goal."

I asked, "What do you mean, turning on each other?"

"You don't think Mr. Jonah killed himself, do you? I know I didn't do it. There may be honor among thieves, but I've never seen it. And while the newspaper said Mr. Prather's death was connected to a prostitution ring, we all know better, don't we?"

"What are you talking about?" Donnie said, a little too quickly. "*You* killed them."

Frost chuckled, stepping down onto the cement floor.

"Oh, come on, we both know better," he said. "If I may guess, you were determined to keep the split as small as possible, to maximize your return."

That's when I realized how bad Donnie had gotten. Was that how Donnie got the key? He took it from Jonah after he shot him?

Donnie said, "I don't know what you're talking about."

"Of course you can't admit it in front of your compatriot. I assume you've taken care of Mr. Quinn as well?"

"Nope," Quinn said as he smashed the butt of his gun down on Frost's head.

THIRTY-NINE

Donnie looked for duct tape on the workbench and returned with a bunch of industrial-size cable ties instead. By the time Frost came around, Donnie and Quinn had relieved him of his coat and gun and bound him to a dusty ladder-back chair found in the pile.

I imagined spending the rest of my life in prison.

Note to self: Learn "Folsom Prison Blues."

"Congratulations on the surprise," Frost said, one eye blinking uncontrollably. "I didn't see Mr. Quinn when I looked in the windows."

"You fucked up," Quinn said.

"Yes, I did. My tradecraft has gotten rusty over the years. I'm seventy-six, you know."

"You snuck up on us pretty good."

"It didn't take much. I parked at Island Convenience and walked back."

Donnie rubbed the toe of his shoe on the cement, suddenly shy. "How did you know we were here at all?"

"Oh, I've been waiting ever since Mr. Jonah began snooping. I don't know how you knew the money was here, but I knew you were coming for it. I assumed it would be sooner rather than later. I actually expected a frontal assault, but when I was going out to my car, I heard you on the beach, and I knew."

"Why are you here in the first place?" I asked. "Why the island?"

He got the blinking under control with an effort. "My mother was born in town. We lived in Worcester during the year, that's where my father was from, but my maternal grandparents owned a camp down in what's now the refuge. When I was a kid – this was the forties, early fifties – my mother and I would come down for the whole summer, and my father would turn up on weekends, when he could. We were surrounded by nature. I suppose it was beautiful."

"Get to the point," Quinn said.

Frost continued, unruffled. "I spent quite a bit of time on my own. But I wasn't much of an outdoorsy child, and I spent a lot of time hiding out, reading comic books. It's where I developed my interest in the law. Thank you, Dick Tracy. About the time I started high school, my grandparents died within two months of each other, and poof, the camp was gone. The government took the land for a low price to add to the refuge. My mother bought this place, which was new construction at the time."

Quinn walked over and pressed the barrel of the gun against Frost's forehead. "We don't care about all that."

Frost just looked annoyed with this breach of manners. "Fine. I just thought some context would be appropriate. After high school, then, I went to college and law school, then joined the Marshal Service. I was head of the Albany office by the time they pulled off the armored car heist."

Quinn backed away and lowered the gun.

"One of the robbers left a fingerprint in the second getaway car, and we traced it to one of their safe houses, and we went in with guns drawn and got Spano. I flipped him in an hour. We rolled up the rest of the crew. It wasn't his guys, he didn't care. The deal was, he walked and got witness protection, if he testified. And he did. Put the other guys away for long stretches. Swore up and down that the two guys who were missing had the rest of the money.

"He got nervous. He told me he'd heard there was a leak, either in the bureau office or at the prosecutor. I, of course, started those rumors. He knew the outfit would be coming after him for testifying, and he was afraid someone in the office would set him up before he could get hidden. I suggested he could just vanish, without witness protection. I said I knew a place. This was it."

"OK, you're an evil genius," Quinn said. "What about the money?"

"We only found a little of it when we rolled up the robbery crew. They all flipped on each other, and everyone claimed one of the other guys was holding it, including Spano. He swore to me it wasn't him. I figured he had hidden it away and was looking for the quickest way to get out and get to it"

He shrugged and smiled.

"Spano stayed here for about eighteen months, cooperated nicely, always showed up to Albany to testify when needed. My superiors weren't happy that he had gone off on his own, or so they thought, but there wasn't much they could do about it. At first he was quite paranoid, always expecting a member of the gang or someone from the outfit to come in the door, guns blazing. But gradually he settled in and came to trust me as his protector. And there was no sign of the money. I was beginning to wonder if I had him all wrong, until one night he made a plane reservation, Miami to Panama City. He was skipping out. Which meant he must have finally retrieved the cash from wherever it was stashed. Apparently he'd gotten so comfortable here at the beach that he didn't think I could be tapping his phone."

"Keep talking," Quinn said.

"Well, I was not about to let him or the money slip through my fingers. I took a few personal days, drove here and watched him. He had let his guard down and failed to spot my surveillance. A couple of nights before his flight, he went into town to buy some clothes. And when he came back, I was waiting for him."

His eyes were bright with the memory.

"Did you have a nice conversation, like we're having now?"

"I shot him before he got a word out."

I expected this news, but it still felt like a part of my past had been cut off.

Frost saw my expression and sneered, "What do you want, tears?"

Quinn beckoned with his gun for the rest of the story.

Frost said, "He had the money crammed into two duffel bags stuffed up in the crawl space, which was accessed through a trap door in the bedroom closet. I found it in about two minutes. A few years ago, I moved it down here. Getting up into that crawl space at my age was becoming a problem."

"It won't be a problem anymore." Quinn held the gun a foot from Frost's face. "We're gonna make this look like a suicide. I'll print out a nice note. You'll confess to whacking the other two. And then you'll be overcome by guilt."

"I'm sure the authorities will believe that," Frost said with a smile. "But there's one more thing you should know."

Donnie shook his head at this blatant stall. "What?"

"The money's marked."

FORTY

Donnie punched Frost in the side of the head, then walked away shaking his hand. "Shit that hurts!"

Frost sagged against his bonds. He was an old man and I didn't know how many shots to the head he could take. He came back blinking again but unbowed.

"Yes, hitting me will fix everything," he said.

"Are you fucking kidding me? The money's *marked*?" Donnie grabbed a stack of bills and held a hundred up to the light bulb. "I don't see anything."

"Not literally marked, of course." Frost spoke as if to a small and rather stupid child. "The serial numbers were recorded, thirty or forty percent of them. There's no way to tell which ones, so you're rolling the dice every time you spend some."

"You didn't know?"

"The FBI didn't tell anyone, even other law enforcement. This was the seventies, remember. No one trusted anyone. After Watergate, we were all being investigated by Congress and the press. Everyone was turning on each other. Why do you think I wanted out? Spano provided me with an opportunity. But I didn't find out they had the serials until I tried to pass some of it. Luckily I'd chosen this little Indian casino in Michigan that had rather poor security. Their cameras weren't recording, only feeding live pictures to the security office. But I was literally checking out when the agents pulled up to the front entrance. It was a close call."

"That's why there's so much money left," I said.

Quinn and Donnie looked at me as if they'd forgotten I was there.

"Precisely," Frost said. "I didn't do what I did to live out my days on this island. I had plans like anyone. Instead I've had to be extraordinarily careful. I've spent just enough to allow myself a vacation each winter. In fact, I'm leaving next week. Or I was."

"What does that mean for us?" Donnie sounded as if he actually expected the old man to help us. "What do we do?"

Frost laughed in his face.

"It means you're doomed. When you start spending the money, they're going to come looking for you. I suspect it won't take them long."

Quinn riffled through a bundle of bills with an unreadable expression. "We'll be careful." He squatted by the bucket and began counting.

"You wouldn't know how. I should have kept my mouth shut and let you spend it. You're going to kill me anyway. You wouldn't have lasted two weeks. You'd never see daylight again." He chuckled. The prospect of us going to prison genuinely amused him, even though he'd be dead when it happened.

Donnie spoke first. "How much? How much is left?"

Frost smiled. "I started with a million-four hundred. In twenty years I've managed to get rid of almost half a mil, so there's just under a million left. It would be a great haul if you could spend it. But you need to keep me alive to help you wash it."

Donnie said, "Bullshit."

"I'm smarter than you are. I've lasted this long without getting caught. I can help you."

Quinn kept counting.

"How would we do it?" Donnie asked.

"How do I do what?"

"Wash it. Spend it. Whatever."

"Oh, you want to tap my expertise before you shoot me? You cretins couldn't possibly pull it off by yourselves. You might get lucky once or twice, but you'll screw it up eventually."

"Just tell me."

"You'll need false identities. Have you got that? No, I didn't think so. Good ID is a lot harder to get post-9/11. Holograms and all that. But let's say you manage it somehow. Then you'll need to fly or drive someplace with casinos, all using your fake ID. I recommend driving to another city, leaving your car in the long-term lot at the airport, then flying. Not someplace on the ball like Foxwoods or Vegas, but some minor island in the Caribbean or the Indian casino in East

Overshoe, Idaho. Someplace where the money's not going to get to a big bank to get scanned for a few days."

"Then what?"

"You might want to think about disguises, because even the dumpiest casino has cameras these days. If you're lucky you'll get one that only keeps the tapes for seventy-two hours. Go to the window, buy some chips. Not the smallest denominations, not the largest. Go to, say, the blackjack tables. Not the highest limit, not the lowest. Try not to lose much. Stay long enough that it won't attract attention when you get up again and cash out. If you feel lucky, do that two days in a row. Or maybe go to the next casino down the road. Try not to touch things, in case they come for fingerprints. It won't matter in the casino, but in your room. Wipe it down when you check out, of course. Then fly back to your car by a different route, with different ID. Drive home by a different route, too. Pay for gas and meals with clean cash of your own."

"Seriously?" Donnie said.

"And then when you get home, lie in bed at night and wonder if you did everything right. Wonder if you left any clues. Wonder if they're going to find you." Frost began to laugh but stopped abruptly when Donnie punched him again.

"Don't scramble his brains until we get everything we can out of him," Quinn said.

"We're screwed." Donnie looked like he was about to cry. "All this for nothing."

"Shut up, Donnie."

"And you haven't even discussed the murders of your compatriots," Frost said.

"You killed them," Donnie said.

"Not me."

"He's full of shit," Donnie said to me and Quinn.

"I'm not sure," Quinn said. "Seems like he doesn't have much to lose by telling us the truth."

"They were our friends! I wouldn't do that."

"Them being your friends makes it even worse," Frost said. "If I were these two gentlemen, I would worry that you-"

Donnie punched him again and this time it looked he might be out for good. His chin sagged against his chest. Donnie paced in circles while Quinn went back to counting.

Someone had to ask, and I was the only one who seemed interested. "Did you do what he said?"

Donnie groaned and grabbed his head with both hands. Finally he let out a sigh and seemed to relax. "OK, it was me. Phil was a fucking asshole. Always giving me orders. He was going to take the money for himself. He had me meet him at the refuge just so he could tell me to keep my mouth shut. He said he needed it worse than me and Chris. He was going to give us each ten grand to keep our mouths shut, like it was some big favor. He showed me the gun he was going to use. I asked him if I could take a look at it. He actually told me to be careful, like I was a moron. That's when I decided. But afterward I was glad I did it."

He was trying not to cry and almost succeeding. Despite everything, I couldn't help thinking, *poor Donnie.*

"What about Chris?"

"I finally told him what happened with Phil. And he wanted to tell the cops. He wanted me to confess the whole thing. He said better to make a clean breast of it than get in deeper. He said the money wasn't worth it." Donnie laughed, hardening himself. "He was soft. And stupid. I wasn't going to jail. We argued, and I hit him with something. I was just trying to shut him up, but I guess I hit him too hard."

"More for us." Quinn looked at me, eyes flat as a lizard's.

I began to doubt I would get out of this basement alive.

"It wasn't just about the money," I said, tap-dancing for my life. "You weren't greedy. Otherwise, why did you bring me in?"

"Right," Donnie said. "This was respect, and about two guys from the old days on the island, sticking together. Hell, you even met the guy that money belonged to in the first place. I figured you were in at the beginning, you deserve to be in at the end."

"I don't need money that bad."

"You don't?" Donnie stared at me, genuinely puzzled. "I thought you were in trouble."

"I am. But I'm not doing this."

Now, of all times, I took a stand. What was wrong with me?

Quinn finished counting and stood up. "Nine hundred eighty grand, just like the asshole said."

"Great," Donnie said and shot him.

FORTY-ONE

My hearing came back slowly, accompanied by a high-pitched whine like a malfunctioning speaker. Quinn lay crumpled against the wall, blood spreading down his shirt. Finally my brain kicked in.

"Donnie, what the fuck?"

"He told me he was going to shoot you before we left. Probably he was going to do me, too, and take all the money. It's you and me now," Donnie said. "Two old friends who trust each other."

"Donnie-" I couldn't think of the next word. I thought I was going to throw up.

"We're fine, really, we're fine." His face said otherwise.

"You morons could screw up a one-car funeral," Frost said.

Maybe the shot had woken him up. I wondered how many other cellars like this one he'd seen. No doubt in all other cases he was the one with duct tape and a gun.

I turned back to Donnie. "The police will be coming soon. I bet they're already on the way." I hoped so, anyhow.

"Out here? They don't come unless someone calls. No one's home across the street. No one heard the shot. We can do whatever we want."

He was probably right. I didn't know what to do now.

In the silence that followed, the *tink* of an Exact-o blade hitting the cement floor sounded clearly.

Frost stood in front of the chair, the plastic ties cut and fallen behind him. He had a gun in his hand, a snub-nosed revolver I had seen once before.

"We *searched* you," Donnie whined like a frustrated child.

"You never checked under the chair."

Frost edged behind one of the narrow steel columns that held up the first floor. Not much cover, but all there was. Donnie moved behind me, aiming over my shoulder, using me as a shield. So much for friendship.

"Maybe you can get me before I get you, but I doubt it," Frost said. "And I really have no problem shooting your friend here, too."

Channeling my father's calm, I said, "Why don't we all just take a second and -"

"Shut up." Donnie's breathing behind me was ragged with panic. "I've got to think."

Frost smiled. Donnie loudly licked his lips. He didn't know what to say or do next.

I had to ask.

"What happened to Mike Spano after you shot him?"

Frost chuckled, a sound colder than the wind outside.

"What a coincidence," he said. "You're standing on him."

The floor under my feet was a grave-sized patch of cement slightly darker than the rest.

Donnie whispered, "Sorry," then smashed me in the head with his gun and shoved me toward Frost. Both of them fired as I fell backward down the well toward unconsciousness.

"So they really did it, huh?"

The first thing I saw when I opened my eyes was a pair of thermal pajamas patterned with '57 Chevys, the legs stuffed into L.L. Bean boots. Ronnie helped me to my feet, both of us groaning with the effort. My head was killing me, and my back wasn't so great either.

"You knew."

"Sure, John and I knew," he said, wheezing. "They been hinting, and then they tried to get us to join them. It was the first night you played poker, right before you came in the door."

I'd stood on the deck, watching their tense conversation and thinking it was about me.

"We said no way, of course. I never thought they'd go through with it. Or that they'd pull you in. But when I looked out the window tonight and saw the three of you leaving, I thought I'd better come after you. I'm sorry, it took me a while to get dressed."

My ears rang and my head pounded. The copper smell of blood hung in the air. Quinn still lay heaped against the wall.

"He's dead," Ronnie said. "Did Donnie do that?"

I nodded.

"They never liked each other. Quinn's been riding him for years. I knew something like this would happen. That's one reason I stayed out of it."

There were other blood drops that couldn't have been Quinn's.

Going up the cellar stairs, Ronnie had a hard time getting his breath. He seemed about ten years older than the day I signed the lease. Maybe I did too.

The front door hung open to the porch. A cold wind had sprung up from the ocean, and the storm door to the outside swung back and forth in the gusts, frigid air streaming into the house, stirring the curtains, fluttering papers. The furnace kicked on.

"C'mon," Ronnie said and coughed. "We gotta see how it ends."

The surf pounded the beach. As we went down the front steps, gunshots sounded out there in the dark. Two different sounds, two guns. We walked around the guardrail and onto the sand.

"They're headed for John's house," Ronnie rasped. "Maybe Donnie thinks he'll change his mind now when he sees the money."

"One of them's hit, too."

As soon as we hit deep sand, Ronnie pace slowed. "Go ahead without me. I can't. My heart."

"What?"

"Need a pill." He fumbled an orange bottle from a jacket pocket. "Go on."

I left him.

A figure emerged from the darkness, running toward me along the water line. I dropped to a crouch, but it was just a jogger, running head down, huffing breaths as rhythmically as a steam train. He wasn't going to alter his run just because of a gunfight. Or maybe the music in his earbuds was so loud he didn't hear it. He didn't notice me, either, or at least he pretended he didn't. You learned to mind your own business on the beach at night.

When he was past, I got up and kept going. I couldn't quite run, because of my back, but I went as fast as I could. After a couple of minutes trudging through the sand, two shadowy figures emerged from the blackness beyond the center. In the empty parking lot, the door of the Dumpster banged in the wind.

The smaller figure was nearer: Mel Frost, with his back to me, in a combat shooting stance. How many shots had he fired? How many were in the gun? And how was a folksinger supposed to know stuff like that? His feet were spread too wide, though, as if he was trying to prop himself up, and he swayed in the wind.

Beyond him, facing my way, Donnie stood with a bucket of money in one hand and his gun pointed at Frost. Another bucket lay tipped over at his feet.

"Bax, get out of the way," he yelled. But yelling made him double over in pain. He dropped the money and pressed his hand over his side. He was wounded, though it was hard to see against his dark jacket. He kept his gun aimed, though. I sidestepped toward the ocean out of his line of fire.

Frost paid me no attention. The left knee of his pants was torn and bleeding, another wound visible near his shoulder. His eyes were blank. He was too far gone to do anything but aim at Donnie.

The shootout was a tie so far.

A siren sounded in the distance, then another. Someone had finally heard the gunfire on the beach.

I said, "Why don't you both put the guns down and I'll call an ambulance?"

Donnie said, "Dammit, Bax. No way."

"I never should have gone along with you," I said.

"It's too late to get out."

"In, out, I'll bury you morons," Frost said. He started to walk straight at Donnie, the gun leading.

They pulled their triggers at the same time.

Frost's gun clicked.

Donnie's gun barked.

Frost took one more step and fell face down in the sand.

Knees bent, gun in hand, Donnie began stuffing handfuls of money into his jacket pockets, more of it blowing away than he was catching.

I went to Frost and turned him over. One of Donnie's shots had caught him in the throat. The amount of blood alone told me there wasn't anything I could do

"Tell them I forced you to come along because you knew what we were doing," Donnie said. "Tell them you were kidnapped at gun-point, and you wanted nothing to do with it."

It might work.

Rising and falling on gusts of wind, the sirens were getting near. Someone gasped behind me. Ronnie trudged toward us, wobbling like a drunk in the soft sand. He looked panicked, one hand to his chest. His breath was ragged.

Donnie tried to walk, stumbled in the sand and dropped the money again, hand slick with his own blood. The bucket tipped on its side. A few bills slipped out and fluttered across the sand.

"Oops," he said mildly, as if he'd dropped his keys. "Little help?"

Before I could move, the wind howled over the beach, whip-ping sand into the air. I reflexively turned my face inland, but its stung me through my jacket and jeans like a swarm of bees. The wind grabbed the loose bills from the bucket and flung them into the air, swirling around Donnie and scattering across the beach. Donnie tried to grab them without success, squinting against the blowing sand. "Stop it! Stop it!"

While Donnie danced, Ronnie grunted and clutched his chest with both hands. He slowly fell forward as he walked, landing face down on the sand. The sirens were close now, the first reflections of their blue lights visible on the windows of the houses atop the dune.

Donnie grabbed the half-empty bucket and began to stagger away down the beach, gun in the other hand. He hadn't gone very far when the first cruiser drove across the parking lot and onto the beach, blue lights strobing across the sand. It jolted to a stop and the two cops jumped out drawing their guns and took cover behind their doors. One of them aimed a spotlight at Donnie, running awkwardly, money blow-ing out of the bucket and swirling around him in the wind like a flock of angry gulls. The cruiser's public address system buzzed to life.

"Freeze! Stop right there! Hands up!"

Donnie turned toward them and almost smiled.

"Don't-" I shouted, but it was too late.

Donnie raised his gun and the cops fired. He fell back in the sand as if yanked by some giant cord. No one moved for a second. A gust of wind came then and snatched more money from the bucket, tossing bills into the air, a tornado of cash whirling down the beach into the darkness until it disappeared.

FORTY-TWO

The town guys had spent so many days and nights outside in the cold digging up water mains that they stripped down to t-shirts in the unheated basement, sweating as they broke through the cement floor. The division of labor was the same as on the streets: One ran the jackhammer, one pulled away debris with a shovel, and three supervised. We all wore foam earplugs, as if at a heavy metal concert.

Wankum had questioned me in the kitchen at midnight, speaking quietly so none of the people going in and out of the house could hear.

"They forced you to come along?"

"Donnie and Quinn showed up at my door with guns. They asked me to join them. They knew I'm having a cash flow problem. They said there was plenty of money for everyone."

He looked me in the eyes for a long moment. "And you said?"

"I said no."

"How'd they take that?"

"They were surprised. But since I knew what they were doing, they said I didn't have a choice."

"We'll see how that plays."

I knew what he meant. Putin and O'Hurley wanted a turn with me eventually, but they were outside on the beach now, examining trajectories.

"You said Donnie used you for a human shield? Nice guy."

"He was pretty messed up. With Waltham Mortgage out of business and a divorce, he didn't have much left to keep him on track. And he had kind of a rough childhood."

"Lots of people have rough childhoods."

"When his father hung himself, Donnie found him."

"Wow. So this was suicide by cop."

"Maybe."

Wankum said, "You got lucky."

"I know. How's Ronnie?"

"He was sitting up when the ambulance took him away, trying

to talk through the oxygen mask."

"That's a good sign."

"For him. For the EMTs, not so much. But at least he'll be able to back up your story."

We fell silent for a moment. Outside the windows, blue flashers and TV lights fought the darkness.

I asked, "How much cash did you find?"

"Don't know yet," he said. "We've got people counting it, but a lot is in the wind. People will be out there combing the beach tomorrow. We'll be watching."

"The money's supposed to be marked."

"No shit?"

"A lot of it, anyway. The serial numbers were recorded."

"That will help."

Now it was almost dawn. Little yellow evidence markers were all over the basement, which had been photographed and videoed from every angle. Quinn's body had been removed hours ago. Wankum didn't understand why I wanted to stay, but he didn't argue.

The jackhammer stopped abruptly. The guy with the shovel stepped forward and removed a chunk of cement from the edge of the hole. The state evidence techs moved in, incongruous in their white paper jumpsuits. They troweled out the dirt, brushed and fussed for a few minutes, then backed away. Wankum stepped forward and squatted down by the hole.

"Hello there," he said.

I looked over his shoulder. The sight was a shock, even though I knew it was coming. In the hole, amid the tattered remains of a black plastic garbage bag, were bones and a half-buried skull, along with scraps of a black sweatshirt with a gold logo on the chest.

We stepped back. The evidence techs moved in again, and one started taking pictures. As his camera flashed, I said a silent thanks to Mike Spano for not pulling the trigger on that snowy night so long ago.

FORTY-THREE

"Please hold for Mr. Polio."

I only had to wait ten seconds before he came on the line.

"I read about that shit you're all up in," he said and laughed. "I gotta admit I'm impressed. You're an O.G., though you sure don't look the part on that YouTube."

"That's an old video," I said.

"You know the Grammys are coming up, right? I got three nominations for Song of the Year and shit like that. You wanna join up, hit some parties, help me push my brand? People see you with me, you'll move some product too."

I explained that the District Attorney had warned me not to leave town, pending possible criminal charges.

"That ain't no thing, they just tryin' to scare you. I been there. Get yourself a good Jew lawyer, get it straightened out, and then hit me back."

I said I'd do that.

I didn't do that.

Lily called me later the same day. Possibly she planned it that way.

She said she was worried about me. I told her don't be. She had me take her through the whole story, interrupting only occasionally to ask how I could have been so stupid.

"Thank God you weren't hurt. Have you thought about what I said? About calling ConcertSquad and getting on those gigs? The mid-Atlantic run down to Florida?"

"I thought about it."

"Have you told them you're in?"

"I haven't decided yet."

"Goddamn it, sweetie, what is going through that head of yours? I know you need the money, if this latest escapade didn't make it clear enough."

"Escapade?"

"It's not funny. Think about all the ways you could have been hurt, or worse. Never mind going to prison. But somehow you got through it and now you need to think clearly. Focus. Get your life back on track. And start playing some gigs."

"Maybe."

"Maybe, nothing. I'm trying to help you here, honey, but you aren't hearing it. You need to clean out your ears."

She hung up.

Rumors about my role spread wildly, according to Davey, who heard them all at the Rum House. His favorite was that I had been tutored in crime by Polio, who gave me the machinegun I used in the shootout.

Davey may have started that one himself.

The upside was that Billy Walston believed I was some kind of badass, despite all evidence to the contrary. At my house, I found a large crew working with a renewed sense of purpose, workers skittering over the half-finished roof like insects. And he came out the door to greet me, rather than making me track him down inside.

"Great to see you, man! I'm glad you're OK."

Even his body language was different. He turned toward me no matter where I went, rather than looking off in some other direction.

"Thanks, Billy."

"Sounds like you had an exciting time, but I guess that could be traumatic too, Quinn getting killed in front of you and everything. Even though he *was* kind of a prick. I want to hear all about it, but not till you're ready to talk."

"I'm not sure I'll ever feel like-"

"That's fine, really. You're OK, that's the important thing. And don't worry about the money. I know you're good for it. Just pay me whenever you can, that's fine."

"Thanks, Billy."

"I don't want any more trouble between us. Friends got to stick together in this world, am I right?"

"You bet," I said. "Now about those pendant lights-"

Abigail didn't do so well in mainland precincts, but turnout there for a winter special election was predictably low. Islanders motivating by the plumbing crisis showed up in droves, though, and gave her a thirty-vote win in citywide totals.

After the ballot boxes and voting booths had been trundled away, Abigail held her victory party at PITH, instead of a traditional downtown spot like the Thirsty Lobster or the Rum House. I had to see it, although I'm not sure why.

The room was packed. Everybody loves a winner. And free alcohol. Coolers held cans of domestic beer and soda and bottles of cheap prosecco on ice, next to stacks of red Solo cups. A DJ played what passes for country music today. Miles Allgood's old Scout troop had hung red, white and blue bunting.

"Congratulations, Miles."

"Thank you. We've won a great victory here, and I hope this is only the beginning for the people of Libertyport."

"You sound like you're running for something yourself."

"I'll be back in a year and a half, with my degree. We'll see then." He leaned toward me, glowing with ambition like a nuclear core. "I'll be needing friends. People with special skills. People who know how to get things done. Which recent events have shown you do."

"You're mistaken," I said "But good luck." I turned away.

The candidate wore a red suit. Her face was bright with triumph, lit by an unfamiliar grin.

"Congratulations, Abigail. I'm sure you'll do great."

"Thank you, Mr. McLean. But I'm afraid this means I won't be available to you anymore. I can't be seen to associate with the criminal element."

"I'm not the-"

"Our communications from now on will have to be strictly official. The Freedom of Information Act is quite specific. Everything has to be on the up-and-up. No more whispering, no more favors."

"I just meant-"

"I'm afraid I can't be in the streets protesting, either. I will have to fight the people's fight from within the corridors of power."

Grandiose, true, but now the island's problems, the whole town's in fact, were hers to solve. Of all the fates that had befallen her in the last few years, this was the worst. But if anyone could face down global warming...

I told Zack that he could take the Sunbird to Bonnaroo. The car presented so many safety and reliability issues that I knew Amy would fold, and she did. She told him he could use her Volvo, pending a long list of conditions. She didn't actually want him to go, of course. She admitted to me that she was betting he and Kayla would break up by then.

I wasn't so sure. The girl seemed like she might be around for a while. Zack had borrowed one of my backup guitars, and she was teaching him to play.

Hedwig began to make herself scarce shortly after the events on Lilac Lane. Probably more of a seasonal thing than concern about stray gunshots, but who knows?

She still appeared on the roof next door every couple of days, but her visits were shorter, her head always on a swivel. She would be leaving soon, flying back to Arctic solitude, so she spent more time hunting, storing up calories for her journey. I had the feeling she was going to miss the birders trailing her everywhere, although she would never admit it.

FORTY-FOUR

Waking up on the island, I always heard the ocean first. Even at low tide, with no breakers, it made a sound, white noise like a distant crowd.

What I heard now was an actual crowd.

The sound crept through the walls and hollow spaces of the old Baltimore theater, all the way down to my surprisingly nice if small dressing room, a floor below the stage. I tuned and re-tuned my guitar, holding the Berwyn D8 tight, my lucky charm. Riding out my first butterflies in years.

This gig was different than the bars and parks I'd headlined for a decade or more. This was a theater, with chandeliers under a domed ceiling, and the audience of a thousand or more music lovers with high expectations, even for the opening act.

Mixed with the crowd noise was the Dixieland jazz that Lily's crew played before every show. A nod to authentic American roots and the things that really mattered. Was it too late for me to matter again?

The stage manager knocked. "It's time."

I patted the check in my pocket and stood. When I opened the door to the corridor, the volume rose a notch. One foot in front of the other. I was halfway up the narrow stairs when the music cut off abruptly and the crowd roared. The house lights must have gone off.

As I entered the wings, I heard Lily talking, though I couldn't make out the words. She didn't have to introduce me, it was above and beyond for a star of her magnitude, but she had insisted. Maybe she thought she needed to remind the crowd who I was.

The crew looked at me with mild curiosity as I approached the stage through the maze of equipment and road cases. A grizzled roadie with a headset and flashlight led me to a spot behind the amps, where we stood in the dark. A spotlight illuminated center stage from on high. I couldn't see Lily, but I heard her shout, "Please welcome Baxter McLean!" The crowd cheered.

This was it.

The roadie mouthed, *You're on,* then swung his flash to show me the path to center stage. This was it. The roadie raised his eyebrows. *What are you waiting for?*

Good question.

I took a deep breath and walked out into the light.#

Acknowledgements

Once again, much gratitude to my early readers – Bill, Ben, Brian and Heather – for their time and insights. All mistakes are mine alone.

Thanks to the people who let me climb their wind turbine in Gloucester, and to my editors at the *Boston Globe,* who said yes to a story about it. I knew about halfway up that Baxter was going to make the same climb.

I can never say enough thanks to Greg, who created another fantastic cover and as usual showed infinite patience in the process. I am also grateful to Kim In Sherl, who gave permission all the way from Seoul for us to use his owl photo in the design.

Many thanks to the independent bookstore owners and other North Shore retailers who have enabled me. Long may you run.

Thanks to all my readers, who make this worth doing.

Thanks to Roe for your patience and so much else.

Finally, as always, thanks to my mother and father for books and newspapers, paper and pens.

JB 3/30/17

45708664R00144

Made in the USA
Middletown, DE
11 July 2017